ZACHARY'S GOLD

Zachary's Gold

Being a recounting
of certain remarkable events
in the Barkerville Goldfields, 1864

Stan Krumm

oolichan books
Lantzville, British Columbia, Canada
1994

Publication of this book has been financially assisted by the Canada Council.

Canadian Cataloguing in Publication Data

Krumm, Stan, 1954-
Zachary's Gold

ISBN 0-88982-138-0

I. Title.
PS8571.R85Z12 1994   C813'.54   C94-910624-0
PR9199.3.K78Z12 1994

Published by
OOLICHAN BOOKS
P.O. Box 10
Lantzville, B.C.
Canada V0R 2H0

Printed in Canada by
Hignell Printing Limited
Winnipeg, Manitoba

For my friend, Paul Soetopo

CHAPTER ONE

I WAS RAISED IN the hill country of New Hampshire, my parents being second generation American farmers and moderately successful as such. My father was able and determined to see that I received an education better than his own, and to that end dispatched me to Chicago at the age of nineteen years to study law.

"Lawyers," he pronounced more than once, "are the roosters in the henhouse of this world." There was some truth in this quaint observation, although within the metaphor of a henhouse, I believe that foxes would be the animals more relevant to that profession.

Knowing his hopes for my life as I did, I was rather surprised at his great displeasure two years later when I announced that I had taken employment as a Pinkerton agent. I had assumed that he would quickly see the similarity between the two careers, both being in the field of law and its maintenance, and consider that my scholastic goal had been more or less reached, but this was not the case. His protestations were all the more hurtful to me in that I had been forced to falsify several letters of recommendation to secure the job. At that point in my life, the idea of cheating in order to become an enforcer of the law did not seem paradoxical at all.

The temptation is to state that my father refused to speak to me from that day on, but in fairness, I myself never found opportunity to communicate to him, and he had no idea of my whereabouts after I left school. I liked my family well enough, but as a group we were always too busy to form those poetic bonds that cannot be broken, or at least ignored.

My three years as a Pinkerton man accomplished two things. Firstly, it taught me to use a Colt revolver a third as long as my leg, thereby convincing me that I was a fully redoubtable young bull and a challenge to all comers. Secondly, it showed me that not every occupation that promises challenge and adventure can fulfil that promise. For approximately thirty-four months I was based in various hotels and railway stations, endlessly asking questions and searching, usually in vain, for scoundrels and swindlers. The greatest excitement I experienced was in being lost twice in snowstorms, and the only time I actually used my revolver, I shot out all the windows and most of the door of a small house. I discovered later that my desperado had never actually occupied the place.

I was only a slightly more cynical and experienced young fellow, however, as I headed west for California in the summer of 1863. There was still a challenge available there for a young man, was the surety, and chances for more than a meagre salary and bunions. I had some vague notions of rounding up wild horses or discovering and conquering some lost tribe of very rich Indians, but by the time I reached San Francisco gold and rumours of gold were the only thoughts that I would entertain. In this, I followed much of the population, for while the greatest finds in the region were becoming or had become depleted, the dream remained. New Eldorados were reported from here and there as well — Idaho and Montana were interesting to me, at first.

I decided to winter in San Francisco, though. I had found work on the docks, and desired to build up enough capital to endure a short period of careful prospecting with no income to cover expenses, before I became fabulously rich. Each evening as I squirrelled away my resources, I would gaze longingly towards the Montana hills, where my empire was waiting to reveal itself. I amassed quite a collection of maps, and pored over them diligently, as if sufficient study would reveal the secrets of the future.

Longshoremen are a rough lot generally, and the people I encountered that winter on the docks were mostly as shameless an amalgam of liars and storytellers as one could hope to find, but mixed with the falsehood and phantasms was a theme I could not ignore — that the relatively instant fortunes of the day were being made not in Montana, but far north of me in the new English colony of British Columbia. British Columbia was where the real gold and the real gold seeker were to be found.

I was reluctant at first to consider the trip, for anyone familiar with the region described it as the Devil's own region to travel. I had hoped to encounter a more hospitable form of wilderness for my journeys, but as the months passed, so did my reservations.

Thus it was that on April 3, 1864, I took passage on the paddlewheel steamship *Commodore* to Fort Victoria, colony of British Columbia. Because of my connections with the stevedores I was able to work for my fare as a non-skilled crewman, my duty being to clean the decks, to sweep and swab continuously. We were so grossly overladen with passengers, however, that there was scarcely a free patch of deck, bench, or bunk that was not covered either by an itinerant miner or his stack of gear. Therefore, I managed to find time to do a fair amount of posing on the foredeck with my eyes on the horizon and my scraggly bronze moustache fluttering in the wind. I was a tall and skinny creature, but fancied myself something of an inspirational portrait piece in that posture.

From Fort Victoria, another steamer — this one so old that it was hardly seaworthy — carried our small horde of humanity across the gulf waters to the mainland and about thirty miles up the Fraser River to Fort Langley, where the next segment of my journey began.

I disembarked from the boat in the early afternoon, optimistic and only mildly nauseous from the ship's motion, so I determined to shoulder my pack and make some distance towards Fort Hope. By nightfall I had covered twenty miles along a most pleasant road, and as I lay rolled in my blanket by a cheery fire, I felt sure that the stories of the road's treachery and danger had been grossly exaggerated.

The next day, in bright spring sunshine, I walked the forty miles to Fort Hope, camping just north of the settlement in ease and good spirits. I remember this quite well, for it was the last I saw of ease and good spirits for some time.

The ten or twelve miles to Fort Yale introduced me to the realities of the odyssey I had undertaken. A fine, cold rain fell steadily and seemed to double the weight of my pack. I spent much of my time cursing the foul capriciousness of road surveyors. When a straight path through the forest was quite obviously available, they chose to make it meander like a prairie stream, and when a really formidable obstacle presented itself, they forced the traveller directly up its face, rather than divert him around it.

It was also at this time that I first glimpsed the River's malicious rage. The flat grey maelstrom twisted along the base of the slate cliff looking as deceptively slow as a coiling serpent until it struck some exposed rock, and spat up sheets of rabid foam. (To this day I recall seeing, at a spot twenty miles or so above Fort Yale, a pair of fallen trees fully thirty feet in length being borne swiftly down the swirling waterway. I watched them hurtle to the edge of a great whirlpool, whereupon they flipped up on their ends like twigs and were swallowed in a single gulp.)

It was nightfall when I straggled into Fort Yale, and I immediately took the chance to emulate the Christ child by seeking refuge in a stable. I remained there the following day, it being a Sunday. Like most of the travellers, I was grateful for a Sabbath rest, even though my own expedition had scarcely begun. A trader with four pack mules was due to leave Monday morning — a French Canadian whose name I now forget. Along with a half-dozen other apprehensive adventurers, I chose to accompany him. We would give him the safety found in numbers, and he, for his part, could supply us from his stocks with certain items we would otherwise have had to carry on our backs. It was a fortuitous arrangement and kept those unpleasant weeks of sojourning from being totally impossible for me. The journey was more than a week and a half of cold, aching bones and misery which I shall not describe at length.

One vivid picture remains in my mind, though, from the celebrated Royal Engineers' road through the wicked lower regions of the Fraser Canyon. I remember being forced to venture out onto what the Frenchman called "cat's paths" — hanging slings of boards suspended from ropes above and shored up by random logs underneath. Dangling there against the sheer slate face, I found the view of watery death far below me was too much to endure and too near to ignore, and I was forced to creep along with my eyes tightly shut, one hand holding a mule's packstrap. It was an undignified posture, but, as I say, a memorable one.

I could easily spend a great deal of time describing our travel north through river canyons, over mountain ridges, swamps, and deserts. It was an eventful journey. I recall vividly the night we expelled an Englishman named Alexander from our company for cheating at cards, barely refraining from hanging the scoundrel. I remember equally, at another point, how disgusted I was to witness the lengthy funeral the papist Frenchman gave his favourite packhorse when it broke a leg and had to be shot.

It is a country that breeds memorable images and strange stories, although the strangest and most memorable still awaited me, weeks later, and farther north.

After travelling for about ten days, we reached the outpost of Soda Creek, some sixty or seventy miles down the Fraser from Quesnelle Mouth. That stretch of the river is safely navigable, and, as luck would have it, we were able to gain passage on the sternwheeler next day.

The operators of that vessel proved to be as wild a lot as any dock workers in San Francisco, and I arrived at the beginning of the last leg of my expedition quite drunk. Indeed, in my attempt to disembark I almost drowned in about three feet of water before I could extricate myself from beneath my river-soaked pack. By sleeping in a shed owned by the shipping company, I was able to keep the frost off my blanket, but I awoke very cold and ill-disposed to the world next day.

I set out alone and travelled nearly twenty miles — as far as Cottonwood House — where I ate good beefsteak and potatoes, then retired immediately to the stables where, warmed by hay and horse breath, I slept a full twelve hours.

In the morning I was much invigorated. Checking my accounts, I found I still had several days of rough grub and thirty-five American dollars, while being within thirty-odd miles of my destination. After having covered roughly four hundred, it seemed such a short distance that I expected to reach the gold-fields that day, but that majestic and malevolent country had more than one surprise in store for newcomers.

The wagon road from Quesnelle Mouth to Barkerville and Cameronton was barely begun at that time, Mr. Gustavus Blin Wright having lately arrived with his crew of men, and I was working my way through the forest along a path four to six feet in width which seemed to have been directed either by a madman or a jack rabbit. It wound and twisted through an otherwise trackless region that managed to be both of extremely steep relief, and covered by swamp. When the forest allowed any dis-

---

tance of vision, snow could be seen on the heights, and after climbing only a short while, I found snow on each side of the trail.

I camped that night on frozen ground between high, white drifts, wondering as I went to sleep whether I would be frozen and blown over before morning. In the following weeks and months I was to grow used to that as my retiring thought, for in that land the snow can come in any week of the year, and the nights are never warm.

There was, of course, no question of turning back.

CHAPTER TWO

AN OMNIPRESENT COLD pervades all recollections of my early days in the Cariboo. Cold crept up into my bones at night from the ground where I slept. Cold fell down silently from the dark sky to surround me in the morning. If I found respite by a fire or in some warm building, the relief was only momentary. The cold was patiently waiting for me when I started on my way again, down the slippery clay streets and the boggy creek banks.

The town did not lend itself to flowery descriptions or fond memories. Situated in the shallow valley of Williams Creek, it more resembled a desolate battleground or the sight of some horrific natural disaster than a planned community boasting to be the "largest city west of Chicago and north of San Francisco."

The lower slopes of both hillsides had been more or less completely denuded, and were simply a vast expanse of mud and slush dotted with mine shafts and shanties – crisscrossed with footpaths and a spiderweb network of troughs and wooden flumes directing the water of the creek to run a myriad of pumps and

Cornish wheels. What trees still remained could not hope for a much longer existence. The sound of chopping and sawing as these were transformed into lumber and firewood was incessant during daylight hours, and a white veil of woodsmoke across the valley's roof was the only testimony to the past existence of smaller forms of vegetation. Scattered across this bleak panorama were the places of human habitation, so small and squalid that they could easily be missed at a casual glance.

While little of beauty could be credited to the town, it could certainly boast great energy and constant activity. The noise of logging, digging, building, pumping, pounding, shouting and cursing lasted all day and well into the night. Indeed, even during the hours of darkness, the valley bottom was covered with spots of light — lanterns glowing over the wet shafts which had to be worked twenty-four hours of each day.

The buildings of Barkerville proper were strung along one long main street and one back street — a few decent structures serving as stores, hotels, and saloons, while the living quarters of most common miners were ramshackle affairs set up with little care and no intention of longevity. Each builder had the same thought — that his cabin only needed to last a few months before he was rich enough to leave. Work time was too precious to squander on personal comfort, and almost none of them had wives or family to consider.

My naivety and lack of foresight was remarkable, in hindsight, and it was to my great discredit that I had thought only as far as making the trek to the land of promise and little of what would be required upon my arrival. I suppose I expected to find some cheap boarding house or bunk-down arrangement, a short season of leisure while I chose the most obvious site to begin my harvest of mineral bounty. Needless to say, no such accommodation existed. The choice was between absolutely exorbitant rates in hotel rooms or a squatter's chances wherever the ground was dry. Luckily, many of the buildings were constructed two or three feet off the ground on wooden pillars, and I spent my first two nights underneath a general store in cold but comparatively dry conditions.

The search for a claim site was more complicated than I had anticipated – the whole of Williams Creek and all the more promising side gulches being completely staked long before my arrival. Newcomers like myself hoped that we might get a chance to pick up a lapsed claim in a good location. Each miner was required to live continuously on site to retain title, and speculation was that some claim holders might not return from their legally permitted winter lay-off, but they were not required to do so until June first, and talk was that the allowance might even be extended to the first of July.

It was a huge country in which I stood, and a withering prospect to have to choose one particular hundred-foot square where a dream might be nurtured into reality.

As I wrapped myself in my blanket that first night under the general store, my mind was like a cauldron, boiling with sundry unpleasant opinions and emotions. I was physically exhausted after my long journey, however, and I was quickly asleep, in spite of the constant noise of boots booming like a drum along the boardwalk not far from my head.

It was not noise that dragged me up and out of my slumbers in the middle of that night, but a small sharp pain near my belly. When enough of my consciousness returned, I realized that some small animal – a mouse, in fact – had managed to crawl inside my clothing and was currently scurrying along my skin, biting where he deemed necessary. This appreciable discomfort caused me to sit up abruptly in the dark, or rather to attempt to sit up, for my head cracked into the floorboards above me with a sound like someone dropping a watermelon, and I sprawled prostrate once more. On the mouse, who bit me again.

By the time this situation had finally been corrected I was, of course, wide awake. I am no more afraid of rodents than any

16

man, but the sensation of sharing one's undergarments with the lower beasts can be quite disconcerting. I couldn't blame the little fellow much, for like myself he was only searching for the warmest available place to sleep, but I confess that when I extracted him from my shirt I did not set him free to bother me again, but summarily dispatched him to meet his mousey Maker.

I resolved to find better accommodation as quickly as possible.

I began the next day with a breakfast of dried beef strips warmed over a fire some fellows had set up behind a corral on Back Street. Conversing with this small group for a short time, I quickly became aware of the protocol that governs talk among prospectors and miners. The first rule on this line is that one may hold forth about great fortune or complain bitterly about the fickleness of life with impunity, and with little risk, in either case, that anyone will believe a single word. Where questions to another person are concerned, however, great care must be exercised. Facetious or jesting enquiries are perfectly fine, as are opinions about technique, background facts, or the superstitions that help to make many decisions. It is forbidden, however, to ask anyone how much gold they have, where they found it, or any variation on those two questions.

I escaped that breakfast time with no new friendships made, but no blows exchanged, and straightaway walked the three miles to the Gold Commissioner's office in Richfield, where maps of Barkerville, Cameronton, Antler Creek, Stout's Gulch, and all other sections of the region lined the walls.

I considered myself to be rather knowledgeable about maps by this time, but after studying these for an hour, I was none the wiser. I walked and pondered, then returned to examine them further, but with no better luck. Other men came and went continually, many checking the same diagrams I found so incomprehensible, then nodding sagely and departing while I tried in vain to decipher the codes of four-figure numbers, pencil scratches over curving lines, and curious abbreviations.

After most of another hour, I departed the offices again, and had just paused on the boardwalk outside the main doors when a small man with an enormous red beard accosted me.

"All right then. I'll take pity on you, lad," he said in an accent that I couldn't place.

"What's that?" said I.

"Come. Over there," he grunted, and I dutifully followed him across the road, where he dropped his huge pack (even bigger than my own) onto a wooden box beside a shed.

"I seen you in there, lad. Half the morning and you comes out all starry-eyed like the minin' maps was writ in Chinese." As he spoke, he rummaged deep into his kit, piling shirts and stale bread on the box beside him. At last he withdrew a wrinkled and worn piece of paper which he clenched in his fist while he repacked his bag and continued. "Yessir, I seen the story enough to know it good, and it's a sad one for sure. You're young and anxious and now you're way out here, and you're lost, and you don't have a clue where to start. Am I right?"

While he addressed me, he wiggled his fingers continually through his great beard, as if he were searching for something lost therein. I bridled at both the man and his approach. The fellow had several times referred to my youth, and twice called me "lad," and although I could see that he was many years my senior, I resented the implication of his constant reminders. His remarks thus far were likewise quite true, but I was not about to admit as much.

"I know my way around quite nicely thank you, and — "

"No you don't!" He spat the words out without waiting for me to finish what I meant to say.

"What?"

"You need my map."

"What? No! I don't need any maps, old man!"

"Where's Pinnacle Creek?"

"What?"

18

"Where's the Welshmen got the new diggins? Is the ground good on the south o' Cow Mountain?"

He could show that he knew the area better than I, quite certainly, but that was a small trick.

"You need my map!" he repeated.

I found his patronizing air insufferable, and I could distinguish the beginnings of a fraud in him as well. I turned away, and dismissed him with a wave of my hand or attempted to, at least. He left his pack where it was and kept pace with me as I followed the path along the creek.

"You ain't got no place neither, to start figurin' this all out, save some fella like me is gonna help you, lad. Cost you three dollars is all, and this map shows you everything. Everything!" He waved his piece of paper in my face like a weapon.

"So how come you're out here peddling maps, instead of getting rich yourself, if you know so much?"

"It's the backbone of it," he lamented. "I ain't young, and I ain't got the back. You got the backbone, you see, and I got the know-how."

"I know well enough how to find my way around the gold-fields without your filthy map!"

"No you don't!"

"And how would you know?" I demanded, turning on him.

"You don't stink enough," he explained with a complacent, vaguely schoolmasterish attitude. He glanced once at me, then examined whatever it was he had finally discovered deep in the confines of his facial hair.

"What? You're saying I smell good? I doubt that very much."

"Oh, not like you're clean and pretty or nothin', lad. You stink o' bad food and dirt and the like, sure enough, but not like gold."

"Gold?"

"The stuff in the ground, young fella! Good gold miners got their own stink — gold stink, a real ugly stink, and you ain't got it, no sir!"

———

One can hardly argue with an explanation like that, so I gave the appearance of relenting.

"So you're going to show me where to start prospecting?"

"Three dollars and you got the smartest map you ever did see."

"Well, let me take a look at it then," I suggested. I still knew him for a fraud. I was only playing along at his game to see where it took me.

"That ain't the point, is it, young fella? You don't know much about business neither, do you? You come up with the money, and then you sees the map."

This last insult brought my anger to the boil. Showing great restraint, I drew out a couple of American coins, but as he reached for them, I closed my hand, reached across, and snatched the wrinkled sheet of paper out of his grip. Turning my back to him, I held it up out of his reach, and began to read some of the markings out loud, while he sputtered objections.

"'Yank's Peak at the quarter mile marker', you say! Quarter mile from what, I wonder?"

"Give it back, you!" he demanded, scratching at my coat sleeve.

"'Don't bother south of here', it reads. You've examined the whole of this valley, have you? You're quite the miner, Mr. Weskit!"

He pushed and grabbed at me, but he was so much smaller and older that it took no effort on my part to hold him off while I perused and critiqued his map. Out of the corner of my eye I saw more than one passerby watching us and chuckling, as I rolled the map into a crumpled ball and tossed it into the creek.

"Now, if you'll kindly leave me alone," I said, "I have things to do."

He stood cursing and pulling at his beard, while I walked away in one direction and his map floated off in another.

As is usual when a person vents his frustration at the expense of someone else, my feeling of satisfaction was short-lived. Within a minute or two I was once again aware that I had no idea of what to do next. The confrontation with Weskit left me irritated, and so self-conscious that when I sat down on the boardwalk to think, I felt everyone's eyes on me, and resumed my aimless promenade, trying to look purposeful and confident. I went all the way down Front Street to Cameronton like this. By the time I turned around and headed back along the path that skirts the creek, I had come to the conclusion that I really did need some sort of advice from a more experienced prospector, although I still maintained that I had acted correctly with Miller Weskit, who was obviously a sham.

The life of a gold seeker was turning out to be more complicated than I had thought. Once more I strolled the length of Barkerville, looking for inspiration. Striking up conversations with strangers in saloons was always a possibility, but it seemed a rather unpromising one. Walking blindly into the hills and starting to dig at some random gully deep in the barrens was equally unpalatable to me, but after a while I began to think it might be unavoidable.

At that point, I spotted a sign next to a doorway in an alley that could, I thought, hold some promise. It was a painted wood sandwich board sign announcing, *Taylor Cunningham – Barber*. Below this title were advertised, *Expert haircuts, shaves, and proper gentleman's grooming. Tonics and poultices available*. At the bottom, evidently added as an afterthought, the sign read, *Polite conversation and advice*. I didn't know exactly what was meant by this, but it did not seem too unlikely that someone might see a way to make an honest profit from the obvious need of newcomers such as myself. In spite of my vaunted scepticism of strangers, I had little to lose by asking. My only other option was to go back to the creek and see if Miller Weskit's map had washed up somewhere on the bank.

The man was alone when I entered, a tall, slim negro with white hair and full sideburns. He had been sharpening his razors, and looked up expectantly when the door opened.

"Haircut, sir?"

I was uncertain where to begin, or how to phrase my question. "I understand you might be able to advise me regarding possible prospecting areas. I'm new to the area, you see."

He nodded his head gravely and with great dignity replied. "To my customers, I am most happy to supply what information I have at my disposal."

As I have said, I was feeling a trifle sceptical after my experience with Miller Weskit, and felt entitled to ask, "What exactly makes you an authority on such matters, Mr. Cunningham?"

His air became one not so much offended as disdainful, and his simple reply carried a tone of the most patrician self-respect I have ever heard.

"I, sir, am a barber," and he lifted the customer's cape from his chair.

When I was seated, he set to clipping and snipping and squinting and waving his scissors without saying a word, so that at first I thought he was going to do nothing but cut my hair — a good enough project, but not high on my list of priorities. At last he spoke. "You are new then to our fair city, sir?"

"I am."

"And you wish to pursue a career as a gold miner, but are unsure of where to begin your search?"

"I've seen a number of good possibilities," I assured him, "but I saw your advertisement there on the street, and I wondered if you might have any additional snippets of information."

"What possibility seems most attractive to you so far, sir?" Glancing at his face in the mirror, I could detect no sign of sarcasm, so I replied, "I think I'd rather just hear what suggestion you would give to a newcomer these days."

Once again he went about his work in silence. He was certainly a good barber. I took a genuine pleasure in watching the dextrous manoeuvring of his long fingers. As he made a few final deft jabs with his scissors at an occasional out-of-place hair, he gave me his judgement.

"No one has been opening up new areas of late, of course —
too early in the year. Only the best claims and the deeper shafts
have been operating over the winter." He sighed sympathetically.
"The best locations are all duly claimed and registered, and from
past experience I would say that virtually all the owners will return to take possession of these within the next few weeks. I am
afraid that right now even *rumours* of good new ground are
scarce, and I believe you are faced with entering virgin territory
and trusting kind Providence."

Once again it seemed that any hope I had held for assistance
had been quashed and I was back to the point where I would
have to pick a compass bearing and begin to stumble ahead. As
I stood up, though, the barber added one more idea.

"If you are not afraid of rough travel, you might try a bit of
prospecting in the Binder Creek area, where it joins Antler
Creek farther down, north of Mt. Tinsdale — toward the Cariboo River and Babcock Lake. You'll make decent wages with any
luck at all out there, and your chances of finding a windfall are
as good as you can hope for anywhere, I believe."

He charged fifty cents, making it easily the most expensive
haircut of my life, but well worth it for the knowledge gained. It
was all I asked. I had not expected anyone to tell me where to
go to get rich — only to point me in a decent direction to start
looking, and from there I was ready to work hard and take my
chances.

My money was fast disappearing. Prices of the simplest goods
were atrocious in Barkerville — even a box of candles or a block
of cheese took a substantial bite out of a dollar, but I felt a certain satisfaction as I prepared to patronize the store under which
I had slept the night before. The general goods store was a single twenty-foot-square room piled from one wall to the other
with commodities of every conceivable sort — unsorted and often dirty. The air was thick with a mixture of sharp odours,
about half of which were pleasant. At the rear, a squat man with

a pointed nose argued in some foreign language with a companion dressed for the street. They seemed close to blows, but then broke into uproarious laughter, after which they argued angrily again.

I purchased a quantity of food, a large tarpaulin, rope, and other small items, thinking as I paid for them that this trade entitled me to one more night beneath the floor.

Since I was venturing next day into the wilderness, I decided to sample properly the food and drink of the city that night. I joined a group of five others in the dining room of the Imperial Hotel to feast at a table laden with beef, ham, venison, vegetables, and numerous sorts of fruit pie. After eating more than I had in several days combined, I stumbled next door to the saloon bar and treated myself to an after-dinner tot of rum. The small room was soon crowded with jovial fellows celebrating their day's good luck. With only the prospect of the cold and dark under the general store ahead, I found it rather difficult to leave. After an hour or two I found myself deep in a bottle of spirits with a spendthrift Greek or Italian. I never learned his nationality for certain, but he spoke no English. I remember a man playing dance tunes on a fiddle, and I recall winding up behind my general store digs with my foreign friend and the remains of our bottle. He talked to me at great length and I listened sympathetically, although, as I say, not a word was comprehensible to me.

It occurred to me later that perhaps this was a sort of preface to a time in the near future when I would have a corpse as my only partner in conversation.

I awoke with the flames of Gomorrah and Gehenna bursting behind my eyes, and flowing the length of my body so as to boil my gastric juices. I drank deeply from a rain barrel on the street, sharing it with a horse who surveyed my condition with sombre disapproval. Then I left Barkerville.

Somehow I forced myself all the way down the valley and through a steep and snowy pass that eventually intersected with the watershed of Antler Creek. Going was hard and slow, but I regarded it only as a fitting penitence for my previous evening's folly, and proceeded with hardly a moment's rest from morning until evening. By nightfall, I had covered the route to my future claim more than double, I thought. Several known landmarks seemed to have disappeared. The creek seemed to have altered its course, and my distinct impression was that Binder Creek did not exist. The sun had just set in the northeast. My misery was complete.

The fact of the matter was that I was soon to be a rich man, but even if I had known this for a surety at that point, I doubt whether I could have summoned up any enthusiasm for life.

I didn't bother to light a fire — merely burrowed into a clear spot at the base of a large fir tree and collapsed into exhausted sleep.

CHAPTER THREE

WHEN I CRAWLED out of my little nest, the morning frost was already gone, and the sun so bright and warm that it seemed the day had been born full grown. With the clear vision of a new day I was able to find with no great difficulty the diminutive trickle that was here called Binder Creek, and I started up its course with a feeling of optimism and rejuvenation.

There was a sharp bend to the creek bed just up from the junction, then a narrow stretch where the spruce and pine branches from each side nearly touched, before the ravine widened into something that might be called a valley. Here I found that a small group of Chinese had staked claims. I saw three sets of newly cut and pounded markers on both sides of the creek, so I presumed that was how many men were there. One fellow was seated on a stump beside a fire in front of a pair of lean-tos back against the trees, and he waved an arm in greeting as I passed.

It was the first claim I had come across in several miles, the country this far down Antler being considered more or less a lost cause by the majority of miners — a situation that sat quite nicely with me. I had no desire to be in a hub of activity. Experience told me that the greatest discoveries were given to the solitary adventurer, and I would be not be satisfied with only moderate success.

A few hundred yards farther along, the stream bed doglegged sharply around a high outcropping of grey slate rock, and in this bend I found the first of another set of claim stakes. Many miners prefer these cul-de-sacs in the water's course, reasoning that washed gold will land there in pockets.

Another fire had been built around the corner and a man in a long green coat was seated beside it, tin cup in hand and a Winchester 30-30 resting close to his knee. I could see that he had a full bucket of tea on the boil, so I chimed out cheerfully:

"Good morning, sir. Zachary Beddoes is my name. Would your hospitality stretch so far as to share a cup of that fine smelling tea?"

He spoke not a word, so that at first I thought he hadn't heard me, although he acknowledged my presence by scowling and setting his cup on the ground. He was a sombre fellow — grey of hair, beard, and skin, although I doubt that he was as old as he looked. The Cariboo is not a home for the elderly.

I tried to put on a cheerful outlook.

"You have yourself a good-looking claim site here, I must remark," I began.

He stood up then, nodded in an upstream direction and said simply, "Come." It seemed to me that he held his rifle rather purposefully in his left hand as he began to lead.

I prepared to unshoulder my burden, but he spoke again.

"Bring your pack," he said, and I did, annoyed at the man's bad manners, but not yet willing to make an issue of it.

He took me a stone's throw distance and stood solemnly beside his upper marking post while I caught up.

"This is my top stake," he stated as if I might not be aware of the fact, then, "Stand on that side of it," waving his gun barrel in an onward direction. I did so.

"Now, then — you've walked once across my property and I suggest it's the last time you try it, or I just might have to blow your head off, which is my right and my practice with trespassers." Speaking thus, he walked away. At that point in my life, I was either quite forgiving or rather easily bullied, for after a moment's hesitation, I did the same, not even considering a violent response to his rudeness. I never learned his name, but always thought of him as Mr. Greencoat.

Binder Creek was not large, particularly at that season of the year, but its course stretched and curled for a good number of miles from where I began to follow it, closer to the Spectacle Lakes than Babcock, as the Negro barber had supposed. As I walked upward and away from previously broken ground, I wondered where that fellow had acquired his information and if he ever ventured out to inspect these wild places himself.

I believe that I may have been less than complimentary in some of my descriptions of the colony of British Columbia, and this is far from fair, for it is a magnificent and beautiful land, even though admittedly an unforgiving one in climate and terrain.

Since leaving Fort Victoria I had seen a good deal of beautiful and majestic country, but nothing on the entire journey was lovelier or more awe-inspiring than the borders of the alpine meadows at the headwaters of Binder Creek.

When I view them now in my mind's eye, I see them green with moss and wild grass, scattered with tiny bright flowers and lichen-coated rocks, but when I first surveyed them on that early May afternoon, they were almost totally white with snow, and beautiful enough at that.

Depositing my pack, I spent most of the remaining daylight hours exploring that high, shallow basin that formed Binder's source. There was actually less snow up there than lower down, as the trees were more widely spaced and the sun was more able to warm the ground.

The vistas open to the eye were, as I have said, quite spectacular. High mountains to the far north sparkled with glacial snowpack — the upper levels of the unexplored earth. To the east, no civilization bespotted the wilderness before Fort Athabasca and the Canadian prairies. When I sat on the rocks with my little telescope out, peering at the land valley by valley, and speculating on what each might hold, time seemed to hesitate, and the world to hold its breath. I do not claim to be a poet, but I maintain that any man of even moderate sensitivity might well find himself so captivated by that landscape that he neglects mundane labours to some extent. Partially as a result of this, it might be noted that the majority of the most successful miners are a crude and callous lot.

My favourite viewpoint was a ridge from which one could look northward and survey a broad, flat valley — largely muskeg and always alive with wild creatures. A silver thread glimmered in the sunshine along the far side of the valley — one of Antler's countless tributaries — and coming out of the dense forest at the far side were many more streams feeding it. I suspect that a shift of geography had at some stage caused much of the drainage to flow north into this valley rather than into Binder Creek, which had become a largely dormant watercourse, compared to the size of the ravines that held it.

I was excited when I considered this — that perhaps a large stream had once cleared its path of overburden, washed the gold veins nicely, then disappeared to allow easy access to the itinerant miner. My theory probably had no basis in fact, but neither do many of the established beliefs of prospectors.

It was mid-afternoon when I looked down from the ridge and first caught sight of the trapper in the distance. At that stage I took him for a prospector, and I paid him little heed. My only impression was that the fellow was a long way afield, and walked with the determination of someone who still had a distance to go.

I wasted too much time that day admiring and exploring the topography of my new home, and I ended up making camp mostly in the dark. Eventually I managed to start a decent fire, cook a grouse I had shot in the morning, and bunk down comfortably enough under some deadfall with my tarpaulin draped above me.

The next week offered continuous clear, sunny weather — it's rare that any sort of weather continues more than a half day in those mountains — and I accomplished a good deal.

I consider myself an orderly and systematic sort of person (although the recounting of certain points of my history may make that difficult to believe) and I approached the work ahead of me in that manner.

I passed the first day in laying out a base camp and my temporary domicile — a lean-to hut constructed from a tarpaulin and existing willow trees. Three more days I used to map out the terrain all the way from the ridge meadow to the bottleneck in the canyon that I felt to be the limit to my territory. Anything below that spot I mentally acknowledged to be in the sphere of influence of Greencoat.

In one hand I took an inkpen and in the other a goldpan, and by week's end I had a large, albeit roughly sketched map of the territory, and a corresponding set of notes. Nowhere did I find what one might call an indication of rich paydirt, but each pan yielded at least some colour. I was averaging twenty to thirty cents, which I considered promising enough to proceed further with my explorations. Only one channel on the north, closest to my downstream boundary, was lacking in any appreciable show of gold.

As had always been my practice, I did not attempt to accomplish much the next day, as it was Sunday, and although I am not a deeply religious man, the habit of a Sabbath rest has proven to be a good one, I think. Towards evening I did, however, shoot a bear, who had come to inspect my residence without invitation, and was forced to drag that carcass upstream and away as far as I could manage, as the meat was too wormy for me to eat. No such inhibitions applied to the coyotes though, whom I heard up there having a tremendous funeral party through much of the night. Their howling sounded most mournful, but I am sure there wasn't much honest sorrow on their part at the demise of the big black fellow, which suggests that even creatures of the wild may tend towards hypocrisy.

Monday morning I started early for Barkerville with an empty pack on my back. I wasn't yet in the proper mood to begin mucking in earnest. I did not wish to be hasty in my choice of a claim as long as competition was slim, so I decided to purchase a full complement of supplies and study the possibilities at leisure before I specified my piece of ground.

At the bottleneck, I crossed the creek and followed a game trail for a while, so as to bypass Greencoat's property, then angled down to meet with Antler just below the junction, crossing the Chinamen's claim as I went. There were indeed three of them, each with his own shelter, and they nodded me politely past in a most neighbourly fashion.

The route to town was much easier on a pleasant day with an empty pack, although the level of the creek had noticeably risen in the few days since I had been through, and in more than one spot the creek bed was flooded and I was forced to detour through the trees. I covered the distance in good time, though, arriving in the early afternoon with time to buy my supplies before the stores began to close. From a blacksmith I bought two pounds of nails and a piece of iron grating I would use for cooking purposes. At a general store I purchased foodstuffs, paper, ink, candles, fishhooks, a swede saw, an adze, and miscellany. Lastly, after checking my finances, I moved on to a dry goods store where I allowed myself the luxury of another blanket. I was

31

close enough to a future flow of income, I thought, to run my savings low.

Since the day I left home I have always kept a brief daily journal, including a record of my earnings and expenses, and the entries made in those Barkerville days are quite remarkable, prices being unconscionably high for any product whatever. Flour was thirty-five cents a pound, coffee a dollar, and my two pounds of nails cost me four dollars American. Quite astonishingly, the storekeepers and miners alike carried on at great length about how low the prices were, now that so much of the road had been completed. I had heard the same sort of talk from fellow-travellers on my journey north, regarding the road itself. "How wonderful," it was said, "that the highway north is now so easy! What a marvel of workmanship!" For my part, I thought the roadway was treacherous and crude, and the cost of living, while perhaps understandable, was no less disgusting.

I now possessed only a few dollars of my savings, which had once seemed so expansive, and I realized that soon my payments must be made in gold dust. That was not such a frightening idea to me, though, and I dispensed another nickel to have a hotel keeper watch over my goods while I walked to Richfield, where I visited the gold commissioner's office. I passed a pleasant half hour examining the official map of the area around my property. Then I returned to Barkerville.

At dusk, when the lanterns were being lit and the workers began to straggle in from the goldfields, tired and exhilarated, hungry and thirsty, Barkerville was truly a sight to behold. It was a beehive of organized confusion, and as strange an admixture of humanity as you could wish to see. On the one hand, every nationality in the world seemed to be represented — Englishman and Scot next to Oriental; Frenchman, Italian, and German babbling in musical polyglot. Conversely, there were almost no women in that crowd, and an equal scarcity of both the very young and the elderly. It was a cracker barrel jammed full of young men, bearded and dirty for the most part, and every one in a hurry.

I took my dinner of cured ham and store-bought bread that night on a bench on the boardwalk. There I met and made conversation with a trio of fellows, as yet with no claim of their own, who were squatting in an unused cabin down the creek, and hoping that the owner would not re-appear before the first of June, so they could take over his workings. We drank a glass of beer together and they invited me to their temporary dwelling, where I spent a more comfortable night than in my usual home under the grocer's floorboards.

That night, I did an unusual thing among miners, for I told them the truth about my own endeavours, although I did not name the location, of course, only that it was some distance to the north and east. They told me with the confidence of the well-travelled and experienced that I had no hope whatsoever. By now I was feeling much more confident of my surroundings, though. I had heard a few local stories myself, and I countered with the remark that before Billy Barker and John A. Cameron had the audacity to search downstream, no one believed for a minute that gold existed on Williams Creek below the canyon. This, of course, was quite true. For that matter, several years went by when local miners never bothered to venture deeper than the blue clay layer they encountered at about fifteen feet, supposing it to be a solid bedrock. Then one day on the Abbott and Jourdan claim, while Jourdan was travelling for supplies, Abbott dug beneath, and had three thousand dollars in gold to show his partner two days later.

These stories seemed marvellous, and the figures astronomical at the time. I was not the sort to even dream that one day soon I would experience such things as would make them all seem pale.

The trio had their own set of stories, statistics, and superstitions, and we talked long into the night. I enjoyed the conversation so much that I had half decided to spend another day with my new-found companions, until one of them happened to mention that an acquaintance of theirs had been suffering from stomach cramps for two days, and there was a possibility that it was influenza.

I was on the path out of town down Conklin Gulch within the hour. I would take no risk with any form of sickness while I was living alone in the cold and damp, and a town overcrowded with unwashed peasants was an invitation to disease. Who could say what sort of poisonous vapours were filtering up from those honeycombs of shaftwork?

On my return to Binder Creek, as I cut across the back side of the Chinamen's claims, I noticed a minor change in the laying out of things. One of them had left the others and had laid stakes at a new location, closer to my own area of exploration. Whether he had a falling out with his partners, or was simply taking their interests to a new locale, I didn't know, but I decided to monitor the situation closely, as I had not yet done my own pounding and paperwork, and did not intend to hurry unless forced to. My hope was that either the negro barber was very selective in giving out his recommendations, or that no one but myself would put stock in his words.

I have never led an easy life, but those six weeks rank as the hardest I have ever spent. I panned the gravel every twenty feet or so, washing away what seemed like tons of mud in the freezing water until I thought my hands would never melt and my knees never straighten. Each result was carefully plotted on my tattered map. At a half-dozen promising spots, I went deeper into the ground, panning out the muck from the pit, level by level, and analyzing my finds. It was back-breaking work, and though my little poke of dust and nuggets was beginning to swell a certain amount, it was scarcely enough to light the fires of excitement I needed to keep me warm and full of steam.

In addition to the toil of prospecting I had to put in some long hours of other work to maintain my survival. Wood had to be chopped, game had to be shot if I wished to eat meat, and planks had to be laboriously sawed from green timber if I meant to build implements such as sluice boxes or a wheelbarrow.

I set up my first sluice box near the top of the main channel in early July. I had been greatly excited to find two nuggets, each the size of a thimble, in a pan of dirt from one of the pits I had dug at about the four-foot level. I felt the fever of expectation upon me, and I pushed myself unmercifully, washing the equivalent of about two hundred pans from that pit, dragging it up one shovel full at a time. After all my exertions, I found nothing more than a small puddle of shiny dust.

More than once, feeling I was on the verge of hitting real paydirt, I experienced this rush of optimism, only for it to bubble away, with myself none the richer. I had expected to find excitement by following the gold rush, but there was now nothing for me but hours of drudgery, punctuated by these frequent disenchantments.

I have failed so far to mention one other of the great joys of living in that wild wonderland — the insects. Once the weather became warm enough to sustain a decent form of human life, it also gave birth to a myriad of species of flies — most of which seemed to be both gregarious and carnivorous. There were horseflies the size of robins, mosquitoes as big as butterflies, and tiny black flies that bit like terriers. Even the ones whose appetites did not lean towards man-flesh seemed to wish to swarm about as spectators or explore the inner regions of my ears and nose. The hum of tiny wings served as my lullaby at night, and greeted me with every new morning.

For long periods I became numb to the dreadful creatures, and of necessity learned to ignore the stinging pinpricks, but from time to time, the song of the black cloud would suddenly impinge upon my senses, and a brief claustrophobic panic would cause me to scream and run down the creek bank for a few seconds of relief.

As I have said, it was a time of great labour and hardship for me, and my moods would sometimes fall into a sullen melancholy, when it was impossible to make myself work. I would be forced to conjure up unlikely fantasies of sudden wealth, and dwell on them for some time before I once again felt sufficiently interested in my claim to recommence the tedious task of shovelling gravel. It is sometimes postulated that hard manual labour teaches a man the truth about himself. The only things I learned were that I hated to work with a shovel, and that my feet deteriorate badly when they are kept constantly wet.

A very short entry in my journal dated July 28 (although my exact figuring of dates was inaccurate at that stage), brings back less than fond memories for me. It says simply "Spoke to Greencoat," and I had no heart then to expand on our meeting.

I had reached the five-foot level of my sixth and last exploratory pit, beside the junction of the main stream and a lower tributary, across the way from the one the Chinaman was working. I was seated on the sluicebox, poring over my figures, when I suddenly became aware of the other man's presence at the edge of the bush behind me.

"You'll be getting close to ten dollars out a hundred pounds right through here, I imagine," he said, as if we were in the middle of a discussion already. I was somewhat taken aback, as that was almost exactly what I myself had figured. I wished immediately that I could mutter something threatening and order him off, but both my rifle and revolver were back in my shelter. Besides, I was only prospecting there — I had no legal authority over the premises.

I nodded and shrugged noncommittally.

"There's better, farther along," I said.

He nodded.

"A little, but not much. Up on the northern-most corner, close to the swamp, where the slate runs parallel to the surface, the gravel is good — good as where I'm at, I suppose, but that's as

------

36

rich as this gully gets." He had approached me casually and was now staring at the chart on my lap. "I see you've got it all marked down. That's good."

I folded the sheet quickly and stood up.

"Fine-looking map," he continued. "You've put a lot of work in, stranger."

"I don't suppose I need your comments or advice, thank you. I'm quite aware of the lay of this land."

"Could have told you what was there for the finding if you'd have asked, you know."

I found that comment both deflating and annoying.

"Yes," I said, "if I'd managed to ask you without getting shot."

"True," replied Greencoat thoughtfully. "True enough, there would be that to consider."

I wasn't sure whether he meant to mock me, but I had enough of his talk.

"You're no longer on your claim, sir, and any rash talk might lead me towards my rifle."

He shrugged.

"Nor are we on your claim," he said with a philosophical tone. "I don't think you've staked one, have you?"

"When I do," I growled, "I might easily drag your body to the edge of my boundary to bury you as a claim jumper."

He didn't answer, but strolled away in the direction from which he had come, leaving me frustrated and angry. Granted, there was no real reason for me to have spoken in such a bellicose fashion, but Greencoat's arrogance, combined with his confirmation that I was not about to unearth the mother lode, had sunk me to the very depths of disappointment and disillusionment. I never doubted that he was telling the truth. It was a little as if he had already used my dreams once, and now they were soiled goods.

For two days I did nothing but hunt, stare at my map, sleep, and wander about. Sitting on the crest of the ridge above my camp with my telescope and my rifle, I would leaf through my options over and over.

I could choose the best hundred feet of Binder Creek and carry on my work as dutifully and systematically as I was able, but that would leave me with only a few hundred dollars — perhaps a thousand, by winter. It seemed scarcely enough to justify a hellish winter camping in ten to twelve feet of snow, nor again the thousand miles of hard travel it had taken to reach it, should I decide to return south before the real cold hit.

I could pack up, call my past weeks of prospecting a bad venture, and try a new location, but chances were that whatever new gulch or gully I moved to would be no more kind to me than this, and I would only have wasted the time I had already spent preparing my camp and building my tools.

Neither of these choices was very desirable, and the third was not much better — namely to return to Barkerville, and see what other opportunities arose. For a while, I persisted with the coarse, dull work of gold mining, but my thoughts began to return more and more to this last possibility.

There must, I thought, be other ways to earn a good living in this country than shovelling muck. Where ten men can become wealthy digging up gold, one more must be able to draw good pay looking after their needs in some endurable way. There would not be much call for dockworkers, Pinkerton agents, or student lawyers in Barkerville, but I decided that before I committed myself to working a claim in that isolated little valley, I would see what work was available in the great gold-rush city.

I believe it was the first day of August when I started for town.

CHAPTER FOUR

I SUPPOSE THAT MY retreat to the relative civilization of Barkerville was due to boredom more than anything else. We human beings carry on a strange relationship with the unknown that allows it to control us in both positive and negative fashions. It is the unknown that fills us with the greatest fear, and again it is the unknown — the gambler's unknown, and the explorer's — that spurs a man on to strive for more than the bare necessities.

Once Binder Creek had become to me a known quantity, I found it difficult to keep her as my wife and only love. I had no plan to abandon her, but the joy of the place had gone with its mystery. Nonetheless, when I arrived in town, my first stop was the gold commissioner's office in Richfield, where a government clerk — tall and very dour — had me sign a form, give descriptions of the terrain, and trace a location on a counter map. I assured him that my stakes were carefully placed in an obvious location, although I had completely forgotten to put them in before I left. I promised myself to do so immediately on my return.

I next proceeded to the far end of the active section of Williams Creek, where I looked for the three friends I had made on my last trip in. I found instead that the owner of the claim had returned from his winter absence and was now alone there, carrying on his work. He was a polite and friendly Scotsman who seemed to bear no ill will toward the fellows he had found on his territory. In fact, he was able to inform me that one of the trio was, to the best of his knowledge, working in a mine on Stout's Gulch. I got the impression from the man that he had been taken on as a partner, which was an impressive achievement, as the claims along Stout's Gulch were, as a rule, more than decently rich. Since most men were not interested in working for wages in the goldfields, accepting a partner was sometimes the only way for an operation to get help.

I looked him up there — the oldest of the three companions, a man named Carl — and waited for him to quit for the day. The other two were brothers, and had returned to Upper Canada after receiving news that their father had passed away.

Carl had the build of a bulldog — low to the ground and very muscular, with a decisive spring to his step, even when he was at his ease. He wore rather thick spectacles, which he tied behind his ears with string, making his blond hair stick up like a rooster's comb. He was not yet in fact a partner in the Stout's Gulch operation, but had agreed to work for wages for one year with the promise that he would become a full partner the next season. This would still be a good arrangement, he thought, as the mine showed no sign of being depleted at all, so five or six months of work would leave him with several hundred dollars in pocket, and a sixth part of a prosperous enterprise.

To emphasize his point, he stood me to a good meal at a hotel, then spent the evening putting beer into me and several other fellows who suddenly seemed to know him well. After this I followed him home and curled up in the corner of his new living quarters — the tool shed at his place of employment.

—

During those hours of food and drink Carl advised me strongly that I should try to make an arrangement such as his. He even said he knew of a place that needed men and might turn out to be a good opportunity. I was convinced, and next day followed his suggestion to a large underground outfit on Lightning Creek, which employed at that time eleven men.

I lasted exactly one day, working in the cold and dark alongside a bunch of Frenchmen from Canada. At some point in the middle of the afternoon I came to my senses and remembered that I had come to town to escape the toil and tedium of mining, not to pursue it in a more repugnant form. I took my wages at the end of the shift.

There were indeed other occupations to try, and I hired on at a couple more over the next few days. It took me again only one morning as a tinsmith's assistant to realize that it would be a most unsatisfactory career, particularly if one were apprenticed to a pompous buffoon who drank while he worked and wept about the wife he had left in California.

I lasted twice that long as a carpenter, working for the firm of Masters and Carson, putting shakes on the roof of a new hotel. The work was better, the air was cleaner, and I got along well with the men. The bulk of them spoke English, and did not smell worse than myself or carry any more exotic forms of vermin on their persons.

My sojourn in the city was going well enough. Whether at work or at leisure, I felt a certain enjoyment in the company of my peers. In the evenings, men would eat and drink in crowded saloon bars, or stand around open fires on the backstreets, or just sit on the planks of the sidewalks and talk pleasant nonsense, but I found myself spending much of my time in quiet contemplation.

On one particularly pleasant evening I found myself standing outside the back door of Top George's saloon, watching a group of fellows toss coins. I fell into conversation with the fellow next to me, a miner of some years' experience named Ben, whom I had met briefly on a previous occasion. He had the habit of cursing so foully and continuously that I dare not transcribe his exact words, but he expressed great surprise when I happened to mention that I was not working my claim at present.

"There's plenty good gold country all different directions," he suggested. "Head yourself out and find a new claim if the first one don't work out!"

"Oh, I don't suppose I'd be likely to do much better at any other spot."

"Then you wasn't gettin' totally left dry at your claim?"

"Not at all."

"You was makin' wages?"

"Good wages, sure enough."

"Then you're plain stupid, ain't ya?"

Ben had a way of saying this that made it seem unlike an insult. In fact, I had a good laugh over it, even while I tried to defend my actions. "Looking for gold is not the only thing a man can do in the world," I said. "Right now I'm making good money as a carpenter. I'm enjoying the job, too. It's something different."

"It won't be something different after you done it for a week or so," Ben replied, and I had to agree.

"There's always something new to try my hand at if I get fed up with building hotels, though."

"But why would you come all the way up to the goldfields to do that for? That's plain stupid! You think you're gonna get lucky and get yourself rich in one day, poundin' nails? Not a chance! But you get back to workin' that claim of yours, and you just might!"

And with that, Ben proceeded to launch into an hour or more of stories of miners who had been on the verge of abandoning their efforts when they finally made the big strike.

I returned to Binder Creek the next day, and the inference might easily be taken that the old mucker had convinced me of the error of my ways. In reality, he had only reminded me of what I already knew to be true, and I would soon have followed that route with or without his advice.

I was being paid six dollars per day — three times what I would make in San Francisco, but good wages were not what I came north to find. I had come for excitement, plain and simple, and it was the idea of sticking a pan in the ground and lifting it up as a suddenly rich man that had seemed exciting. Ben's stories had been effective in one way, of course. As I trudged my way back up the valley, I was once again filled with a dreamy sort of expectancy. Unfortunately the attitude did not last. Within a few days of my return, I had reverted to my habit of spending every third or fourth day away from the business at hand — hunting when I really had no need of meat, or exploring territory I had no real need to know.

My creek-bank operation rewarded me well enough — yielding some days an ounce and a half of gold, which at sixteen dollars per ounce amounted to ten times a good day's wages where I was born and raised. Still, it was too predictable for me, and I say this to my discredit, for I know I should have been more than happy to spend every waking moment toiling for those returns. I did not, though — usually leaning my shovel against the sluicebox long before darkness compelled me to do so, and spending the last hours of each day eating a leisurely meal, or sitting on the ridge of land upstream from me, where I could watch the setting sun plate the broad valley to the north with that more ethereal form of gold.

In late August I took a few days away from my labours to travel down into that valley and prospect down some of the creeks and gulches along its near side. Some places I found no colour at all when I panned, while in others the tantalizing flecks of brightness would appear, but never in any amount greater than Binder Creek had to offer. As far as I could tell, the Negro barber had been correctly informed.

———

Returning from one of these forays, about four or five o'clock on an afternoon of cold spitting rain, I was just about to start up the hillside towards the ridge boundary of Binder Creek, when I saw a man leading a pair of mules along the far side of the swampy meadows. It was the same man I had seen a couple of times before, the man I originally had taken to be a prospector but later had recognized as a trapper. Again, both his mules were laden with pelts. He was evidently on his way to town to sell them. Uncharacteristically for me, perhaps, I felt like a bit of casual conversation, and I shouted across to him, setting down my pack under a stunted pine tree. At first it looked like he might ignore me and carry on, but after a second look in my direction, he stopped. He didn't speak or take a step towards me, but he half-saluted with one hand and spun the animals' lead ropes around a twig while he waited.

Because of the scattered swampy pools that dotted the meadow, I was slow covering the ground between us, and had to keep both eyes on the path ahead, so that after five minutes, I was only halfway across. Looking up, I saw him waiting patiently, twisting the strands of his beard between two fingers. He seemed to be thinking, perhaps smiling, although I couldn't say for sure, at that distance. As I approached, he circled behind the near mule, and began to rummage around in the saddlebag. The idea crossed my mind that he might be looking for a bottle, or a flask, and the notion of sharing a drink was quite appealing, cold and tired as I was. Then suddenly he caught sight of something behind me and straightened up abruptly. Without a word, he took hold of his mules and started away down the valley at a brisk pace, ignoring my further calls to him. I turned my eyes to see what he had spied behind me, and found that it was none other than Greencoat, looking down at us from that particular viewpoint I considered part of my personal domain. His presence there irritated me greatly, although I could not have done anything about it, even if he had still been around when I got there.

Two uneventful days of work passed, and once again I happened to be seated on a log on the ridge eating an evening meal of cold grouse meat and bannock when I chanced to see someone far across the valley moving eastward along the creek. I had my telescope with me, and in the failing light I was able to see the same trapper, this time accompanied by only one mule, still carrying furs, or so it seemed at that distance.

His progress across my field of sight was slow, and I was given ample time to wonder at the sequence of events that might bring him back along that path in that manner. Why with one less animal, I thought, and why should the remaining one still carry its full load of goods? My best speculation was that he must have disposed of both his beast of burden and his furs at the same time, and was unable, for some reason, to sell the remainder. It was too late in the day to pursue the matter, and I returned down the creek bed to my claim, guessing that I would never know what the true story was.

As usual, time proved me wrong.

Two days later I decided to weigh my gold stores as accurately as I could. I was fairly close, I think, considering that my scales were made of a teapot lid, a straight stick, catgut fishing line, and a lump of lead I knew to weigh a half ounce. I discovered that my coffee can contained just over thirty-five ounces of mixed flake, flour and nuggets. I gave myself one more day of working after that and headed in to town to celebrate my reaching the sum of three pounds of gold discovered.

Summer was already fading away. I wanted to be south of Quesnelle Mouth before serious snow fell, which meant that I must plan on being gone somewhere in the middle of October — a thought that should have caused me to use every day with careful stewardship as long as I was earning money so quickly. Mind you, I was already wealthy by the standards of my limited experience of life, and this made me ever ready to dole myself out another luxury. One day off to lie in the sun would be nothing to a rich man like myself, I thought. And what was the use of gold in the poke, if I couldn't buy myself a pound of bacon for a dollar and a half, or a jar of maple syrup for two dollars?

On a Saturday night somewhere around the thirtieth of August, I paid twenty-five cents and allowed myself to be boiled and steamed in a Chinese bathhouse, then met my friend Carl for supper in the George Washington Hotel. The meal was delicious, and after several pieces of pie, we sat for another half hour smoking cigars before exiting into the shadowy evening.

Barkerville was sometimes referred to as *Middletown* because the main street more or less continued south to Richfield and north to Cameronton without a sharp break, and Carl and I strolled leisurely the entire length that evening, enjoying the cool late summer breeze, and ended up, as darkness became complete, in a saloon in Cameronton. My friend recognized some people there, and we were soon seated at a table of six, drinking and talking.

The man next to me was a fellow named Hector Simmonds — sometimes miner and sometimes deputy to Sheriff John Stevenson. I happened to mention that I had once worked for the Pinkerton law enforcement agency, and he proceeded to hold forth for the next hour as if we were longstanding colleagues, telling me what a tedious dandy Stevenson was, and how Judge Begbie would no doubt soon give him the job of making the region safe for civilized persons.

In every profession there are men like Hec Simmonds — men who must promote their own greatness without cessation, more often than not to convince themselves that they are not the failures that they appear. To be fair, it would have been difficult to do a law officer's job in that region, for petty crime was rampant, major crime abundant, and resources to enforce the law limited indeed. There was a wildness in the air, bred by greed, and one could see where a young buck like Hector would find the situation exciting and challenging. He thought it a shame that he was given only occasional employment as a deputy, and then with no real responsibility, but few people in that money-loving populace were willing to part with taxes to pay for any substantial security force. Instead, they did their best to protect themselves and settle their own disputes.

The real law of the goldfields was Judge Matthew Bailey Begbie – a man who no one failed to respect, and who was generally feared more than he was respected. He was called a hanging judge, but he was never known to hang a man not given a proper trial by his peers, nor was he ever accused of being harsher than necessary – necessity, of course, demanding a very harsh attitude.

"He's the smartest, best looking, best speaking, strongest and toughest man in the Cariboo," was Hector Simmonds' deduction. I don't know whether he ever met the good magistrate, but he admired the fellow so much he tried to mention the name regularly, linking it with his own in some tenuous fashion.

"Judge Begbie sent me and Stevenson down to Van Winkle on Tuesday to investigate the robbery of the Barnard's Express wagon. Curious affair, that – real curious. We talked a spell to the driver and the swamper at the roadhouse there, then went with them to a place almost at Beaver Pass, where the holdup took place. One man. Scarf over his mouth. Driver says tall; swamper says medium/short. Driver says Winchester .30-.30; swamper says army carbine.

"He picked his spot good. Just over the top of a ravine there, the beavers have dammed up the crick, and to get around the pond, they got to take the wagon kind of up on the side of the slope, you see. And the land being swampy, they're all three of them – there was a passenger along – they're all three watching the wagon so as it don't tip over into the beaver pond, and this guy with his rifle just ambles up behind and hollers at them. It's a lonely spot to meet your maker, so none of them makes a fuss."

Hec's greatest joy in his part-time occupation appeared to be palming a beer and telling a story, and this one seemed particularly pleasurable to him, even if I was his only listener.

"This guy was clever, you see, a good planner. First he gets the driver to unhitch the horses, and he spooks them off south — takes a shot at their heels and they're halfways to Cottonwood. Then he gets the three men — this passenger, you know, he's an Englishman from England, and I think he thought the whole affair was a bit of a lark. Anyway, the outlaw sends the three of them — after they'd emptied their pockets — he sends 'em walking back towards Van Winkle. From the top of that rise he can see 'em for most of a mile, so he knows they aren't gonna head back and sneak up on him. He's got all day, pretty much, to root through that wagon and take whatever he likes."

At this point, Simmonds leaned forward conspiratorially and spoke in a low voice, not that the other men at our table were at all interested in the story. It was probably a matter of general knowledge by now for everyone but me.

"He got lucky," was the word. "That wagon carried two gold bars — each thirty pounds — and a strongbox with twenty more pounds of dust and nuggets. The Ne'er Do Well Company was shipping it down to the Bank of British Columbia at Quesnelle Mouth."

I found this interesting indeed.

"Eighty pounds of gold! That's fourteen, fifteen thousand dollars," I estimated, and he corrected me with a nod and a grin.

"Better than fifteen thousand."

"And they were shipping all that on a wagon with one driver and one swamper to guard it? How could they do such a thing?"

Simmonds shrugged.

"What else are they going to do? The Cariboo Gold Escort was gave up a couple years ago 'cause no one used it. No one trusted a half-dozen hired guns they didn't know and that the government wouldn't even guarantee, so now everyone pretty much trusts to good luck. Good luck, Judge Begbie, and the

---

48

hangman, of course. Anyway, where's a robber going to go with his loot anyway? Like this fellow — he's got a good-sized lump of gold, but he's also got a troop of deputies checking every man on the trail between here and Lillooet. Every roadhouse will be checking out travellers too — tall and short alike."

"Did you try to track the man? How was he transporting the gold?" I inquired.

"He had a mule — two mules actually, and Stevenson and I did track them as far as Jawbone Creek but once he got on the creek bed — well, you can't do much."

I had to agree with him. The courses of those creeks are like cobblestone — hard and rough, with shallow water spread out to erase what little sign might be left. But Hector Simmonds did have one more piece of information that I found most interesting.

"We trailed him right up to the creek and we found one of his mules there — he'd shot it dead. We guessed it had gone lame and he ditched it with the clothes and whisky and such that he'd taken from the wagon along with the gold. He shot it and ditched it and carried on. We searched down the creek for several miles, but he either stayed on it or covered his trail too good for us, so Stevenson ordered some Indian trackers from Quesnelle Mouth. They should be here tomorrow."

I remembered something I had seen not long previous.

"The mule you found — what all was left with it? " I inquired. "Just clothes and miscellany? No furs?"

"Furs?" he said, and squinted at me through the smoky gaslight. "Curious enough, there was some furs, yes. How'd you guess that, stranger?"

Mercifully my mind was quicker, even after several glasses of beer, than the self-important deputy's. I told him that I had heard some parts of the story from someone else earlier, and he reluctantly accepted that explanation.

I asked no more questions of Hector Simmonds.

———

CHAPTER FIVE

WITH MORNING LIGHT I left the gold-rush town on a new sort of search, although I felt the same expectant high hopes I'd had as a prospector.

In retrospect, I cannot say with certainty what my exact plans were, nor claim to be sure of my motives. My goals were not illegal ones, but I must admit that neither was any altruism involved. I set out to find a bad man who seemed to elude all other legal pursuit. In this I smelled a definite opportunity for personal gain, a gain I hoped would be substantial and readily converted into American dollars.

I started out on a Sunday morning. There was a light frost on the ground.

I had originally thought of travelling past my camp and down into the valley, but it was mid-afternoon when I reached Binder Creek, and the sun was already settling behind Mt. Greenberry, so I satisfied myself with collecting and cleaning both my rifle and my Colt revolver and making up a light pack, suitable for one or two days' journey. After examining it, and thinking things over, I discarded some of the food and replaced it with extra ammunition for both weapons.

I made an early start in the morning, and was able to see the sun rise into a clear blue sky as I rounded the ridge and began the descent into the low flat valley that angles down from where Summit Creek joins Antler and eventually runs parallel to and west of the Spectacle Lakes.

When I describe it as marsh or swamp land, I hope no picture arises of gloomy, foul-smelling bogs, for it is more accurately a sort of pleasant and lovely lowland — water meadow entwined with higher ground of shale, and all blanketed with a thick layer of moss and lichen. The leaves of the few birch trees were turning yellow, and an unearthly sort of mist coiled and skirted on the ground as I broke the silence of that morning with my heavy tread. My spirits were light. Once again I was on the edge of the unknown — a pleasant place to spend an autumn day.

It amused me to think of the more official search party. The sheriff and his Indians would all be trying to pick up the bandit's spoor going downstream and to the south. Their logic was good enough. Who would want to take ill-gotten gains anywhere but south, towards cities, civilization, comfort, and freedom?

I happened to know that the trail led north and east, through the wildest of wilderness, over Mt. Nelson, then probably via the Willow River valley and Summit Creek until it reached the place where I would begin. By that time, I supposed that my quarry would have dropped a certain amount of his caution, and I would be in no need of Indian experts to track him.

My entire train of thought was speculation, but it seemed reasonable to me to believe that if my fur trapper friend was actually returning from a hold up, then he was headed for a hideout in this region. This mountainous route led to nothing but more mountains, so I didn't think he was merely passing through. In point of fact, I thought that his lair was probably relatively close.

———

Following this direction, the country became almost totally impassable within only a few miles.

If my suspicions were correct, he was hiding his criminal activities behind the facade of a simple mountain man, and his cabin might be just around the next bend. He was certainly not being secretive about his path. Almost at the spot where I had spied him a few days previous, I found a whopping stack of mule dung – a blatant, malodorous roadmarker.

As I walked, I toyed with the idea of walking up to him quite openly and in a friendly manner when I found his abode, then quietly checking out the place for anything suspicious, but the memory of Greencoat's threat when I innocently crossed his claim made me review the plan with caution. What, after all, did I know about this man? I could not be sure that he was indeed a highwayman, but neither had I any reason to think that he would have reservations about blasting anyone who crossed his path unexpectedly.

I decided to follow the rules I had been given when working for the Pinkerton Agency in Illinois, the first of which was always to assume that the suspect was armed and dangerous. (This is a redundancy that never ceased to amuse me, for anyone who is armed is also dangerous. The bishop's grandmother is dangerous if she has a revolver.)

Examine at leisure, I was always told, and approach with caution. Be quick to get your firearms at the ready, but slow to shoot.

In three years at that job, I had hunted down a dozen men, alone or with partners, but I had never been fired upon. This new errand was more exciting for me because I was embarking on it for my own benefit and of my own volition, but there was no reason to believe that I was in any greater danger. If I couldn't find this fellow, or if he turned out to be nothing more than he appeared, then I could return to my work at Binder Creek with nothing to regret but a day or two of pleasant travel.

Man and mule were following the little creek bed in an easterly direction and their tracks were easily spotted in any of the sandy stretches, so I was able to make good time and enjoy the sunshine for several hours. As if their footprints were not obvious enough, the pack animal continued to drop memorials at regular intervals. I marvelled at the digestive capacity of that brave animal!

By noon I had covered about eight or ten miles, and I was thinking about stopping to have something to eat, when I found myself at a dead end — a sort of *cul de sac* — where the stream widened into a shallow lake, with tangled dead spruce all around its border. I could see where the valley would continue farther ahead, but not how I could get there, let alone how I might lead a mule through the bog and brush. After looking the area over carefully, I decided that I must have lost the track earlier on and needed to backtrack.

About a half mile back I found the spot where the trapper had given me the slip. It was a simple manoeuvre, but nicely done in a well-chosen spot. If the way had not been so fully blocked farther downstream I might have ambled on for hours. Here, only a single reversed hoofprint by the water's edge told me that the deception had taken place.

They had cut across along the top of a sandbar, leaving a trail a blind man could have found with his cane; then, when the ground was rocky again, they had walked into the creek and stayed in the shallow water as they returned westward.

This is the point in the hunt where a tracker must use his logic, as well as a quality some would claim as intuition and others call luck. I had no way of knowing where man and beast had emerged from the stream — whether upstream or down, north side or south, and there were plenty of places all along where the signs could be easily hidden. These signs were now four days old as well. Far from discouraging me, however, this new development gave me extra enthusiasm, and confidence in my assumptions. What reason to disguise his trail did my man have, unless he was afraid of pursuit?

The hoofprint I had seen led me to believe that they had turned back upstream, and logic told me that he would most likely have his base camp somewhere in the higher ground to the north of these lowlands, so I concentrated my search along that bank, thinking as well that he would probably not have doubled back too far.

As it turned out, all three of my guesses were correct, but it still took me several hours to once again pick up their route. They left few signs of their passing, but to my good fortune, the mule once again proved his singular talent for defecation. Beside a scarcely visible game trail heading straight up the hillside, I was pleased to see a small brown cairn of organic matter.

The trail from there was easily followed, albeit a bit steep and slippery with wet birch and poplar leaves, and I must admit that at that stage I was enjoying myself immensely. The feeling was something I had not felt for years. It was what I had hoped for years before when I had first joined Pinkerton's detective agency – excitement, expectation, and a pleasant sense of danger. Alan Pinkerton, on the one occasion when I met the man, had commented that "Whenever you can find something everyone else considers lost, or catch up with someone that everyone else has given up on, you can expect to command a good reward." I think that on that cool, sun-speckled autumn afternoon as I strolled through the mountain forest, my mind was more on the prospect of that reward than the situation at hand. As a matter of fact, I remember reprimanding myself for not asking Hec Simmonds about the express company reward, as if it were already my due.

I followed the game trail farther than I would have expected, up hill and down, through poplar then pine forest, until I came out on the crest of a ravine centred on a small stream flowing east, which would probably flow into the little lake I had been stopped by at noon. I stood there for a long moment, wondering whether I should turn left or right, upstream or down, when

I suddenly noticed that the much-travelled mule was grazing unconcernedly in a clearing directly across from me. Fifty yards from him was a cabin, half hidden by trees.

Mentally cursing myself, I dodged back out of sight and peered more carefully through the branches at the scene across the creek. There was no smoke coming from the little tin chimney, but that was normal for this season and time of day. The mule continued to graze as if he had not noticed me, but those beasts do not normally pay attention to anything they do not intend to eat or anyone who is not threatening them with a stick.

I watched for about ten minutes, which seemed a very long time, and nothing stirred to indicate any life on the premises. A small window faced me, but at a hundred yards distance, it was only a black square. Ideas and plans tumbled through my mind three and four at a time, but nothing ideally suited to the moment stood out, except to try for a closer look at the little building.

I circled carefully to my right through the bush, crossed the little creek several hundred yards upstream, and worked my way as close as I dared to the far side. There was not enough water in the creek flow to make sufficient noise to disguise my approach, and the ground was well-scattered with leaves and debris, so I was slow in my progress and not altogether silent, but I was satisfied that I had not been heard or spotted by the time I was crouched in a thicket of willows on the far side of the cabin, watching the door.

Again I waited while nothing happened.

It is one thing to know that patience and care are advisable, but another matter completely to actually spend any amount of time staring at a static scene. One of my legs went to sleep. It wasn't easy, trying to shake and flex some feeling into it, without making any noise, and for a moment I recalled some of the frustrating aspects of my former employment with Mr. Pinkerton. After a certain length of time, a person feels downright foolish just watching and waiting — like a man fishing in a rainbarrel.

I made another short circle, positioned myself behind a large, rotten poplar stump, and got a third view of total inactivity for another few minutes.

It seemed fairly obvious that the man was either away from home or asleep within, so I released the safety catch on my rifle, hunched slightly forward, and started towards the cabin.

I had taken precisely one step when a deafening roar split the still air — an overpowering blast that seemed to come from all directions at once. I would not have believed that my reflexes were so good, but I was instantly behind my poplar stump again, just as another shot was fired and a chunk of rotten wood the size of a frying pan flew up into the air. It was definitely not a .30-.30 he was shooting. The gun sounded like it was being fired from inside a well.

I fell to my knees, stabbing my rifle barrel into the dirt, then realized that my backside was exposed and stood up. Flattened thus against the poplar trunk I sensed that my head was sticking up, and I half crouched. Then, amongst all the other thoughts rushing at me was the recognition that I did not know where my attacker was, and where he was shooting from. For that matter, was he sitting still, or was he at that moment stealing through the trees to get a clear view of my back? I had no experience of being the hunted party, rather than the hunter. I didn't like it.

"Wait!"

Irrationally I shouted it, as if we were friends playing a game. Then again — "Wait!"

I hoped this might make him pause for a second or two — long enough for me to think. No clever new plan arrived, so I had to settle for an old, very risky one.

"Don't shoot!" I hollered once again. "Just hang on and don't shoot, 'cause I'm coming out. I'm going to throw my gun out onto the ground, and then I'm coming out into the open. I just want to talk, all right then, friend?"

He did not answer, but I did not expect him to. As I was shouting, I was removing the big Colt .45 revolver from the holster that held it tucked against my chest under my jacket.

"Is that okay, friend?" I called good and loud to cover the sound of the handgun being cocked. Then I slid it into the back of my boot top, very gently. I was already in a tight spot, and it would do me no good to shoot my own foot off.

"Come on out, then." The voice sounded reasonably human. He was somewhere to the left of the cabin door.

I threw my rifle onto the ground, well away from my position, took a long, deep breath, which I knew might well be one of a very few left to me, and sidled out of my cover like a frightened dog, keeping my right arm slightly behind me, and half dragging my right leg.

Two paces into the open I paused, and I knew that one great hurdle had been cleared. He evidently wasn't going to blast me from cover immediately. I tried to look innocent and feel relaxed during those long few heartbeats, and finally he stepped out from behind a pile of cordwood.

He was of medium height and very thick, with a bushel of black hair and beard surrounding eyes that looked like they had been sharpened to a point. Wool trousers and checkered shirt; homemade leather jacket with rabbit fur trim; wool socks — I had come upon him with his boots off.

He could have been any miner or trapper in the Cariboo except for the long-barrelled cannon he swung at his hip. There was a hint of a crouch to his posture and his eyes darted left and right quickly as he walked forward, although he never completely looked away from me.

"You alone?" he asked finally in a low voice. It was a liquid drawl that spoke to me of regions far to the south.

My mouth opened, but I didn't answer. I couldn't decide quickly enough whether it was to my advantage to say yes or no; I was too intent on looking for an opening to safely pull out the

Colt. If I could convince him to take me inside, I thought, I might get a chance as he went through the door.

"I'm alone," I admitted.

He remained on the balls of his feet, ready to jump to left or right, gun barrel directed straight ahead but weaving just a few inches back and forth. Behind him, I could see the mule, long ears in the air, watching us with great interest.

If the rifle barrel at any time moved more than ninety degrees away from me, I decided, I would try to get the drop on him.

At last, he relaxed.

"You really are alone," he said.

I smiled.

He smiled.

Then he lifted his carbine into a shooting position, gave one bark of laughter, and blew a hole in the side of my right coat pocket. I don't remember if I cried out or not, but I jumped and rolled and tugged at my gun handle, all at the same time. The trapper fired again, and a shower of dirt exploded just beside me.

Then I had the .45 out and pointed in roughly the right direction. I don't recall if my eyes were open or shut, but I kept pulling the trigger and jerking the gun down as it tried to jump out of my grip, over and over, until it refused to fire again.

As the stillness returned to the little valley, I realized that at least one out of that magazine full of bullets had managed to connect with the trapper. He wasn't moving.

In the distance behind his body, I watched the frightened mule disappear somewhere towards the swamplands. For another minute I remained on my belly, brandishing the empty handgun. Then I stood up, sneezed the gunpowder out of my nose, and dusted off my clothes. First I took a long look at the bullet hole in my jacket and pondered its implications; then I walked over to examine the dead trapper.

Dead he very definitely was. The long-barrelled Colt .45 is

named the "Peacemaker," and it does make for a sort of peace efficiently enough.

He was lying on his side — bleeding a small amount from his chest and a great deal more from a fist-sized wound between his shoulder blades. I had plugged him as squarely as if I had known what I was doing, and the result was not a pretty sight. Looking down at the first man I had ever killed brought a confused and distasteful mix of emotions, followed by a wave of dizziness and nausea. I slumped onto his chopping block and kept my head down for a moment until it passed over and through me.

"Your own damned fault," I said quietly. I took a deep breath, stood up, and felt my face go hot and cold in turns so quickly that I had to flop back onto my seat.

"Your own damned fault," I repeated to the dead man.

After a few more minutes, I stood again, and headed down to the creek where I washed my face and hair in the freezing water until my self-control was restored. Unfortunately, this confidence was short-lived. When I returned, and surveyed the scene once again, I felt the same sick dread, along with a vague guilt, although I knew perfectly well that I had fired in self-defense. I stood there, about ten feet away from the man I had killed, facing in his general direction, but not looking directly at his body.

"Why should I worry about doing in a rotten dog like you?" I muttered.

I received no response from the corpse; no communication from his departed spirit; no vaporous voice of explanation from the silent, watching forest. Soon, my feelings of nausea and dread turned to a sense of disgust.

"You are a vicious and an unrepentant varmint," I told him. "You bushwhacked me before I even had a chance to double-cross you, so don't lie there looking so offended. I just did what I had to, and you have only yourself to blame. You're a disgusting, faithless bandit and it's no wonder I feel a bit sick. You should be glad to be dead just for your own self-respect."

For some reason, I felt a little better after blurting this out, although I was still a long way from feeling pleased with myself. The north country was turning out to be a study in depression and frustration. First I had sought gold in the standard way, by means of honest labour on my own claim, and had found the exercise to be unsatisfactory. Now, I had come sneaking through the trees after other men's gold, solved a mystery, killed a man, and experienced an even deeper dissatisfaction at the end of it all.

I stood and looked around, more out of restlessness than genuine curiosity.

His cabin was squat and solid — large logs chinked with moss and roofed with turf, dirt floor, one window. Leaving the door open gave me just enough light to see my way around.

A bed across one wall was made of poles four inches thick and supporting a sort of hide hammock made of bear skin. Two empty blasting powder boxes, one on top of the other, served for shelves, and a small table with a willow pole chair used up most of the remaining floor space, except for the corner by the foot of the bed where a small cast-iron stove was placed.

It was a beauty — two feet square and three high, with fancy legs and the name *Palmer* in raised letters across the door. It made me realize, thinking of him carting that cast-iron contraption all the winding way from Barkerville, that the trapper must have lived in this place for quite some time, and poured out as much of his sweat as any law-abiding pioneer.

A map of British Columbia was pegged to the wall logs. It was curled and yellow-stained where the chinking had allowed moisture. Two or three books sat on his shelves next to the jam tins and plates, along with several copies of the *Cariboo Sentinel*. A canvas backpack and various items of clothing could be seen stuffed under the bed. His boots, slightly larger than mine, I noticed, were behind the door.

On the table, besides a miscellany of buttons and burned matches, were an unlit oil lamp and a kerosene cooker with a pot of stew on it. The stew was cold, but beside the lamp was a ceramic mug full of steaming hot liquid. I had arrived at tea time, it appeared, and with some pleasure I swept off a layer of bearberry leaves and spruce needles, and began to drink the brew.

Standing thus in the doorway of his cabin, I felt obliged to thank my host.

"You make a good cup of spruce tea," I granted, "and I appreciate you keeping it hot. We'll have a frost by morning. Hope you don't mind my using your bed tonight. It's getting late, and I'm sure you'll sleep better than I do anyway.

"I'm only joking, friend — no need to look so upset."

A very slight and cool breeze fluttered the poplar and birch leaves and carried to me the rich smell of the mouldering — an ancient, empty smell.

"You should never have tried to bushwhack me," I told him. "You're a worse shot than I am at close range with that buffalo beater. I was going to get your tea anyway, so you might just as well have invited me in. Now look at yourself — bloody and uncomfortable and two nasty holes in your jacket.

"And let me assure you, I'll find your gold as well, so I hope you didn't go to too much trouble hiding it. You might just as well have left it here on the step, because I'm quite determined. Yes, I'll find it."

Already the sky was shading to a darker blue. The search in earnest would have to wait for the morrow.

CHAPTER SIX

ALTHOUGH I WAS loath to touch it, I knew I would have to do something about the corpse before nightfall. It was either that or be faced with lying on the dead man's bed and listening to the coyotes divvying him up in the dark — and while not a sentimental man, I knew I would find that disturbing.

On the other hand, it seemed unwise to bury the fellow. When I eventually got the sheriff out to the place, he would want to identify the body.

During these deliberations, the unpleasant thought appeared at the back of my mind that if I was unable to discover the gold and stolen goods on the premises, I would have no small problem in explaining why I had shot this solitary trapper. Granted, he had acted strangely over the past week, and had shot at me with intent to cause bodily harm, but we were, after all, situated on his property, and I was the one who had come creeping through the bush with rifle in hand.

Until I had solidified my plan of action, I considered it best not to dispatch my adversary to the devices of worm and beetle.

On the south wall of the cabin, two lynx hides had been stretched, and between these hung a good length of quarter-inch rope. Tying this around the body, I dragged it twenty or thirty yards to the base of a stout poplar tree, just out of sight of the porch and window. Here I could hang him safely enough for the time being without feeling spied upon.

I threw the rope over a thick limb which stuck out from the tree fifteen feet from the ground, and made a lariat loop with one end. At first I intended to hang him thus by the ankles, but the mental picture of him dangling upside down was distasteful to me, so I retied the rope around his chest and under his armpits. I knew he was dead, but somehow I felt he should not have to be uncomfortable as well.

Hoisting him up was more difficult than I had expected. He was a heavy brute, and his arms and legs, which had already started to stiffen up, had a tendency to get caught on rough spots in the bark. Finally, though, he was duly suspended with his back to the poplar trunk, and I tied the long end of the rope to a neighbouring tree.

He made a strange spectacle. The lariat loop had pulled his arms up until they stuck almost straight out, and he looked like a scarecrow, or as if he was about to take off in flight. His eyes were rolled back and wide open, giving him a look of terror, and once again my sense of decorum was offended. I trotted to the cabin and fetched his cloth cap. I was able to scramble high enough up beside him to jam it down over his head, half covering his face.

"There now," I murmured, wiping my hands on my trouser legs, "That's good. Can't expect anything more than that."

By hanging him there, I was acting in what I honestly felt to be the best interests of the deceased, but I couldn't shake the feeling of being a sort of grave desecrater, and I found myself talking to relieve the nervousness.

"That's about all I can do for the moment, I'm afraid. I don't

63

suppose I'm obliged to make you look pretty — just keep the weather and the wildlife off you for the time being. Take it or leave it."

Sometimes in the mountains it seems as if the stars come out before the sky starts to darken. Someone turns up their wicks a little prematurely when the weather is clear and cold, and they are already gleaming at the full when the robin's-egg blue overhead begins to darken towards navy.

The first thing I did when I got back to the cabin was start a fire in the little wood heater. Under a moose hide beside the main woodpile, I found kindling already cut and a stack of birch bark — enough to last a week or two at least. Matches were neatly stored next to the foodstuffs in one of the powder cases. It seemed my late host was an orderly man, and as I waited for the room to heat, I supposed I might as well find out if he could cook, since there was already a good-sized pot of grub ready to be set on the stove top.

I ate two good helpings along with bannock from my own supplies, and mentally congratulated the fellow on his culinary prowess. He made a fine stew from potatoes and some meat with a taste akin to pork — bear perhaps, or porcupine. I didn't let my imagination wander any further than that.

Warmed and fed, I began to inspect his belongings more carefully, hoping for some clue as to where his valuables might be hidden.

The floor was solid earth, smooth and undisturbed as far as I could see, which was disappointing, for if he had buried the gold indoors I should probably have been able to spot something. I was looking for a fairly bulky load, and I quickly searched the ten-foot-square room to no avail.

I did, however, find some things of interest in a small carrying satchel made of soft leather, which was half hidden behind the pile of clothes under the bed.

First I drew out two bottles, and taking them closer to the kerosene lamp, discovered that they were sealed and certified as Scotch whisky, bottled in some distant place with a name that only a Scotsman could pronounce. To say that this was something rarer than gold would be an understatement. There were two brands of whisky produced and bottled in Barkerville, and the miners all agreed that they were "refiners' liquor" – that is to say that if one poured the stuff over gold quartz, it would dissolve the rock and leave behind the pure metal. The precious stuff that the trapper kept under his bed was probably not available in most drinking establishments of San Francisco – certainly not in the nether corners of the Cariboo.

I wasted no time before pouring a sample into a ceramic mug. I was no connoisseur of spirits, but it was most certainly pleasant to the taste and gentle in the throat, and I paused to savour it for a long moment before delving deeper into the leather bag.

All that remained therein was a pair of steel-framed spectacles, two silver dollars, eight fancy brass buttons, and a small, blue clothbound book – Lamb's *Tales From Shakespeare*. It was a well-read volume, wrinkled and dog-eared, marked randomly by pen scratches inside the cover page. The frontispiece was inscribed "To Neddy, on your birthday, 1854," which brought a variety of thoughts and speculations to mind.

That salutation, combined with the nature of the book, implied to me that the recipient might have been a very young man. A gift to a scholarly lad from mother or aunt. That would have made the man I hung from the poplar tree considerably younger than I had supposed. I had assumed him to be older than me, but he could, in fact, have been still in his twenties. A beard can certainly have a misleading effect.

Then again, the inscription could well have been written by a sweetheart to her beau. In that case, where was this darling of ten years past? Were her affections long since alienated and forgotten, or was she now somewhere waiting for the lover whose life I had cut short?

A third, very likely possibility was that the writing on the opening page had never been addressed to my dead trapper at all; that the book was given to another unknown, and I had shot a man named Archibald or Nathaniel.

For convenience, I assumed from that time on that his name was indeed Edward, and I began to mentally refer to him as "Dead Ned." The Lamb's *Tales* was too well handled, and given a very special hiding place; I could not believe it to be only a casual, secondhand possession.

There were three other books in the cabin, but these stood in a row on the back of the table, held between two blocks of quartz/granite amalgam. Baker's *I Discovered Africa*, and a book of some mystic's theories on the end of the world sat on either side of a large publication called *The Trapper and Furrier's Guide*, which alone of the three seemed much-used. It was a sort of almanac issued by the Hudson's Bay Company, containing numerous hints and bits of information on the setting of traps, skinning of animals, and storing of pelts, along with price lists, maps, and diagrams of various tracks.

Did my newly expired acquaintance learn his trade from a book, I wondered? Was the time he spent on the trapline purely a facade to hide his criminal activities, or was he rather a bona fide man of the wilderness, who had dabbled in robbery as a sort of sideline?

Once again the third possibility had to be admitted: that he was entirely what he appeared — a lonely woodsman, made a bit trigger-happy from cabin fever — and that the only criminal was myself — killer of an innocent man.

I poured another cup of whisky and examined the room once again without finding any hint of illegal activity or ill-gotten gains. Only the liquor saved me from worry and depression. Tomorrow, it appeared, I would have to widen the area of search, and scour the campsite and surrounding bush for evidence of a hidey-hole.

I was not totally disheartened, but in that dark and unfamiliar cabin, with only the sound of a strong wind for company, I couldn't help feeling a bit nervous. I knew perfectly well that the trapper had lived alone, and yet some instinctual caution made me listen for sounds of someone returning – a rightful owner, ready to throw me out of this place.

I must admit that my rather childish fear made me carry the lantern outside with me when I found it necessary to attend to the other activity associated with drinking. It was a beautiful night. If one must waste time casting spent liquor onto the ground, I supposed it was best done thus, with shadows dancing and windblown clouds scrolling hastily over a sparkling sky.

Buttoning my trousers, I wandered the few paces through the bush to where my silent companion was dangling.

"Ned, Ned. You're looking better this evening. I think the night air agrees with you."

The ropes had settled around his chest a bit, and his arms had dropped almost to his sides, so he did look a little less daunting. The cloth hat pulled down over his eyes was a great help as well.

"My friend," I continued, "the more I get to know of you, the more I appreciate you. It wasn't actually you, it was your belongings that I was hunting for when I came out here, but that doesn't mean I have no respect for you now. I certainly do. You're evidently a good worker, well organized, you can cook, and ah, yes — you have most excellent taste in whisky. The perfect host! You serve it up unstinted, I must say. Sir, I salute you!"

I daresay I appeared something of an oddity to the owls and raccoons that night – lantern in my left hand, ceramic mug raised to toast my suspended friend.

"My gratitude and my admiration know no bounds, Ned, but there remains one fact which is unarguable. You are a thief. You know it and I know it, and since you have divorced yourself from the cares and desires of this world, you might just as well come clean. Cough up, so to speak, my good man, and tell me where the gold is. Stop being coy, and I have a proposition for you.

"You must pardon me for tinkering with your private possessions, but I had to have a look around, you understand, and I've just by chance come to the knowledge that you have a sweetheart somewhere. All right then — either a sweetheart or a mother. Of course you have a mother — I know that, but I'm guessing that she might be a bit livelier than you, old man. Anyway, mother or sweetheart, I'm sure they could use a chunk of your gold stocks, and I'm willing to share. Now, the sheriff and the judge, they'll have ways of finding out who you are, and I can find out who your next of kin is through them, Ned. A thousand dollars in gold would keep their lamps lit and their chimney smoking for a good long time, and the Ne'er Do Well Company will never miss it. They'll be happy as stuffed geese just to get the main part of it back, and no questions asked. I'm planning to keep a little piece for myself, you see, just in case the idea of a good reward hasn't crossed their minds. That way no one gets offended, and I don't have to go asking please and thank you. Ten percent, maybe — that's fair, and I'll end up with enough to look after whatever woman you've left behind."

My cup was empty and I was cold.

"You let me know, then, but hurry it up. A stiff doesn't get many good opportunities coming his way, you know. I'm going back inside, but you'll like it better out here. Not being unsociable, you understand, but it feels like a real chill blowing in, and that'll keep you, well, held together. Just mind them crows, and keep your hat down over your eyes. Those critters have no sense of decency when mealtime rolls around."

With my third cup of whisky in my hand, I stood again at every angle to the room, and glared at each of the very limited number of nooks and crannies available for inspection. The place could very well have been drawn up in the Hudson's Bay *Guidebook* under the title – "A Well Appointed Trapping Cabin." No log sounded hollow; no piece of furniture covered over a hidden pit; no tin or box contained anything but the proper sort of food. I slouched into the chair, cup on lap.

The bottle of elegant Scotch had, by that stage of the evening, done Hell's own business inside my tired brain, and done it well. Apart from my days in the goldfields, I was never much of a drinker, and I suppose the stuff took me by surprise. When I attempted to lean my chair back and swing my feet up on top of the shelves, I overbalanced and nearly wound up flat on my backside. Instead, I kicked the shelves apart with my flailing feet – one of the powder cases landing beside the stove, spreading its contents on the floor.

I had time to utter only one mild profanity before I saw Dead Ned's hiding place.

Between the two boxes was an almost unnoticeable space about an inch and a half deep – a sort of shallow tray, a foot or so square. He had lined it with a pair of perfect white rabbit skins, and on these were placed a stack of paper money and six pocket watches.

After staring stupidly at the tableau for a moment, I reached out and leafed through the pile of currency. It was a mixture of bills – some British and Canadian, but mostly American; all in all, the equivalent of perhaps a thousand dollars.

I then turned my attention to the timepieces. They were arranged in two careful rows of three – two silver-coloured, and four gold – one with a hinged cover over its face. I picked that one up and opened the cover, and as I did so the wheels within jiggled enough to move the second hand a few notches. Up to that moment it had been stopped at precisely twelve o'clock.

Looking down, I realized that the other five watches were likewise stopped at precisely midnight (or noon, if you prefer). Hour,

---

minute, and second hand on each one were exactly aligned towards the top of the dial.

This discovery unnerved me slightly for some reason, and I replaced the device, its cover closed, and took another drink of whisky. After a moment of puzzled thought, I reached out and shifted one of the other watches slightly with my fingertip. Immediately the longest hand tripped forward a few steps and stopped. The same occurred when I shifted its neighbour. They were precision pieces.

But why such careful settings, I wondered? It would be no simple task to line up those eighteen chronometric arms, although time was obviously in no shortage during the long nights of a trapper's winter. Closer examination revealed that the bottom powder crate had been nailed to both floor and wall to keep it from jiggling, even after such a bang as I had administered to it a few minutes before. That was a good deal of engineering to ensure the arbitrary immobilizing of a batch of clock wheels.

Some very peculiar sort of superstition it had to be, I reasoned, and such was not out of character for the men of that region. The darkness of night is so unfathomably black, and the sounds of the wind and the wilderness are so full of suggestion, that eccentricity begins to sprout from the sanest and most logical of men.

It was another man's superstition entirely, but it affected me as well in some way, for I felt disinclined to tamper with the little tray of personal valuables. I speculated, though, that the assorted types of money and the collection of watches were the sort of things that a highwayman might naturally accumulate. Once again, my confidence was bolstered that I had indeed tracked down the man who had absconded with the Ne'er Do Well Company's gold bars.

The thought was not totally pleasing, however, for with it came the knowledge that he had crossed twenty-five miles of mountain on his way home from the robbery, and he might well have stashed his booty anywhere along the way.

It took my liquor-fogged eyes a lengthy time to register the corner of a sheet of paper protruding slightly from under the rabbit skin. I drew it out carefully, shifting the little white fur blanket, and setting all the watches in motion. It might take an hour to realign all six. At that point I realized why it had originally been done.

"So now you know," I whispered to Dead Ned. "I've found your secret, my friend."

It was a single sheet of good quality paper — five inches by eight, marked with red ink. Two long, wandering lines crossed the page, one small square was drawn near the bottom, and six stars, each encircled, were connected by a dotted line that formed a diagonal loop.

"Your watches are ticking, Ned. I've found your treasure, and it's too late for you to do anything. But maybe you can relax a bit now. You're a suspicious man — careful and suspicious. I'll bet that tonight will be the first really sound sleep you've had in years."

It took no genius to figure that the little square was the cabin wherein I sat, and the irregular lines a pair of creeks. What lay where the dead man drew the stars I would discover on the morrow.

Daylight was not a pleasant thing, when it next penetrated my senses. As soon as I shifted my weight in the leather hammock bed, I began to suffer the unavoidable after-effects of poisonous quantities of liquor. I remained half-seated, leaned against the log wall until I was certain I would not immediately disgorge my previous evening's meal, and tried to make sense of my surroundings. My brain was like a whirlpool, and as I reached into its swirling patterns, I came up with only random, scattered thoughts and impressions. I remembered discovering the hidden map, and the promise of gold bars to be found, but at the same time I recalled standing over the corpse of a stranger, dead by my own hand. It was a poor trade-off of memories, first thing in the morning.

As my thoughts became marginally more coherent, the outlook for the day deteriorated even further. The light that came through the cabin window had an unmistakeable pallid luminescence. I did not need to look outside to know that it had snowed.

Even with a treasure map in one's possession, there are times when it is impossible to feel excited. I managed to pull on my boots, find a cup other than the one I had used the night before, and stumble and slide over the white-sheeted clearing to the creek, where there was hope that I might extinguish my flaming thirst.

The wind had blown in the cold of winter with this early snow, and the shallow creek — only an inch deep in most places where it needled its way between the rocks — was frozen. Desperately I bashed at the surface with my cup until I finally found a deep enough pocket of liquid water to yield a decent drink.

Standing there in my boots and underwear, cup in hand, I felt much closer to being a poor, sick beggar than a rich, young adventurer or a fearless bounty hunter.

It was at that point that I once again remembered that I had killed a man. The fact registered in my mind, then slowly curdled in my belly. It was no longer just the alcohol that sickened me. There was a disruption — an affliction of soul and spirit that could not help but manifest itself in bodily fashion. I had not broken the law of the land, if the truth were told, and before God, who presses a higher standard than any court of man, I could defend all my actions and most of my intentions. Still, there was a bleak uncertainty within me.

Through a screen of branches up the slope, I could see the outline of Ned's body, and at that moment I was glad that I did not have to approach nearer. I had a sense that I had inadvertently become involved in matters too great for me, matters best left to God alone.

The mule had returned and was standing at the edge of the trees, watching me with laid-back ears and a solemn expression. I suppose a man has nearly hit bottom when he receives pity from a hungry mule.

I drank a couple of quarts of water and dragged on my trousers. Even the mental image of a pair of heavy gold bars was incapable of rousing any enthusiasm from me. Work was a better cure. Against one outside wall, between the woodpile and the cabin, was a large stack of dried marsh grass which I took to be the animal's winter feed. He seemed grateful for it, at any rate, and allowed me to tie him by a long rope to a stake near the cabin. I expected to use him soon, and I had no wish for him to try his chances in the bush again.

After that, I chopped some wood, forced myself to swallow a few bites of bannock, and felt a bit more human. The sun speared through the clouds from time to time, and it appeared that the snow might not last the day. I shouldered my rifle, folded the map into a shirt pocket, and started out for the trapper's line of stars.

The near end of the dotted line lay due west of the cabin, but rough ground and dense underbrush forced me to circle south to approach it. Taking this route, I found that the bottom of my map roughly corresponded to the edge of a large marsh or shallow lake into which several of the creeks in that area flowed. Of necessity, I followed its meandering margin, although it was by no means easy walking. It was often a tangle of snaky willow and alder brush along with the dead spruce and balsam that some previous high water had smothered, and the light fall of snow added to my troubles by disguising the potholes and ditches full of icy water.

It took me two hours or so to negotiate the semi-circle to the spot less than a mile from the cabin where the first star was marked. I suppose I was tired, and my feet were surely soaked, but in the full current of excitement I didn't notice these details much.

The map gave me two points of reference with which to find my goal — the place where the creek met the swamp, and a well travelled game trail, for that was what I discovered the dotted line to be.

I don't know exactly what I expected to find when I got to that point. Obviously there would not be a sign saying *Gold Hidden Here* nailed to a tree, but I suppose I assumed that something obvious would present itself when I reached the general vicinity.

Several times I reviewed the map, even walking some distance down the game trail to ensure that it did indeed follow the route marked by a dotted line. The spot where I returned to stand was not large enough to call a clearing, but it was definitely the opening of the path where it met the swamp, and that was where the bright-red circled star was placed.

I criss-crossed the ground repeatedly, kicking at the snow, gazing up into every tree, and using my rifle butt as a broom to open up the smallest windfall, but I found not the slightest piece of evidence.

I was squatted down at the icy edge of the marsh, grumbling to myself, when I noticed a pair of beaver swimming through the shallows fifty feet from me. Standing up and looking farther into the water itself, I realized that Ned had set beaver traps almost within arm's reach of where I crouched.

I was suddenly afraid that I had discovered the unpleasant truth about my treasure map.

I fairly ran down the game trail from there — a veritable Roman highway compared to what I had just struggled through, and within ten or fifteen minutes had reached the junction of the path and the creek, where another star had been sketched. Now that I knew what I was looking for, it took me no time at all to spot what I expected to find. A pair of marten or mink sets had been laid just up from the stream bank beside the trail.

What I had in my possession, it seemed, was not a guide to buried treasure, but a diagram of a dead man's trap line. He had died, it seemed, defending the location of his traps.

I carried on farther down the rough track that corresponded with the dotted line, but no longer with hurried steps – no longer with eyes wide in anticipation.

The next two stars were placed quite close together at a point which, if Ned's scale and bearings could be trusted, would be about a mile due north of the cabin. Again I found the traps without much difficulty. In the first, I discovered a marten peacefully stretched out, but I couldn't be bothered to collect him at that moment. At the next star there were placed a pair of traps – one close to each side of the path.

These demanded more of my attention, but not because of any hope for gold.

Both traps were empty, but they had been sprung. Not only that, they had been dragged to the end of their restraining chains, and thrust into the undergrowth. The ground around each was scratched up as if with some gardening tool, and dirt and snow were scattered on the traps. As if to provide a final insult, between the two was a pile of animal droppings, still steaming slightly.

Although I had never before seen the type of tracks which surrounded the spot – much like a marten, but larger – almost six inches in length, I could identify them easily enough. Even before I checked them, I knew that only one animal indigenous to that area would treat the work of human hands with such contempt.

Certain supposed experts would testify that the lower animals do not experience such emotions as anger, hatred, or malice. Such experts have had no contact with the wolverine. The Indians exhibited a deeper knowledge of the beast when they classed it as a fur-bearing devil – an evil spirit incarnated and set loose among the trees. Wolverine are not numerous in any region, but a trapper or a settler would readily decree that one wolverine in

75

a thousand square miles is simply one too many. They feed on whatever is available, and will kill whatever crosses their path. Sixty pounds of wolverine is a match for any living thing in the wilderness, including man, for they possess a demonic cleverness that compensates for any advantage that human intelligence might give.

I had no desire whatsoever to prove my manhood against such an adversary. I had barely survived my last attempt at tracking down a resident of that region, and my initial impulse was to return to the safety of the cabin to plan my next step carefully. A superstitious image crossed my mind — a bear-like wraith guarding the dead man's cursed gold.

Common sense told me that I was a well-armed superior being, and that the wolverine was only a potential hazard — a doomed one, if I kept my eyes open. It was almost unavoidable that I should confront and destroy him, for we were quite close to the cabin, and there I had a dead body strung up a tree, and a mule tethered to a post. I couldn't have chosen better bait to draw him.

I make no pretence at being a master tracker, but with a fresh light snow and relatively open country, I had no trouble in following him. As was evidenced by the still-warm droppings on the trap, he was no more than a few minutes ahead of me. I walked with my rifle at the ready — safety off, bullet in the chamber.

The beast's tracks went up an incline in a general northwest direction to begin with, then he circled back to his left — parallel to the game trail I had originally followed, but skirting the ridge a quarter mile away and above it. His trail wandered back and forth as he sniffed and rooted into every windfall and hollow, and the expectation that I was probably gaining on him made my caution even keener.

A sort of bowl-shaped hollow filled with bog and bulrushes presented itself, and my quarry skirted its eastern side, rummaging for any sign of nest or burrow in the high leathery grasses.

Even with the fresh snowfall I did not find it easy to discern his spoor through that rough vegetation. An amazing thing it is to me that a creature of such a stocky, bearish build can creep through the forest with only the occasional broken twig and split branch behind him.

I wasn't much worried about losing my way, although I stopped to regain my bearings quite regularly, for I knew that travelling thus, either west or south, I would soon be intercepted by one of the bodies of water that could be followed back to the cabin. Should the animal decide to carry on north, I would follow him only long enough to see him out of my sphere of concern.

As it was, he turned to his left again, and headed downhill and to the west. When his route crossed the trapline he continued his counter-clockwise circuit, back towards the place I had begun to pursue him.

As I passed the third trap I saw the marten that had been held in its jaws when I first passed that way an hour earlier. It had been ripped in two. The wolverine had not stopped to eat it, but had only paused before carrying on.

He was tracking other game — more lively and challenging to him. Once again my belly constricted.

I only walked a few more paces before I stopped to consider. I was now travelling a circular route, along with another well armed killer, and exactly who was pursuing and who being pursued was a matter of arbitrary viewpoint. The main difference between the two of us was that he was in familiar territory, and probably feeling in much better health. Viewed thus, the odds were definitely in his favour.

I gave up, turned around and took two, or at the most, three steps towards home before I heard a sound like a low bark or a harsh cough — a sound that I couldn't locate, unfortunately. Mentally, I had pictured the wolverine behind me at that stage, so I was starting to turn myself when he burst out of a thicket of juniper and willow ahead of me.

I was just able to shift and face the attack before the brute hit me, knocking me backwards so far that it felt as if I had fallen off the roof of a house. Even as I landed with all my wind burst out and my senses stunned, his jaws clamped into the flesh between my shoulder and my neck. The heavy cloth of my jacket might have been thin silk, so easily did those knife-sharp teeth shred it and pin themselves into my muscle and sinew.

The pain was overwhelming — a horrible fire bleeding down my back and up into my face, where I could feel the wiry fur of his cheek pressed against my own.

Two facts loomed clearly enough in those long seconds to take control of my consciousness. First, I recognized that the animal was trying to get a grip on my body with his forepaws. After that, he would either chew out my throat or scrabble my intestines onto the ground with the claws of his hind legs. To stop this, I tried to keep rolling, batting at him with my free left arm, hoping to stop him from gaining any firm purchase.

Secondly, I realized that I still held my rifle. My hand was on the trigger, and my grip was firm, amazingly enough, but as we rolled around I had no way of telling for sure where the barrel was pointing. My right arm and the gun were both sandwiched between our bodies. In that death grip there was no chance of working it free to aim it, nor would there be any second shot to fire. One of us would die before then. As pain and fear became unbearable, I knew that I would have to fire, and hope for the best, but years of practice and instinct made it very difficult, even at that critical moment, for me to discharge a firearm that seemed to be pointed quite directly at my own head.

Whichever of our heads the bullet contacted, I would gain from the outcome.

I fired, and immediately realized that I had lost in my gamble, and had shot myself in the belly. New fire burned my flesh, making me squirm and writhe in wild twists. I rolled and crawled and pawed at my chest. It took a long moment to reach the knowledge that I was not only still alive, but free of the carnivore that had sought my life.

The wolverine lay about three feet distant, his back to me. The two yellowish stripes that ran the length of his black body seemed to be pointing at a reddish tuft of fur hanging to one side at the base of the animal's skull, still dripping blood.

I looked down at the powder burns where the muzzle of the Winchester had lain against my chest, and considered that I was on the better end of the exchange.

Then, for a time, I was unconscious.

CHAPTER SEVEN

W HEN I AWOKE I saw broad spatters of blood on the
snow, and a good deal more had soaked my shirt and coat. Not
much of this belonged to my erstwhile friend of long tooth and
fur. I was badly injured, and on this I blame the irrationality of
my next decision – to depart from my roundabout route and
head across country, straight south to the cabin.

Soldiers wounded in the war with the South were known to
do much the same sort of thing – begin to walk aimlessly and
without fear of being lost, until they simply dropped dead in
their tracks. It is a physical sickness that infects the mind – a
delirium that caused me on that occasion to lose much of my
sensation of pain, while robbing me of my intellect. At the best
of times I would have had to be very careful in that trackless
bush to avoid losing myself forever, but when I left the dead
wolverine behind me, I stumbled straight forward – down ra-
vine-side and up again, through bog and bramble with no caution and no reference to guide me except the vague feeling that
home was somewhere up ahead.

It is to this day miraculous to me that I reached my destination. So vague was my grasp of reality during that trek, that as I staggered down the creek-side I eventually encountered, looking only at the rocks and gravel under my boots, I stumbled right past the cabin — thirty feet away — without recognizing the spot. Luckily the mule began to bray loudly enough to catch my attention. I'm not sure whether it was the odour of blood or the scent of the wolverine on me that frightened him so, but I mumbled deep thanks to the poor creature as I tottered past and into the cabin.

Reaching that refuge revived my faculties to some degree — at least long enough for me to use my good arm to throw a few more pieces of wood onto the coals that remained in the heater.

I pulled off my clothes and was about to collapse onto the bed, but a glance at my bloody and unclean shoulder convinced me of one more thing I ought first to do. Returning to the tag end of the bottle of whisky I had befriended the night before, I poured a full cup. Half of that I downed in a couple of graceless gulps. The other half I poured into the open wound at the base of my neck.

I gave voice to my pain loudly and poetically for a few moments, then coiled my body into the blankets on the bed, where I spent the rest of that day and night.

All I remember of those hours is successively being very hot, then freezing cold. Later, in the blackness of the cabin, with only orange needles of half-light escaping from the cracks in the stove, my fever gave me visions of devils and leaping carnivores at the foot of my bed.

Morning found me miserably weak and consumed by thirst, but with my coherence returned, at least. Whatever poison had been spat into my body by the villainous wolverine had worked its way through without killing me, and now all I needed was a day or two to regain my strength.

Virtually all my clothing except my trousers, socks, and boots had been destroyed in the attack — shredded, bloodsoaked, or lost on the path. I was forced to rummage among dead Ned's effects and to wear what I could of his clothes, wishing at the time that cleanliness was rated a little higher among the priorities of trappers and miners.

He was a shorter man than myself, but thankfully his second pair of underdrawers was a two piece set — not the combination type that I normally preferred. Undersize combinations would have put a pressure on my shoulders that I could not have endured, but since he was a heavier man than I, his chemise draped over my injury quite loosely. It was short of course, and my navel was exposed to drafts, but beggars, as they say, must not be choosy.

My entire upper body ached and protested at the slightest movement. My left arm and side were frozen and useless. Already, though, the open flesh had begun to crust over and there were no signs of it becoming septic — none of the angry redness that signals poison working its way into the blood. I considered dousing it with alcohol again, but even the thought of that brought tears to my eyes, and I promised myself to wash it when I had hot water.

Once I had managed to dress, I set about the necessary chores with Spartan dedication and frequent rest stops when I became tired and dizzy.

First I needed water, and I carried two pots full from the creek, placing one on top of the woodstove, along with the remains of the stew. Next I managed to hack one block of spruce into kindling-sized pieces and start a fire. Lastly, I reached deep into my stores of compassion and used the last of my strength to drag an armload of strawy marsh grass to the mule. The poor beast was tethered on stony ground with little to eat.

By the time I went back indoors, the cabin was mostly warm, and I felt quite proud of myself, albeit exhausted.

Half of that day I spent sleeping. When awake, I forced myself to eat a bit, drink water, and cleanse my wound. In the afternoon I sat in the doorway for a while, taking the air and allowing the healing rays of sunshine to work on me, even as they mopped away the remnants of snow. I tried to keep my mind on a positive track — away from the unanswered questions about my current predicament, but the unpleasant truth kept returning to my shadowy thoughts.

There could be no neutral outcome to this affair. If I succeeded in proving Ned's guilt by finding the stolen gold, then I would be a hero in the eyes of the law, and a tidy bit richer. If I could not prove my suspicions with concrete evidence, however, I would be viewed as a glory-seeking fool who shot an innocent man before the poor fellow could explain himself. Feeling as miserable as I did, I would readily have admitted the latter, at that stage.

My fever returned with nightfall, and I spent another night fighting with phantoms.

I slept late next day — a good sign for my recovery. Not so pleasant, though, was the arrival of a new malady — a foul bout of diarrhea. I don't know how long the trapper had been working on the pot of stew that I had eaten for two days, but I blamed the stew for my gastric distress. I threw it as far as I could into the bushes, pot and all.

Squatted down in the weeds beyond the woodpile I shouted at Ned, "The game is over, and I had the last laugh, you scoundrel! If you think this is some kind of revenge, you're being cruel and unfair."

Needless to say, I did not feel terribly energetic that day. Neither could I come up with an obvious next place to carry on my search, so I contented myself with rest and recuperation.

For matters of diet, I boiled a batch of red beans and potatoes into a tasteless muck, which improved greatly when I threw in the crumpled leaves of certain weeds that were hanging upside down in one corner of the room. Whether he was a real woodsman, or only a desperado in disguise, I couldn't say, but Ned obviously knew something about edible plants. Not many of God's little green things can hope to make boiled beans and potatoes palatable.

I no longer felt a soul-sickening guilt when I pondered the fact that I had killed the man, but it was still an oppressive thought, for practical as well as emotional reasons. I wished at least that I had been able to interrogate him before I shot him. At times I felt sure that the fellow could not have been the outlaw I had taken him for, but when I thought it through, my original hypothesis was supported by too much evidence, circumstantial though it was. New questions presented themselves as well. This was a prime season for furs, so why, if what I had in my coat pocket was a map of his trapline, was he using only a dozen or so traps? For that matter, several of the ones I had seen were not even set. Why was the map hidden so carefully? Why would an honest man be so secretive and suspicious about his trapline? Undoubtedly, Ned was more than the simple trapper he wished to appear.

After rolling all this over and over in my thoughts, I was as exhausted mentally as I was physically.

To pass the time, I read whatever was available — the trappers' handbook, which was entirely tedious, apart from the illustrations, and Lamb's *Tales* — a most enjoyable volume.

Turning to the book's frontispiece, I read the inscription written there and once again regretted that I hadn't tried my alternate plan when I tracked Ned down — to come upon him openly as a friend.

Was "Neddy" really lovable? I tried to imagine him fresh-faced, smiling and in love, but I could not. The picture in my mind's eye showed his smile as a wily grin, and he still held a gun behind his back.

Seated on the bed with a cup of strong tea, I took note for the first time of the few other random markings across from the dedication. These consisted of four short, curved lines, several inches apart, with a number and abbreviation beside each. Next to the longest line was carefully printed "50 p.," while "20 p.," "15 p.," and "10 p." were inscribed beside the other segments.

The "p." I understood to be the English abbreviation for "pence," and thought that these jottings were some type of accounting figures. Perhaps as a child he had thus kept track of his petty debts. At first, I decided it was one more facet of this intriguing character's history that I would never have a chance to clarify — young Edward as a tiny lad in an English country village.

Thinking again, I remembered the brief words I had heard him speak, and recalled that his accent was not English at all — it was American. Also, the printing was too fresh — done, as a matter of fact, in the same colour ink as my map.

My curiosity was up. I pulled the dirty, folded paper from the pocket of my discarded shirt, and held it in one hand, Lamb's *Tales* in the other. Examining the two, I discovered that not only was the ink the same, but each piece of paper was the same size, with a matching blot of ink covering one corner, where evidently the pen had been laid down and had leaked.

As I moved from the bed to the table for better light, I knew there was a link to be made here that held a great deal of importance, but it remained indecipherable for a time.

Finally, I began to laugh — chuckling at first, then breaking into a deep and joyful laughter that I found difficult to stop. When at last I gained some control, I strode to the door, swung it wide open, and shouted.

"I've got you, Ned! I finally got you all the way, you mouldy old rascal!"

Then, leisurely and confidently, I picked up the map and the book, which I held by the frontispiece page. Placing one on top of the other, I pressed the two sheets against the window and observed how the lines traced each other.

When I set up the ink blots in the corner so the one on the book's page exactly covered the one on the map, the four short lines aligned themselves perfectly with four segments of the trapline's dotted path. Each of the little curves began at one of the stars that marked a trap set, and wound along the game trail for a portion of the distance to the next star. It took little imagination to guess that the "p." abbreviation stood for paces, and all that was needed to find the first designated location was to step off fifty paces, or twenty, or whatever.

And what would I find at each of these points? I was quite sure I knew, but to say I was anxious to view it with my own eyes would be the grossest understatement.

The only problem was that the nearest cache was most of an hour away, and darkness would be complete long before I could make it back.

I was still tempted. I had been over the route once, and I had a lantern and matches, but the penalty to be paid if I lost my way in the darkness was too hard. I was weak, the ground was slimy with new-melted snow, and the breeze would likely extinguish my lamp.

I looked at my watch as if it were a note from my worst enemy. Twelve hours it would be before I could start out. Although my tired body could well use another half day of rehabilitation, the momentary excitement had left a void when it passed, and I felt cheated.

I thought of a celebration drink to pass the time, but the very smell of the whisky was repulsive to me — sour and medicinal. I contented myself with tea made from more of the trapper's weeds, and warmed-over potatoes and beans, which by now had developed a crust the thickness of bacon rind.

Disappointment and impatience led to melancholy, which turned to a feeling of nervousness that I could not shake. I tried to raise my spirits by visualizing my moment of victory as I returned to civilization leading a mule carrying Dead Ned and the gold. People along the street would catch the odour of decay, see the iron set of my expression, and turn silently to follow me with their eyes.

I would confront Sheriff John Stevenson in the open air outside his offices, with a crowd of the curious around us taking in every word.

"There's the man. Here's the gold." He would look ruffled and confused while he examined my goods. Then suspicion would cloud his gaze.

"There was loose gold taken along with this, and one of the bricks has had some pieces carved away," he would say. "Where would they be, Mr. Beddoes?"

"I undertook the search only after you had given it up, Sheriff," I would reply with a hint of contempt. "The outlaw must have stashed that portion before I reached him, while you were looking down south."

If there was any question that total public support was behind me, I might then and there bare the wolverine wounds, and describe the hardships undergone while furthering the cause of justice. No mention need be made of the whisky.

If there was a reward forthcoming, I would accept it gracefully as my due. If not, I would be no man's beggar, but retrieve at a later date what I had invested in a safe place on my way into town.

The scenario was satisfying to some extent, but it did not compare with the exhilaration of actual discovery, and it did not help much with passing the time. Three or four times during the night I got out of bed and checked the time by the faint fingers of light that escaped from the wood stove.

Never in my life had I carried a watch; now I referred to one every other hour. I had claimed it as the finest of the six watches in Ned's secret drawer, and I appreciated its fine decoration and smooth, heavy feel. I wished only that it would move faster.

Morning finally came, and found me dressed and drinking tea at the table. When the light was good enough to distinguish between the mule and his pile of feed, I started across the meadow. In one hand I held my rifle, in the other I carried a shovel. On my back, my pack was empty except for Lamb's *Tales From Shakespeare*, with a map between its pages.

In the poor light, I tripped and skidded my way over the wet grass and clay, but I made good time. By six o'clock I was at the first set of traps — fifty paces away from my initial discovery.

Where exactly, though, did I first place my foot? How long were my paces compared to those of the dead trapper? When I got there, did I look to right or left? Were the goods buried or cached up a tree?

I was getting sick of these questions. For weeks and months, I had ordered my life according to the pull of mystery, the glittering unknown, and the thrill of the chase, but enough was enough, and as I stomped out the fifty paces, I yearned desperately for some end to it all.

At a slight curve in the path next to a large rock, I set down my rifle and began to rummage in the undergrowth on both sides of the path.

It didn't take long.

Five feet from where I had leaned my gun, I swung the shovel against what appeared to be a tangle of fallen spruce branches and heard a hollow, drumlike sound. Under a thin layer of boughs and needles was a wooden box, three feet wide, one deep, and four feet long. It was constructed of hand-hewn lumber, but carefully built, with very few cracks at the joins.

I had trouble manoeuvring the tip of the shovel head between two of the boards, but after that it pried open easily, and I was able to reach the contents — all wrapped in oily cloths.

Guns.

There was a Maynard rifle, and two identical Henrys. A Sharps buffalo gun with a handsome, carved stock caught my eye, as well as a Winchester like my own, and several more rifles I didn't recognize, both muzzleloaders and breechloaders. Handguns also had a place in the box — Smith & Wesson and Colt, both army and naval issue, as well as models with more obscure names engraved on butt plate or trigger guard. There were single-shot guns, repeaters, and revolvers, and to correspond with every rifle or pistol, it seemed there was at least one small pouch or box of ammunition, as carefully weatherproofed as the weapon itself.

I appreciate a well-made firearm as much as any man, but at that particular time, the sight of those worthy machines made me feel a chilly disappointment and a growing anxiety.

What had the maniac done with the gold? I didn't want a ton of weapons; the Ne'er Do Well Company didn't want them, and the Sheriff in Barkerville didn't want them. Who would want them? Had Ned sold the gold to outfit some army of brigands? Had I shot some outlaw general planning to take over the Cariboo goldfields by force?

I left the guns unwrapped and the case open, and headed off briskly down the trail towards the next spot marked on the map. It was a mile or more distant, but I wager I was there in not more than ten minutes.

I stepped off the twenty paces so quickly that I went more than the proper distance, and only after fifteen minutes of tedious circling and thrashing in the undergrowth did I discover a small nail keg, half buried in the soft duff of needles at the base of a fir tree.

I made no attempt to be neat, but crashed my shovel head repeatedly onto the wooden lid until it shattered. At first glance inside I was disappointed to see the familiar dirty brown of oilcloth, but when I reached into the keg and grasped the material, I found a double-sided pouch, such as express men use to carry mail. From its reassuring weight, I knew that this pouch was not full of mail.

I braced myself, and lifted it out. When I spread it on the ground and opened the flaps, I beheld two rough gold bars — approximately sixty pounds in total weight, and most probably ninety to ninety-five percent pure.

I sat back on my haunches and just enjoyed the sight for several minutes, like a farmer surveying a well-ploughed field after a long day of work. Only after that did the memory return to me that a strongbox of loose gold had also been taken in the robbery. No trace of it was to be found, neither in the keg, nor in the immediate surrounding area.

The next box was more easily found than the previous two. Most of the spruce boughs that had originally covered it were scattered by the wind. It was built of rough lumber, as the first had been, and measured about three by three by one and a half feet deep.

When I had pried the top off I involuntarily caught my breath. As a matter of fact I believe I may have stopped breathing altogether for a minute or two.

I had hoped to find the strongbox holding twenty odd pounds of loose gold, and that I did find. What shocked me was that it was sitting on a stack of a dozen or more assorted other containers, and they likewise appeared to be full of gold — fine to rough dust, rice grains, and nuggets the size of walnuts. The stuff was loaded into leather pouches and canvas pokes, coffee cans, glass sealer jars, and boxes both metal and wood.

Once my momentary stunned surprise had passed, I lifted them out of the crate and spread them on the ground, guessing at weights as I went. If the strongbox was twenty pounds, I thought, then the jars must each be ten, and the largest canvas sack better than thirty.

When I had emptied the box completely and peered into each individual container, I made an accounting and reached a total of roughly one hundred and twenty pounds of raw gold. Including the two bricks a half mile behind me, I now possessed about a hundred and eighty pounds.

Rapid arithmetic spun out a figure of fifty thousand dollars. For some reason, my immediate thought was that for that sum I might very likely be able to buy the San Francisco City Hall.

As if in a dream, I carefully restacked the odd-shaped bundles of wealth into the wooden box. I felt like a child rewrapping his Christmas gifts and replacing them under the tree. One leather poke, filled with a pound or two of small nuggets, I retained and dropped into my pack before recommencing my tour.

There was one more drop-off point marked on the Lamb's *Tales* frontispiece, and that was another half mile distant. To reach it, I had to cross a wide gully with boggy ground and twisted underbrush along its floor, and I twice lost the path completely and had to retrace my steps. On the other side, the route wound along parallel to the gorge, and where it narrowed to a crack I found the trap set — three small traps for marten or mink, all of them sprung and inactive.

Carefully I walked off the prescribed distance of ten paces, then took my shovel and hacked at the bases of the trees and among the clumps of deadfall.

After a half hour I had no luck at all and was totally mystified. I had rechecked the map, repaced the distance, and rescoured the ground on both sides of the track, but no box, barrel, or burrow presented itself.

I had already discovered more than I had hoped for originally, so I should have been happy to abandon the site without regret, but my curiosity had again been roused. It appeared that the deceased miscreant had very deliberately sorted his ill-gotten goods, and distributed them according to several types — guns, gold bars, and loose gold (although why he found it necessary to spread them over half of God's allotment of wilderness I do not know).

What, then, could he have planted at this last, most distant station?

It was nearly eleven o'clock. I took a bannock biscuit out of my pocket, unstrapped my canteen from my shoulder, and sat down to ponder what I might have missed.

I had finished my meagre lunch and arrived at the conclusion that the trapper had at some time past moved this final stash, when my eyes finally lit on a coil of rope draped on the peg of a broken branch of the spruce directly in front of me.

The coil hung just above my eye level, and leading upwards from it was a six-foot length of rough line and a dun green seaman's bag which dangled easily at hand, yet well camouflaged. With a leap and a pull I had it at my feet.

From the feel of the sack I could tell it contained only paper, so what I expected to find within was paper currency, but I was only partly correct. I found two hundred dollars or so in the bag, but more importantly, I discovered there the personal papers of a half-dozen or ten different souls — all of whose fate I could easily enough guess.

Ned was an even nastier fellow than I had originally supposed.

Inside a leather tube sewn shut at one end I found the laborious accounting lists of an unnamed miner. Month and day were listed on the left, the weight of that day's take on the right. At the end of each month a running total of gold on hand was kept. The only declarative sentence on the document was written at the end of May. It said "I do agree and swar that I will hed for home aftr geting 250 ounses." The last total on the page was 194 oz.

Two diaries rested among the papers, and I pulled these out for later perusal. As I myself keep a journal, I felt a special interest in these. Glancing in one — a black, hardbound volume, I read:

"Am abandoning my share of the workings on French Creek after the dispute with J.W. I will try prospecting on the other side of Cunningham Pass. Even if results are not as good as here, I will at least get away from this ongoing conflict."

Judging from the penmanship, he was an educated man. He made further entries for several weeks before he evidently met Ned, and escaped from all of life's ongoing conflicts.

Also in the bag were a dozen or so letters, a certificate of honourable discharge from The Royal Navy, some newspaper clippings, a deed to a farm in Washington State, and scrips and scraps of other sundry papers. Lastly, there was a small, hinged watch box, and therein two small mother of pearl hair ornaments and a lady's gold ring set with one small diamond. My euphoria of discovery was replaced by an ambivalent gloom as I considered these few oddments of jewellery.

Perhaps my curiosity could be viewed as morbid, but before I departed, I took several items to examine at my leisure. Everything in the cache was intriguing in its own right, but I contented myself with the two diaries, and a couple of long, descriptive letters, as well as the military medals and the lady's ring, the implications of which still bothered me.

The walk home was slow and uneventful. Along the way, I stopped to re-seal the nail keg and the box full of firearms. For the first time that day I took notice of the weather — now raining a thick and chilling rain.

By the time I reached the cabin, fatigue had overtaken excitement, and without even bothering to tend the fire, I collapsed onto the bed, where I spent most of the afternoon.

When I arose at four o'clock, I felt more tired than ever. The exercise of chopping and carrying a few sticks of wood helped a bit, although it was both painful and awkward to do this with my injured shoulder. I boiled water for tea, and while it steeped, took the mule to a new tethering spot farther down the meadow. Returning indoors, I placed the pot of spuds and beans onto the stove, resolved to shoot some meat at the next opportunity, and took my mug of tea outside. It had stopped raining, but the sky was the colour of cold ashes.

Steaming cup in hand, I walked once around the outside of the cabin, once around the clearing that served as a yard, and ended up seated on a stump, looking up at the dead trapper hanging against the poplar trunk. A pair of crows who had dropped by for a bite to eat left when I arrived. "Ned, Ned, Ned —I'm disappointed," I finally said as I sipped my hot brew.

———

93

"Disappointed indeed. Now that we're practically old buddies I could forgive you much, you know. Waylaying all those strangers, mind you — that's a bad business, Ned. You're lucky no one takes much interest in their fellow man up here, or the poor misfortunates would have been missed.

"You picked 'em careful, did you? Travellers on their way, were they? Prospectors who worked a bit too far afield?

"Oh well — who am I to talk? Not exactly perfect myself. Gold and greed — they'll drag the strongest of us off the straight and narrow. And the chance of a bit of adventure — that's just as bad, isn't it? You start off just wanting a little bit of excitement, and where does it take you? Bang! You've killed some joker before you know it. You did them in, and I did you. But, Ned, I found the diamond ring, and that disappoints me terrible. I don't know what your background is or what sort of circumstances got you into your line of work. Maybe bushwhacking your neighbour is what a proper fellow does where you come from, but killing women — that I don't go along with. How did you expect to get away with that?

"I'm sorry. A man has to draw the line somewhere, and that's where it is for me." I spit out a few dregs of tea-leaf, and banged my cup empty against the stump. The crows were getting noisy and impatient for me to be gone, but I had a few more things to say. "Still, I suppose I should thank you. You've made me a very rich man if I can ever get the yellow stuff out of here.

"I really did intend to take the gold bars back, or at least I think I did, but I can't see turning over your stack of dust and nuggets to some pack of politicians and bankers who'll just divide it up amongst themselves.

"So the good news is this, Ned: I've decided to let you go free. I could have turned you in and ruined your good name, but as of now, you're free to do as you please. Of course, since the authorities won't be able to give me your real name now, I won't be able to track down your sweetheart or your next of kin to give her that thousand dollars I mentioned earlier. My apologies.

94

"I've got some worries of my own, you know. Problems. For that matter, I think you might have fretted about the same situation yourself.

"How do I get this stuff out of here and cashed in? I don't dare take it to Barkerville, or even Quesnelle Mouth — too many questions too easily checked. I'll have to carry it, as is, at least to Fort Langley, and preferably all the way across the border. Five hundred miles; two hundred pounds, plus supplies; and me with a gimpy arm. By the time I got back today I couldn't even carry the shovel with this hand.

"How did you plan to manage it? Was that express wagon your last fling? You shouldn't have got greedy; you were already stinking rich.

"And speaking of stink, Ned, the breeze has shifted, and you're none too nice to sit next to anymore.

"I believe I'll do my thinking inside."

CHAPTER EIGHT

*T*HE MORNING I started back to Barkerville began with a filmy mist over the blue sky, but by nine o'clock the sunshine had burned it away, and the day had developed a genuine warmth. As I climbed up and over a rocky bluff, bypassing a wide loop in Antler Creek, I took off my shirt and carried on bare-chested. I was optimistic as I considered the daunting prospect of moving the stolen gold out to civilization. The rays of the sun felt luxurious and cleansing on my bare skin. Mountain weather is capricious, however, and I soon felt the tickling sensation of tiny, cold raindrops on my back. Moments later, the rain turned to light snowflakes. The sky was still blue, with only an occasional knot of cloud, but such, as I say, was normal for that quixotic climate. Once I grew accustomed to it, the feeling of snow on bare skin was not overly unpleasant, and I walked thus — half disrobed, through the falling snow — rejoicing in my good health, which had been so much at hazard of late.

I felt, as I walked, like a man re-emerging into a wider world after a long respite in prison or a hospital room — invigorated by the autumn hillsides: the broad, empty spaces, the expanse of moss and low berry bushes, and the great variety of weeds, herbs, and ferns. In that harsh country, where rock and gravel leave little space for good soil, and where fierce winters rule over half the year, life of small and hardy sorts exerts itself with a beautiful determination. No chunk of slate forces itself out of the ground without being painted over by delicate lichens and ornate fungus; no grey stick of scrub submits to total annihilation until its twisted limbs have sucked every drop of nourishment from the ground. No nameless weed in that airy region exists for its brief moment without bedecking itself in tiny, bright blossoms.

My journey that day was leisurely and contemplative for two reasons. Firstly, as I have said, my aesthetic enjoyment was greatly increased after a week or so of poor health, confinement, and introspection. Secondly, I was still vaguely unsure of my exact plan of action.

My immediate destination was the claim on Binder Creek. I had invested enough time and energy in the place to want to ensure its security, even though I had no longer any intention of carrying on operations there. I also realized that if an explanation was ever required for my possessing large quantities of raw gold, I had best be able to say that I was the owner of an active claim.

In reality, the gold I would be transporting would be easily recognizable as having come from many different locations, since each creek and drift provides ore of distinct appearance — round, well-washed pebbles that have been worn smooth in some pocket of water, or fresh flakes and fingers of metal only lately broken from the quartz that held them. Some of my new-found wealth was brightest yellow and as pure as if it had been refined. Some, from different sources, would be honeycombed with quartz, rust, and sand.

Still, in case of emergency, any plausible explanation might satisfy the authorities, and in that eventuality, I wished to be able to put my best falsehood forward. Binder Creek would be duly registered and open to their investigation.

———

I was only about three miles from Ned's cabin when I noticed campfire smoke just off the course of Antler Creek, down a gully with a trickling side stream. Evidently someone was prospecting, or had set up permanent workings there, and this troubled me slightly, being so close.

I did not stop to investigate, but as I continued on, my thoughts returned for perhaps the hundredth time to a picture I had in my mind of friendly old Ned stopping to chat with a solitary miner on an isolated claim. A bit of talk, a cup of coffee, a joke, a laugh, and a bullet in the back. The trapper would clean up the premises at his leisure, and if anyone actually knew that the unfortunate prospector had ever been there, they would assume that he had called it humbug and gone back south.

Looking at the distant twist of smoke, it struck me that the man who started that fire was a lucky little fly to wander so close to the web now, after the spider was gone.

The snow flurry ceased almost as quickly as it had begun, and the rest of the walk was warm and pleasant. In the early afternoon, I started up the valley side through the trees, and arrived at the ridge meadow to find a pair of grouse waiting like a small feathered sacrifice near the spot where I had been accustomed to sitting and surveying the valley. Not wishing to seem ungrateful, I shot the two of them and carried on, down the course of Binder Creek to my claim site.

While my campfire was heating up a pot of water, I hastily gutted and plucked the two birds. It had been a long walk, I hadn't eaten meat for several days, and the aroma was delicious. To preserve my sanity, I was forced to leave the immediate area, so I strolled down the creek, looking over the familiar ground for any changes that had occurred in my absence. Everything was virtually the same, of course, except that the single Chinaman had gone, leaving only a couple of stacks of gravel tailings and his wood chopping block to show that anyone had ever paused there. I didn't know whether he had left the country, or simply returned to partnership with his brothers, but I didn't then venture far enough downstream to check. Instead I returned to tend my cooking fire.

A Ruffed Grouse makes a pleasant meal for one — sinewy but tasty, with a flavour and texture much like rabbit. Ideally, it should be cooked for a long time to tenderize it, but I'm afraid my hunger got the better of me, and I ate the first half of it nearly raw. The flavour was decent enough, but it was about as tender as a cowhide glove.

While darkness crept into my little camp, I sat on a grey, weathered snag and stared into the orange coals, wishing I could think of some relatively secure way of transporting my new-found wealth. No such idea was forthcoming. Instead, a cool breeze arrived, bearing the moist, chill edge it had picked up from snow on higher ground. Even if I had never gone off in search of the Ne'er Do Well Company's gold bars, I thought, I would be deciding to leave the Cariboo about now.

My little lean-to shanty seemed suddenly very frail and ugly as I bunked down that evening. While Ned's cabin had seemed dark and airless, like some sort of crypt or mausoleum, in comparison, my own home now felt as cold and close as a coffin.

I drifted off to a restless sleep, with the wind blowing right through my makeshift walls and keeping me on the edge of wakefulness. Late autumn is the coldest time of year, when a man's body still feels that it has some right to warmth and comfort. Later it forgets the sensation completely.

When morning came, I was too cold to sleep and too tired to rise, so I lay there a long time, curled up like a snake in winter — too sluggish to squirm. Finally I crawled out of my hole, pushed together a fire, and heated tea in my billy can. It was well after eight before I had the initiative to start for town.

I was not, of course, overly alert. I had spent too much time in thought, not enough in sleep, then huddled against a campfire until my face was baked and my backside frozen. Stumbling down the gulch with rifle and pack on my back, hands deep in pockets, shoulders hunched, I failed to cross over the creek as was my habit.

"You're a man who likes to flirt with danger, young fella." I looked up to see Greencoat glowering at me. His rifle was at the three-quarters position, resting on his left forearm. His right hand held the stock by the hammer, fingers free of the trigger, but looped through the guard. For a long moment we stood there, glaring eye to eye. Finally he spoke again.

"I've already given you a warning, and here you are again — trespassing on my land."

Glancing down, I saw his neat, three-sided marking post not more than four paces from my feet. I had almost completely crossed his claim, but I was still inside the boundary. Rational thought dictated that I should apologize, step lightly, and so end the confrontation. My neighbour did not choose to think along that line, however. I didn't either.

"Is that your stake?" I asked politely.

A second or two passed. He was suspicious, and unsure of the implications of my question. When finally he nodded slowly, I drew my hand out of my side coat pocket holding the Colt .45 already cocked.

Only his eyelids moved.

I took basic aim at the little stake, and blasted it five times, blowing it into splinters, and nearly destroying both our eardrums. When the ringing echoes had died down enough that I could hear myself speak, I said "You'd better cut yourself a new one." Then I turned my back on Greencoat and walked the rest of the way down Binder Creek.

I followed a slightly different route into town than I normally used, and it was three o'clock when I found myself on a high piece of land at the opening of Shy Robin Gulch, just off Grouse Creek. I felt a mixture of relief and excitement as I looked down on the city of Barkerville, with Cameronton just beyond, down the valley, and Richfield around the corner to my left. It was no scene of beauty – just a flat, grey expanse of cabins, shanties, aqueducts, and footpaths spreading up the hillsides cradling Williams Creek, with a ring of smoke hanging there that could never seem to escape from the valley. The grey clouds were draped like a drab woolen scarf about the town's shoulders. After the splendid colour of the autumn forest, this aspect should have been depressing, but at that moment it was to me a wonderful expression of human life and desire. Thousands of men hurried and scurried about down there, vitalized by the hope of finding one special thing.

I had already found it.

Any one of them, of course, would take it from me in a minute if I lowered my guard. Caution and secrecy were the order of the day.

My plan was to purchase one more pack animal and, together with Ned's mule, which I had left back at the cabin, work my way inconspicuously south, keeping up the appearance of a poor, hapless prospector. In addition to my supplies and gold, I would carry a maximum of firearms and ammunition selected from the dead trapper's private armoury. Even if Governor Douglas sent a platoon of infantry after me, they wouldn't stand a chance.

It wasn't a great plan. Two animals take a fair amount of care and attention. There would be heavy lifting and carrying, with long hours of walking involved, and I was still not completely recovered from the wounds inflicted by the wolverine. I would be in danger from law officers and outlaws alike, over six hundred miles of rough roads and rough weather. For great reward, though, great risks must be taken.

To begin with, I wanted a bath, a set of underwear that fit properly, and a meal I could eat from a plate at a table. My first stop was the Bank of British Columbia, where I exchanged three ounces of Binder Creek gold for currency.

The bank was quite unlike those in more civilized cities. The main part of the building was like a warehouse, caged off from the public by strong bars and solid wood countertops. The patrons were left only a small corridor of space across the front where they could wait to do their business with the clerk, who stood at a small gap in the iron barricade. At busy times, the customers would often be forced to line up on the elevated boardwalk outside the front door to wait their turn. It was certainly a secure arrangement, but not at all convivial, particularly when the clerk seemed to be tired and depressed. He was small, pale, and well-dressed — most unsuited to his present locale. I tried my best to mirror his emotions as I played the role of a luckless gully-grubber.

"Horrible, isn't it?" I said to him, "but that little poke is all I have to show for six months' hard work."

"Horrible place, this," he agreed without showing much interest.

"I'll be glad to be shot of it."

"You're lucky, all right, " he grumbled. I felt a bit sorry for the poor young fellow, for unlike myself, he was probably just as miserable as he seemed.

"You expect to stay on for a while, do you?" I inquired politely. He looked up at me with red-rimmed eyes.

"I'm here on contract."

"How long is the contract?"

"Three months."

"And how long have you been here now?"

"Year and a half." He dismissed me by looking over my shoulder to the next customer, and I shuffled off.

After my encounter with this young master of finance, I found it much easier to wear a gloomy countenance. I purchased underwear, a shirt, and a newspaper, then returned to the Colonial Hotel, where I spent a leisurely hour in a hot bath.

I possessed no medical training, and a close inspection of my wound after I cleansed it told me little, except that it was still ugly and sore. The weakness and recurring ache in my shoulder made me suspect that the wolverine had managed to rip some of the muscle completely apart, but I was nervous about doctors at the best of times, so I chose to ignore it for the time being. These things took time to heal, of course, and I was already learning to compensate with the other arm.

I decided to postpone my dinner until I had checked out the availability and price of mules. I was luxuriating not only in the warmth and cleanliness, but also in the atmosphere of the town itself. After the solitary weeks, each face spoke loudly to me — of ambition, success, and failure; of the resentment of the hungry, and the altruistic friendliness of the suddenly rich. It was constantly necessary for me to remind myself that my mask must be that of the disappointed failure.

It was difficult to keep from grinning. I felt like a little boy, delighted with the base-drum sound my boots made on the board sidewalk as I tramped my way towards the stables just down from the hotel. There were a couple of horses for sale there, but no mules. Two other places, both nearby on the back street, gave me the same story.

It was the time of year when a great number of miners packed their belongings and headed to more hospitable climes for the winter, and for some reason or other, mules seemed to be the creature of preference as a pack animal. I myself would gladly have used a horse, but I needed two animals for the size of my burden, and I didn't consider myself a good enough horseman to manage two of them — especially animals with which I was unfamiliar. Beside that, I already found myself the owner of one mule, and I thought it inadvisable to try to use two different species in tandem.

At a fourth stable, I found someone who at least knew of the whereabouts of a pack mule. A negro yard man told me of a blacksmith drunkard who possessed one which he wished to sell. I thanked him, obtained the necessary directions, and found myself ten minutes thereafter behind the blacksmith's shop in what was referred to as a corral, although it was only a foul-smelling outdoor stall.

The farrier himself was a squat, bald Englishman who, true to the stable hand's report, sweated rancid whisky.

"He's a grand little animal," he claimed, with ill-staged pride. "And the only reason I can bring myself to part with him is that he's been so faithful to me these three years that I can't bear to see him suffer through another of these Godforsaken winters. You're going south, are you, brother?"

I replied to the affirmative as I looked the beast over. For once, it was not difficult to appear downcast. He was a sorry-looking old runt indeed, and it depressed me to think that just when I had come into possession of a treasure beyond my greatest hopes, I might be forced to entrust it to this mangy little grey swayback.

The blacksmith must have sensed my dismay.

"Aye, of course you can't reckon a good mule by its looks now, can you? They're not given to great beauty at the best of times, are they? It's character you want now, don't you? Character, courage, strength . . ."

I expected from the sound of things that he had probably named the thing Lord Nelson, and fed it molten iron since it was foaled.

"What's that?" I asked, pointing to a large shaved area on its flank, centred on some sort of sore.

"Oh, that. Yes, that spot." He shrugged. "He's rubbed herself raw against a rail, hasn't he? No worry there, mate. No worry there."

He ran his hand down the mule's back once in a gesture of feigned affection, and I couldn't help but notice that the single stroke removed a noticeable handful of hair, which I did not consider a good sign, even with my limited knowledge of those animals.

The thought that I found most dismaying was that there appeared to be no better mule available in the whole of Barkerville or Cameronton.

I thought that the approved thing to do when purchasing any member of the equine species was to examine the teeth before discussing the matter of price, so at that stage I put one hand on Lord Nelson's jaw, the other over the bridge of his nose, and tried to part his lips.

With a speed I would not have believed possible from the old wretch, he clapped his jaws at my hand like an alligator. I almost matched his speed, and kept the damage to a bit of lost skin, but he locked onto the sleeve of my coat and we enjoined in a battle of tug of war that had everyone momentarily in a frenzy, including his besotted master.

"Hey there, none of that! Let him go! Don't hit him, brother! Let him go! Don't fight him! Easy! Easy!" he wailed.

Suddenly the mule released his grip, I lost my balance and sat in the mud, and the blacksmith and myself exhibited our knowledge of colourful expressions.

"What do you want for him?" I finally shouted, taking the man completely by surprise, for I'm sure he had lost all hope of making a sale.

"Oh, thirty dollars," he ventured, when he had regained his composure.

My response was even louder than anything said up to that point.

"Five dollars, sir! And I'll take blanket, bit, and rope! Also that bag on the rail over there, and if you open your mouth for one more word, I'll chop you into pieces and feed you to this decrepit devil!"

He took my five dollars, and the deal was complete without so much as a handshake. It seemed that my skills as a negotiator improved a great deal when I was angry, but I was not about to gloat over the success of my bargaining. I wrapped my bleeding thumb with a strip of my handkerchief and led my obstreperous new friend down the back street towards the hotel.

For another twenty-five cents I obtained lodging for him at the stable on Main Street, then returned to the hotel to do the same for myself, as it was too late in the day to consider heading out of town. After depositing my pack upstairs in my room, I returned downstairs for a late supper.

Mealtime had officially finished, but in the kitchen I was given a plate, a corner of a serving table, and enough hot food for a crew of six. Afterwards, I lumbered upstairs to my bed, where my excess translated itself into severe internal discomfort.

Unable to consider an early night in spite of my great fatigue, I returned to the kitchen for bicarbonate of soda, then tried to still my boiling gastric juices with a walk in the cool night air.

I strolled as far as the last commercial buildings on the far side of Richfield, then back, past the hotel, and down the strip of saloons in Cameronton that bathed the muddy streets in gaslight and filled the night air with the sounds of the banjo and piano.

Looking in the window of a place called the *Lucky Penny*, I saw a card game in progress, and I decided to rest my legs and watch the gentlemen play a few hands.

I was no more than a foot inside the doorway when someone called my name. It wasn't a big place, but amidst the bright lights and the fog of tobacco smoke, it took me a moment to make out my friend Carl seated with a half-dozen other fellows at a table laden with jugs of yeasty Barkerville brew. I strolled over and stood beside his chair, and he himself took his feet, put a hand theatrically across my shoulders, and introduced me to his mates.

"Gentlemen, we are fortunate enough to have with us tonight my friend Zachary, the richest man in these mountains — a veritable modern Midas."

My mouth fell open into an expression of guilty horror.

In fact, I had arrived while they were in the middle of liquor-loose gossip about who was rich and who was ruined — the most popular sort of discussion in Barkerville — but I was so unprepared to meet up with anyone that I missed the joke. I stared accusingly at my friend, gulped like a dying fish, and turned red.

Everyone, except perhaps Carl, enjoyed my obvious discomfort, but I couldn't think of a thing to do. I realize now, of course, that I should have joined in and laughed it off, but at the time I was incapacitated with amazement that my distant friend had somehow discovered that I was rich.

"I'm not!" I blurted out, "I'm not rich at all!" And I continued to stand there until a friendly arm pushed me into an empty chair.

I sat, but my expression did not change. I was furious with myself for not planning what I would say or do in this situation. I knew I was acting in the worst possible way and dramatically drawing attention to myself, but by now I thought I would only compound matters if I just stood up and left. I glared angrily at Carl, who sat cleaning his spectacles, mystified by my over-reaction. I toyed with the glass of beer someone had poured me.

"You know, I believe we really do have a big winner among us." The speaker sat directly across from me – a red-bearded, bald man who had affected a red bow tie over his grimy woolen shirt. "Buy another pitcher, friend, and tell us," he said, "where did you strike it, and how much did you take?"

There was still some jest in this, but it was a direct contravention of local protocol. I would have been well within my rights to sneer at him and keep silent, but once again I was stupid enough to over-react.

"I tell you, I'm as poor as all of you put together, and if you choose to call me a liar, then you'd best do it outside in the street."

Now even the card players at the next table were interested. Everyone was watching me. A fat Englishman sitting next to the bald man spoke next. I believe he may have been the proprietor, and he tried to calm things.

"No one's saying you've done a thing wrong, Mr. Zachary. It's all just passing conversation, and you're not required to tell us two bits. I'm sure you deserve everything you have." Then with a wink he added, "or anything you don't have."

———

I wasn't sure just what he meant by that, but things were getting worse by the minute, so I stood up, pronouncing angrily that I certainly deserved better than to be harassed by a bunch of drunken strangers, and stomped out.

Carl followed me. He called from the doorway, but I wouldn't stop, so he walked alongside, apologizing and trying to explain the obvious.

"You have to forgive them, old man. You really did sound a bit suspicious, and everybody likes to hear good news, now and then. But it's really as you said in there? Nothing turning out for you at all?"

"Isn't my word good enough for you, Carl? I'm on my way south and out of this useless country, but I thought I could at least remember you as one good friend."

More than anything, I was angry with myself for being so stupid in public, but I allowed my ill humour to be interpreted as annoyance at his mistrust.

Carl continued to exhibit his long-suffering pose.

"Look me straight in the eye then, Zach, and tell me plainly that you're out of luck and broke, and I'll buy a jar of whisky, and we'll drink a last goodbye down at my place," he said.

Without thinking, I replied, "No need for that. I've got a room at the hotel."

I knew I had blundered as soon as I said it, but it was too late. The twinkle returned to Carl's eye and he smiled.

"The American? The Colonial? Kind of expensive, aren't those rooms?"

I turned on my heels, and answered over my shoulder as I walked into the darkness.

"It's a sad thing," I said, "when a man can't trust the word of a friend."

"Trust?" Carl called after me. "You don't know the meaning of the word, Zachary."

I had spent the whole day in anticipation of a soft, sound sleep in a hotel bed, with a feather pillow and a wasteful number of blankets, but the joy of that night of comfort was robbed from me by the implications of my argument with Carl. I was annoyed with both my friend and myself, and worried about the slim but serious chance that someone overhearing our confrontation would have his curiosity tweaked enough to investigate a bit. Needless to say, I could afford no investigation.

I resolved to be up early and on my way, before I had a chance to make things worse. I would have saved myself a great deal of trouble if I had held to that decision.

CHAPTER NINE

*I*T WAS LATE when I awakened. I could tell by the sounds in the hall and outside in the street. Both mentally and physically I felt muddy and blunt. My first thoughts were of my indiscretion the previous evening, and I muttered self-depre-cations all the time I was dressing. I held the irrational but irre-sistible suspicion, as I carried my belongings downstairs, that someone might try to follow me when I left Barkerville. I tried to shake off the feeling, but I could not.

I had become a noticeably more cautious, more suspicious man since my encounter with Ned. Monumental events in the life of a man can change him dramatically and instantaneously, and my experience of homicide and great wealth had certainly produced a change in me. I was not a better man, but neither was I much worse, I suppose. As I looked over Barkerville that day, I was probably braver, stronger, and shrewder, but I was also more selfish, and there was a callous aspect to my personality that no one would be likely to consider a positive characteristic.

The street outside the hotel was already busy – workers working and travellers travelling, but no one gave me a glance or lurked in the shadows. No stranger followed at a discreet distance when I started down Main Street. I was still suspicious and nervous, but gradually the mood subsided, and I walked along, considering my plans for transporting the gold.

I was disturbed by the recollection that Ned himself had once used two mules. The journey that he undertook was much shorter than mine, his burden lighter, and his knowledge of the animals greater, but even so, his expedition ran into calamity, and he was forced to shoot one animal. The independent spirit of mules is well-documented, and the dreadful vision came to me of one gold-laden beast headed off one way, while the other chose an opposite direction, leaving me alone in-between. I then considered the idea of hitching the pair to a wagon — a prospect that was appealing for the main part — but one great drawback prevailed. As the murderous trapper had demonstrated, a wagon invites investigation from all sorts of fellow travellers, and since it must remain on the main road, it is difficult to avoid those investigations. A person could try to disguise the cargo as something cheap and innocent, but what would that be? All goods travel from south to north in that land. The only thing worth bringing back to civilization is gold.

I toiled at the proposition for some time, but by the time I was back at the hotel, I had been forced to give the idea up, and return to my plan of leading two mules. I retrieved my belongings and walked down the street to pick up Lord Nelson.

I had not brought a great deal with me on this trip — change of clothing, a bit of food, a blanket, and a package of the papers and personal effects from Ned's treasure stash. (Originally, I thought I might try to do a bit of detective work — visit the *Cariboo Sentinel* and figure out who some of his victims had been — but the idea now made me too nervous.) In total, I guessed I was asking the mule to carry about five pounds — not much, for a creature commonly referred to as a beast of burden.

111

He was reluctant to cooperate with me, however. In fact, I believe he sneered at me.

"Listen careful, you miserable emasculated ass. I'm the one responsible for seeing that you're dry and well-fed, and I don't ask for thanks, but let it be known that I'm also the one that chooses when we walk and when we stop. If you cross me one more time, I'll show you that I can wield a bigger stick than that drunken Englishman ever owned."

I doubt that the animal even knew that I was addressing him, but it made me feel better, and the creature did indeed clatter along behind me without complaint.

It was nearly noon already, and I was a bit hungry. Rather than reach into my baggage, I stopped at a butcher's, (his name, incidentally, was Baker), and purchased a two-pound slab of moose sausage — rather dry, but very good, with a spicy bite to it. I tethered the mule to a post and carried the sausage into a saloon to eat with a tankard of beer. I brought my little hand pack, but left the rest of my things with Lord Nelson.

On the saloon wall was a poster advertising an evening performance of a musical extravaganza entitled *Goldfield Romance – A Miner's Story*. The advertisement promised that it would be a stimulating entertainment that would please one and all.

I was sure that it would. The amazing thing is that a crowd of gold miners and prospectors find it vastly enjoyable and enlightening to hear in prose, poetry, and music that their life is full of excitement and romance. From hard experience they know this to be totally fallacious — ridiculous, in fact — but they listen to it with rapt attention and hoot and stamp their approval when the spectacle is over.

The truth is, I thought, that for every gold seeker who goes home rich and satisfied, there are two who leave in coffins, if they leave at all.

With that, the great plan hit me: coffins!

I wasn't immediately certain whether it would be necessary to carry a body or bodies, or whether empty coffins would suffice. The gold might be hidden in the coffins, or in concealed compartments within the wagon, with a casket or two on top. With a suitably plausible but gruesome story prepared, I was sure I could deflate the inclination that anyone, inside or outside of the law, might have to search my cargo.

My good humour returned. The odds for success seemed to have increased dramatically.

I checked my watch to see if there was still time to talk to a carpenter about building coffins, and found that it was just after twelve. From my recollection, they took a break at that time to eat. I thought it would be polite to wait for a bit before I approached them. There was plenty of time.

I left the watch, with its cover open, on the table in front of me, cut myself another slice of sausage, and took a long drink of beer. It was a most pleasing pastime to try to visualize every possible problem with my plans, to work out the details of execution, rough out a time table, and so on. I was enjoying myself, and at first paid little attention to the fact that the man at the next table was staring at me.

He was a man of my own age, clean-shaven, dark and tall, and from the way he kept glancing at my table, I assumed he was interested in my food. I thought perhaps he was a proud unfortunate who hadn't eaten in some time, although there was a drink before him. With my hunting knife I chopped off a sizeable chunk of the sausage and offered it to him in a friendly manner.

He pulled himself upright and shook his head in refusal. His eyes opened even wider than they were before, and for the first time, I began to feel uneasy. I decided to leave as soon as I finished my drink.

"That's a nice watch," the stranger said, in a tone that was not perfectly conversational.

I nodded agreement. I had thought, myself, that it was the best of Ned's selection — gold-plated, ornate, and heavy.

"Might I ask where you got that watch?" the tall man continued.

I affected an impatient attitude as I rolled the heel of meat into a scrap of newspaper, and replied that my father had given me the watch for my twenty-first birthday. Before I could stand up, he spoke again.

"No," he said firmly. "No. That watch belonged to my brother. He got it in the navy. You see the coat of arms . . . "

My own eyes were probably a little wide when I looked again at him. To my horror, he was holding a pistol — an ugly beast with a homemade wooden grip — in his hand. It wasn't yet pointed at me, but it was resting on his table.

"My brother. Timothy . He got himself murdered a year or so back, right on his own claim."

I was momentarily unable to speak. The half-dozen other patrons and the bartender were also watching, and listening to the man in grim silence.

Things looked pretty bad. My thoughts about getting a coffin made were assuming a nasty, ironic aspect. The stranger was not likely willing to appreciate the humour in it all.

"You got his watch. You got the nerve to flash it around like you're proud of it. My God! You don't deserve to breathe the same air as he did." The man's voice was becoming high and light, and he had given me a good view of the end of his gun barrel.

My chances of talking my way out of the situation were becoming too slim to consider; my own handgun rested deep in my coat pocket, and there wasn't a friend in the world to stand beside me.

Ned, I thought. You've ruined us both, you detestable dog. Even if I managed to tell the whole truth to the law right now, they'd probably hang me as your double-crossing accomplice, rather than treat me as any friend of justice.

There wasn't much point in worrying about how my explanation might be received, because the man at the next table was obviously within two or three minutes at most of blasting me into the hereafter.

I smiled broadly and, I hoped, confidently.

"Just calm down there a minute, friend." I deliberately picked up the pocket watch and snapped the cover closed. "This watch is not your brother's. It was given to me by my father when I myself entered the navy. It has my name and birthdate engraved on the inside."

A hint of uncertainty appeared on his face like a crack of light entering a dark room.

"Here. Take a look."

Again, very slowly, I flipped the timepiece in his direction, on his gun hand side.

It skidded across the corner of his table, and began to fall to the floor. Like any civilized man, this fellow reflexively followed his impulse to stop a watch from being dropped, and when he grabbed for it, I kicked a chair against his arm.

A half second later, I had overturned both tables on him, knocking him flat on his back on the floor. His gun discharged into the ceiling, spreading gunpowder smoke and sawdust over the patrons, most of whom were howling and diving for cover. My adversary was between me and the front door, trying to regain his feet, so my only path of escape was past the bar and down the hallway, where I expected to find the rear exit. I had no such luck. The perverse designer of that building had ignored the necessity for a back door. There was only the base of a stairway at the end of the hall.

I had no choice, nor any time to choose, so I ran up the stairs three at a time, leaving the shouts and commotion below me, and found myself in another corridor, with doors down each side. The two I tried were locked.

I was running like a rat from a cat, heedless of direction as long as I could keep running. There was a window slightly ajar at the back end of the building and I raced for this, even as I heard the sound of boots pounding up the stairs behind me.

Outside the window was a three-foot-square wooden landing

---

which I had thought would be a fire escape, but instead of a ladder leading down, the demented Barkerville architect had installed three steps leading upwards, onto the roof. Again, I simply followed my own momentum, and climbed up.

My pursuers were almost upon me. The nearest one came through the window just as I was scrambling up the wood shingles on all fours. I reached out and grabbed the tin bucket I found at the roof's peak, and swinging it by its rope, I clobbered the man hard enough to knock him back into the building.

The saloon, like most Barkerville structures, had a high, steeply pitched roof, with a flat walkway two feet wide running down the length of the peak. On this were kept large barrels to catch rainwater, and the aforementioned bucket to lower it down. The system worked both as plumbing and fire protection.

I now found myself stranded up there, twenty-five feet from the ground, with no way down except through an angry mob. Prospects were not pleasant.

The building had a false front on it, and I supposed there might be some possible descent at that end, so I charged madly along the walkway, leaping over the low wooden rain barrels as I went.

My last leap was not successful. I clipped the toe of my boot against the lip of the barrel's rim, bounced once on the walkway, then rolled and skidded down the steep pitch of the shingles in a diagonal line that bumped me head first into the false front at the edge of the roof. Bruised and bewildered, I was able to grasp onto the corner by my fingertips for about one heartbeat, with my legs flailing and searching for purchase beneath me.

I knew I was about to fall a full two stories, and my mind quickly brought back to me the advice of a man I knew who raced horses in California. "Spread out your fall," he advised, "and turn it into a roll, so your bones don't take a full impact."

My grip gave out, and I plunged downwards. Halfway down,

my heels caught on a horizontal flagpole and this spun me up-side down, so that I landed flat on my stomach on the boardwalk.

Gasping and choking, I leaped to my feet and hurtled for-ward — directly into a man who had started towards me. We went down together in a thrashing pile of arms and legs; then we both scrambled quickly to our feet. I had my fist already raised to slug him, intending to one-punch him back down, when I realized I had just knocked over a preacher. It is for instances like these that they wear their collars backwards.

He had a look of confusion and horror on his face, and I con-fess, I was myself taken aback by my own actions.

"Excuse me, Father. Excuse me!" I exclaimed. "I didn't see you, Father, and . . . "

"No, no. Please. I am a Presbyterian. You needn't call me Fa-ther. You may call me . . . "

A gun blast sounded somewhere above me, and once again I was on the fly — across the street, under the boardwalk, and then underneath the buildings. Here I was quite thankful for another of the peculiarities of Cariboo builders. The fact that most larger structures were raised off the ground on posts allowed me to scurry beneath them and out of sight.

Crossing an open space, I was again fired on from behind, but the shot missed its target. My Colt .45 was still in my pocket, banging like a hammer against my knee with every step, but a gunfight with the whole town was not what I wished.

I could hear shouting and commotion in the distance, but whoever was pursuing me was well behind, I supposed.

Hurrying along, first under buildings, then behind them, I covered a long stretch of Main Street, then struck up the hill along a muddy footpath. I tried to stay hunched over and look inconspicuous, which is not easy when you are running as fast as your legs will carry you. At the crest of the first hill, the track turned sharply right and snaked between the posts that held up an overhead aqueduct for a hundred yards or so, before it petered out at a group of shacks and shafts. At that point, even as I started to slow down, someone off to my right hollered something, and I dodged behind a scrubby clump of juniper bushes at the top of a little gully. I was suddenly standing on a very steep incline, treading unsteadily through a sea of greasy, grey clay muck — the discharge of the pumps emptying the nearby mine shafts. I couldn't halt myself, and pitched forward onto my belly, then slid down the hillside like a child on a toboggan, with my face ploughing through soupy mud.

I never knew who had shouted, but I presume it had nothing to do with me. I stood up, dripping filth, and walked away unseen. It might have been a decent disguise, if I needed one. I looked the perfect image of someone who has just come up from wading through a flooded drift.

A half mile away, on the other side of the hill, I holed up in an empty tool hut and waited until it was nearly dark.

Since I no longer had a watch with me, I could only presume that it was six-thirty or seven o'clock when I crawled out of my hole. It was dark enough so that my features would not be distinguished easily by a passer-by, but light enough for me to find my way through that labyrinth of trails and human burrows, where lanterns were too widely spaced to facilitate walking at night.

I headed first to Carl's place. I had some things I needed to say to him, and a question or two to ask as well.

He was still bunking in the equipment shed at his mine, although the tools had gradually been moved out to other locations in deference to his comfort, and enough improvements made to render the building livable for a future partner in the operation. The walls had been filled with sawdust for insulation, a bigger stove installed, and a window cut in the south wall.

When I arrived, darkness was nearly complete, and I felt quite secure lingering about in the shadows of the main bunkhouse, where I had a view of my friend's entrance door. It was more than an hour, or so it seemed, before I saw him approach from the far side of the workings, carrying a lantern and accompanied by another man. I couldn't see their faces, but I easily recognized Carl's walk — a slow stroll, swinging his legs loosely like a seaman. The two men separated, and the other fellow went into the bunkhouse. I intercepted Carl as he reached his own quarters.

I called his name in a low voice, and slipped behind the building, out of sight. He followed me, holding his lamp at shoulder height.

"Well," he ventured at last, "I'm a little surprised to see you."

"I'm sorry about last night. I was rude and thoughtless, and I should have known better. I guess I was tired and not thinking straight, but that's no excuse, I know. Please accept my apology as a friend." I rattled it off, all in one breath.

He set the lamp on the ground, and hunched up against the building. I could see him shaking his head in the dimness. "Last night was no big affair. I suppose I was a little short myself. It wasn't proper to grill you like that, and I shouldn't have let them keep on when I saw you were bothered by it, but..." His voice trailed away.

He wasn't comfortable, in spite of the exchange of regrets.

"That wasn't why you're surprised to see me."

"No."

There was a long pause, during which he drew a chunk of chewing tobacco from a twist of paper. "The sheriff's man was here to see me not two hours ago. Hec Simmonds."

I whistled faintly.

"That's ruddy quick."

Barkerville was not as big a town as I gave it credit for. In the space of an hour or so, they had identified me and determined who my closest associate was.

"What did he ask you?"

Carl shrugged.

"He wanted to know anything I knew about you — what you did, where you lived, where you came from, that sort of thing."

"And what did you tell him?"

"I told him that after I thought it all out, there wasn't much I knew about you — not even where your claim was." The remark had a sad reality about it. "If you're in trouble, you needn't worry about me. I told him what I knew, which was very little. I didn't figure it would hurt you at all. I don't think he actually believed me, since I admitted that we were friends, and you usually stayed with me when you came to town. He said he'd be back again maybe."

This turn of events put me into a quandary. I had been ready, up to that point, to tell Carl the whole story, and to ask him if he wished to take a share in my venture. The two of us would have had a good chance of getting the stolen gold safely out to civilization and disposed of, but if the law had an eye on him, he would be too much of a liability. I myself was still an enigma to the sheriff's office, but Carl could be traced and tracked. He was too well-known in the town.

"This sheriff's man," I asked, "did he tell you why they wanted me?"

Carl's reply was still guarded.

"Well, it was Hec Simmonds, was who it was, so I didn't put a lot of stock in what he had to say, but he said a bit, and somebody who'd been in town said a bit . . . I don't know how much I believe . . . "

"What, then?"

"They say you were in a saloon and you tried to pawn a watch that was known to belong to a dead man — some fellow that had been shot in the back for his gold. Hec says when they asked about the watch, there was a big gun battle, and you escaped. Someone claimed you stopped to beat up a preacher."

He had to smile when he said that, as did I, but I was feeling rather sick. Carl was waiting for a true account.

120

"Someone saw me in possession of the watch. I wasn't trying to pawn it, I just had it. I ran off because I couldn't afford to wait around and explain. There was no gunfight. No preacher was beat up."

Even in the flighty shadows of the kerosene lantern I could see relief on my friend's face.

"Where did you get that watch, then?"

I thought it would be better for both of us if I gave him an abridged account, if any account at all.

"I got it from my partner." Carl nodded, as if that explained many things. "My partner is not altogether a nice fellow. Maybe I shouldn't have taken up with him, but it's too late now. I didn't ask him where the watch came from."

"You have a partner! You should have told me that last night, Zach, when you wouldn't tell us what you'd struck and all that. I would have understood if you'd just said that much. I mean your partner isn't going to be out bragging to all his friends, is he?"

I shook my head. "No, he doesn't say a thing to anyone."

We talked a little longer about this and that, but sidestepped any direct description of the nature of my "lucky strike" or my future plans. When I finally said it wasn't wise for me to stick around, and stood to leave, Carl asked, "You really are leaving the goldfields, then, I presume?"

"Yes," I admitted. "Soon. It's getting colder."

"I reckon I won't see you, then."

"Maybe. Remember to check your mail though, Carl. I promise that at the very least, I'll write a letter when I reach my next home. Just to say I made it."

It was agreed, and we shook hands on it.

There was one more thing.

"Carl, I don't dare stay here tonight, but would you have a blanket you could spare me? I don't have cash, but there's plenty of gold in this poke, so you can replace it."

He gave me what I knew to be his best blanket and said he

would consider it an insult if I suggested that he should accept payment in return.

I never saw the man again, although I saw his name mentioned in a copy of the *Cariboo Sentinel* dated about two weeks later. He was working in a drift at the forty-five-foot level, when the earth chose to exercise its prerogative to act with random malice, and swallowed him, along with two others. I have heard that sort of scene described before, and it holds a horror that is the more intense for its subtlety. The men on the surface hear no roar and see no crashing rock and timber. There is simply a very slight flexing of internal earthen muscle — a ripple almost unnoticeable along the ground skin, and perhaps a whisper of dust floating up from the main shaft. Before anyone can react, the poor creatures down there are dead and buried — sucked into the darkness below.

It was an obvious fate for Carl, for he, unlike myself, was a true gold miner. Many of the men who travelled north in that gold rush — most of them perhaps — were not of that genuine fibre. Some were adventurers, some escapists, and some were desperate characters driven by a greed they could not hope to placate in any other fashion. Some, incredibly, were lazy, and travelled that long, hard road in hopes of finding easy money.

Most of these characters would, like myself, escape at the earliest opportunity, but I'm sure that Carl would have made a home and a long life there, had a more lengthy life been granted him. Barkerville in the sixties was a perfect environment — a heaven on earth — for men of his peculiar caste.

These gold miners had very little in common with, for instance, the New England coal miner. They were much more of a type with the mule-skinners, trappers, guides, and gamblers who formed the northern community. They lived their life in love with the feeling of expectation, and they somehow experienced an ongoing fulfilment from their days spent cold, wet, and muddy, stealing a spoonful of sparkle on a good day.

I stumbled off to find some place in the shadows where I could rest until morning. It was cloudy, and too dark to see even the outline of a footpath except for the storm lanterns which were spotted around the more prosperous claims close to Williams Creek. These operations worked twenty-four hours per day, partly because their daily return was so great, and partly because they flooded so quickly if the pumps were shut down.

I followed the trails from one of these little circles of light to the next, never allowing the full brightness to illuminate me, until I had reached the outskirts of the town proper. There I crawled into a dark thicket and pulled the blanket around me.

I can't say I was able to get comfortable there, with twigs and stones poking at me every time I shifted my weight, but I did manage to manoeuvre myself into a position where I would have been able to sleep if I had not allowed myself to think about my predicament.

I realized I was now well on my way to being a notorious and sought-after criminal. The forces of justice in that country were neither brilliant nor well-organized, but they had my name, and they could therefore find my claim easily enough at the registry. I could not return to Binder Creek. More disturbing to me was the thought of what they would find when they looked through the belongings I had left on the mule tied outside the saloon. After a cursory perusal of Ned's collection of papers — his victims' diaries and letters — Sheriff Stevenson would no doubt come to the conclusion that I had murdered not one, but at least a half-dozen unfortunate souls. He would also assume that I was still in possession of their gold.

CHAPTER TEN

I WAS ON MY feet and moving before it was light, but I still thought it advisable to change my appearance as much as possible. I tucked my trouser legs into my boots, tied my hair back into a pig's tail like a sailor, and removed my coat. I carried it wrapped in my blanket as I skulked past the sleeping small claim holders, around the fringe of Cameronton, and away from civilization.

I was still in possession of my map, and I plotted a course west/southwest, towards Mount Greenberry. This would allow me to skirt around the lower levels of Sliding Mountain, and back down to the course of Antler Creek, not too far from Ned's cabin.

The sun was out when I reached Wendle Lake, but there wasn't yet much warmth to it. The water was freezing cold but I stripped to the buff and waded in, scrubbing myself with black sand, and whooping with anguish and ecstasy. I felt a bit like I was punishing myself for the foolish mistakes that had made my last few days so disastrous, although the chief reason for my oblations was simple personal cleanliness. I smelled even worse than I felt.

The sunshine dried me quickly, and I went to work on my laundry. I rendered my coat in satisfactory condition by banging it against a tree trunk until the caked clay disintegrated, but the rest of my clothing had to be washed or left behind. I flushed out my trousers, shirt, and underwear in the lake, then draped it all over a sturdy willow bush.

I intended to sit there and sort out my plans while I waited for my drawers to dry, but immediately realized that I was becoming uncommonly hungry, and I had a long day's walk before I reached known food supplies. I was therefore compelled to start on my way dressed only in my coat, with my wet laundry dripping from a stick behind me, like a soldier carrying a most undignified flag. I found I could walk just as quickly naked as I could in proper clothing, but even there, in the deep privacy of the wilderness, I found it slightly humiliating.

I deserved to feel humiliated. With a most self-destructive efficiency I had burned my bridges behind me, and destroyed nearly all the options I once had for escaping from the Cariboo with my new-found wealth. It was no longer safe to show my face in town, nor indeed in any roadhouse or village north of Fort Langley if the sheriff and Judge Begbie had decided that I was a thieving murderer, and they had every reason to so believe.

It was now impossible for me to carry out my half-formed plan to ship the gold in coffins, which was most regrettable, for something about that scheme appealed to my sense of poetic mischief. It was now out of the question, though, as were most propositions. I was in trouble.

I had one mule and about one hundred and eighty pounds of gold, and I would need a good stock of supplies to make a six-hundred-mile trip without ever visiting a roadhouse or a general store. This was entirely too much of a burden for a single person at the best of times, and my arm was still too weak and painful to be of much use. It had taken a fresh round of abuse during my flight from justice, and I felt sure that if the muscles had not been ripped completely asunder up to that point, they must be now.

I considered the possibility that I could make two trips. The second time north I would come in disguise and be better prepared.

That idea was repugnant to me, especially after the events of the last forty-eight hours. I didn't want to tempt fate twice. I had recent experience of the number of things that can come from nowhere and spoil a man's carefully laid plans. At the back of my mind, I was afraid that I might never dredge up the courage and resolve to come back for any gold I left behind, and the idea of abandoning wealth in the woods was the most repulsive thing of all. If I hadn't been to some extent a greedy man, I would not have come to the interior of British Columbia.

I couldn't believe that any miner's sudden riches had ever caused him such immediate vexation of spirit.

I travelled at fine speed, all downhill and nearly in a straight line, and it was no more than three o'clock when I reached what I figured to be Two Sisters Creek. At this junction I was able to look out over a broad area of swamp and marsh, at the far side of which ran Antler Creek. Keeping to the contours of Sliding Mountain, I skirted these lowlands, with my eyes open for an animal stupid or slow enough to shoot with a pistol. I had no such luck.

I did, however, see a fine breath of woodsmoke from the same camp I had noticed on my way out to town, and this started a new line of thoughts unravelling in my brain.

While I did not like the idea of a partnership, it was an option that had to be considered if the opportunity came along.

The only person I actually knew and trusted was Carl, and he, of course, could not be used, now that the law was peering over his shoulder. There remained, though, the possibility of hiring on a stranger.

———

The drawbacks were obvious. There would be no way of knowing if the man was trustworthy enough even to carry his own share of the load, let alone resist the temptation to cut and run, and do a doublecross. There was also the matter of sharing. If I took on a helper, would I be required to cut him in for a full share? A half? If I gave him a quarter of the booty, I would be dealing away forty-five pounds of gold, while running the risk of insulting my compatriot because it was unequal in his eyes.

The day was in its latter stages, and I still had several miles to travel. I had to decide something soon.

I came up with a fabricated proposition that might sound plausible to a potential partner whose back was stronger than his brain. I could claim to be an agent for a group of unnamed and slightly mysterious fellows who wished their gold to be discreetly transported as far as the lower Fraser. On behalf of these dubious gentlemen, I would be entitled to hire one more able body who would receive, like myself, 10 percent of the goods. When we reached a place somewhere below Fort Hope, I would claim that it was the designated rendezvous, and I would dismiss my helper, suggesting that our desperado employers might arrive at any minute, and that his best chance for survival was to take his 10 percent and disappear without having to meet them.

As a cover story, it was noticeably riddled with implausibilities, but presented to the right stranger, it might suffice. The plan as a whole was weak, but I deemed that if I talked sweetly and slept with my pistol cocked, I could make it work. If worse came to worst, my partner and I might well come to blows, but I hoped this would not occur before we reached the relative safety of the coastal lowlands. Certain scruples would keep me from shooting the fellow in the back, but I trusted from experience that I could come out the winner in a suitably unfair fight.

I was running out of ideas. It was time to accept the risks and go to it. I decided to sneak up on the camp below me, and take a look at what I could see.

From a clearing on the hillside I could look down and pin-point where the smoke was coming from — a spot on a little creek not significant enough to be even marked, let alone named on the map I kept in my jacket pocket. When I circled around and reached its gully higher up, I found that the bed was dry — water probably running there only in the spring.

I worked my way down slowly until I could smell the burning wood and hear its distant pop and crackle, then moved into the forest border and picked my way stealthily through the spruce and scrub. The trees were tall and the underbrush thick through this area. It seemed to take an inordinate amount of time to cover the last hundred yards.

Finally, though, I glimpsed something white through the screen of branches, and knew that I was on the outskirts of the clearing. I crouched down and waited to see movement, but nothing stirred. Becoming slightly anxious, I crept carefully over to my right to a pair of huge granite boulders, side by side and slightly higher than the open space and the fire. I could squeeze in between the two big rocks and peer over the top lip of the front one to get a good view.

The camp was empty. A sturdy lean-to or temporary cabin, with a moose hide for a door, was nestled under a pair of twisted jackpines, and clothes or pieces of cloth were laid out to dry on a rock the size of the one behind me. A hatchet was stuck into a log near the fire. Over the latter was set a tripod of green willow, wired together, with a blackened pot dangling down over the flames.

No one was in sight. I waited, and felt a prickly sensation rise at the nape of my neck.

Still no one appeared. My mind flashed back to my first arrival at Ned's cabin, and I was thankful that once again I had decided to approach this place under cover. Without even rustling my coat sleeve, I drew my gun from my pocket.

What a horrible country, I thought, where even when you're

sneaking up on someone, you have to worry about getting am-bushed from behind.

I pictured in my mind the tall fellow whose brother had been unfortunate enough to know Trapper Ned. I could still see the immense bore of his homemade revolver.

I couldn't wait and watch anymore. I had to move before I froze with fear, or panicked and ran. Still holding my gun at the ready, I slid down and stepped out from between the boulders. Doing so, I almost ran smack into the man return-ing to his camp.

We both shouted at the same time. I yelled a simple Anglo-Saxon epithet of low character, but I cannot say exactly what his exclamation meant. He shouted it in Chinese.

If a Chinaman's face can go pale with shock, I believe his did at that moment. He was returning, I presumed, from doing what men of all races must go to the bushes to do from time to time, and as he walked he was tying a cloth belt or sash around his waist.

His eyes levelled on my Colt .45, which was pointed directly at the spot where the furrows in his brow met the bridge of his nose, and his arms immediately flew into the air. His pants slid slowly down, until the waistband caught around his knees.

I was surprised to see that he was not wearing long under-wear — only short pants under his trousers. His legs were rather scrawny, without a sprout of hair on them — a sad-looking speci-men as he stood there in the pathway.

It wasn't the sort of first contact with a new culture that any-one would choose. We stood there, open-mouthed and dumb, for a long moment, like a pair of idiots — I staring at his knobby knees, and he at my gun. Finally I lowered my gun and he raised his pants. Common etiquette didn't cover this situation, and nei-ther one of us knew quite what to do.

"Hello," I said.

He nodded with a confused and slightly worried look on his face.

"I was passing by on the creek, and I thought just to be

friendly-like, I should drop up and say hello. See if you had a cup of coffee to share."

He didn't reply.

"You have any coffee, by any chance?"

Still confused. No reply. I slipped my weapon back into my coat pocket.

"Sorry about the gun. I just wasn't thinking, and I was a little . . ."

He didn't have the slightest idea what I was saying.

"No English, eh?"

Finally I had spoken a phrase he understood, and he smiled and nodded proudly.

It was rather disheartening. Once again I had the sensation that I was jinxed. My plan of action was proving itself impossible before I even had a chance to see it fully formed.

The Chinaman asked me some questions in his foreign gibberish and pointed to his camp. I assumed it was an invitation, and allowed him to lead me through an opening in the bushes and into his camp.

He watched nervously and smiled a lot as I sat down on the log beside the hatchet. He was every bit the self-conscious host, especially since he still didn't know why I had blundered into his domain, holding a gun and catching him in an undignified pose. Perhaps my obviously depressed mood put him a bit more at ease, because he eventually quit glancing at my gun pocket, and began to say things in his native language that I had no interest in trying to understand.

There was only one thing capable of drawing me out of my melancholy, and that was directly in front of me, hanging from a willow tripod, and exuding an aroma of boiling grouse or rabbit. No language barrier could disguise the lusting look I directed at the man's dinner, and despite a certain temporary reluctance, he was most gracious in making motions of invitation.

"I'd love to indulge in a bit of dinner," I replied gratefully.

"Haven't eaten since yesterday noon, and I've done a fair piece of work since then."

He removed the pot from the fire and shovelled a serving of a white goulash into a blue and white ceramic bowl. This he gave to me, while himself taking his share in a tin cup, much like the one I had left behind in the Barkerville saloon.

"Looks good," I said, "even if I have heard a few scary stories about what you people eat."

As we sat and ate in silence, I wondered if this might be the same fellow who had a claim just below mine on Binder Creek. He looked basically the same, but I was really unable to distinguish one Oriental from another. I suppose they thought all Caucasians looked the same, apart from the different colours of their beards.

The meal was mostly rice cooked in broth, with little meat in it. I wolfed my first bowlful down in rapture, and since I couldn't make myself understood enough to be polite, I simply helped myself to most of what was left in the pot, smiling thanks to my host and mumbling compliments that I knew he couldn't decipher.

Having taken the frenzied edge off my hunger, I decided to savour the second helping a little more carefully. I had seen the cook drop a small dollop of some sort of relish on his own portion, so I fetched the bottle to try the taste for myself. It was a clear, oily mixture, with seeds and bits of red and green vegetable, almost odourless. I put half a teaspoonful in my mouth and swallowed it before I happened to notice the concerned expression on the Chinaman's face.

The flames that rolled down my throat could not have been hotter if I had stuffed my face with all the coals from the campfire. The water bucket was next to the lean-to, and I attacked it desperately. The pain abated only while I was actually swallowing, so I drank continuously for several minutes, soaking my shirt front in the process.

I give the man credit. He had every right to laugh, but he

maintained an aspect of friendly concern throughout. He did, however, eat my bowl of food after I signified that I had lost my appetite.

I watched him in silence, feeling the skin of my throat turn crisp and flaky, and ruminated on my situation. I found myself in a most unusual state of affairs. It was not just that I was alone, and sharing a meal with a stranger, for the unspoken rule of the backwoods was that any traveller was entitled to whatever form of hospitality he required, without question. Obviously, it was a rule that transcended boundaries of language and race, for notwithstanding my social gaff of pulling a gun on my host, he seemed quite willing to share his home with a weary wanderer.

The wild and unusual thing that struck me about my circumstances was the realization that I was about to take this man as my partner in the most important venture of my life. I had no idea how I was going to manage it, and I fully recognized that it might prove disastrous, but logically or not, I felt I had no other choice. This would be my partner.

I was exhausted, really — emotionally, physically, and mentally. The coherent part of me knew that I was playing the fool, but I also knew that the decision had been made as completely as if I had written it down and registered it with a justice of the peace. A gambler would recognize the feeling. After being at the table too long and calculating probabilities too many times, in the small hours of the morning, knowing full well that the odds are against him, he bets everything he owns on a pair of sevens.

Against all better judgement, I would find a way to make this Oriental wretch understand me, and I would pay him a king's ransom to help me carry my fortune to safety.

Somehow or other, I would do this.

My first task was to get him to accompany me to Ned's cabin. There were maps there, as well as the mule and other objects and tools I could use to get the meaning of my proposition across.

He had finished the last of the rice, and looked just about as tired as I was. No doubt he had been working his claim since daybreak, and was hoping I would leave him to his evening's rest.

"How would you like to come with me and see my place?" I asked. "I've enjoyed your hospitality and I think it's your turn now. We'll let my throat heal up on the way, and fry up some spuds when we get there — how's that?"

He smiled and nodded, but I knew he was totally ignorant of my meaning. I tried repeating myself, this time standing and gesturing — with sweeping arm movements — pointing down the creek and miming a walking motion.

"Come on then, my diminutive friend. We can be there well before dark, but we have to ship out pretty quick."

I hoped he was picking up the amiable tone in my voice, and grinned at him like a patent medicine salesman. He looked in the direction I was pointing and shook his head.

At least I knew that he was taking my basic meaning correctly, and I couldn't blame him for not jumping at this seemingly point-less opportunity, but I refused to give up gracefully. Still talking in my most cheerfully persuasive tone, I strolled over to his makeshift living quarters, lifted the moose hide door, and peered inside.

"You'll like it down my way — quieter, farther away from the hustle and bustle, nice scenery. No gold up this neck of the woods anyway, you realize. Total waste of your time. A short break and a walk in the fresh air will do you a world of good."

I stooped, and reaching into his lean-to, pulled out a kind of straw mat that he had lain across a carpet of spruce boughs, and a pair of green blankets. These I quickly rolled into a rough bun-dle. He jumped to his feet and took them from me with a most discordant-sounding set of objections, which I gave no sign of understanding. I allowed him to scold me in his own tongue, or explain to me the error of my ways, or whatever combination of the two, while I quite deliberately poured his wash-bucket over his campfire.

At this stage, his remonstrations took on a new tone and volume that I could appreciate, but gratefully not specifically translate. He evidently judged me to be a lower form of life, and was considering dire and immediate action against my well-being, but first he intended to put his bedding back in its proper place.

As he turned to do this, he heard me cock the big Colt revolver, and lapsed into immediate silence.

Still holding his mat and blankets, he turned back to face me, and gave me a long and eloquent speech – his personal analysis of our situation. The gist of this was that I was most unfair, and he was most unwilling. As his future partner, I thought it fitting to forgive him for his whining tone of voice and his shortsighted outlook on life.

"Come along," I said. "Not much more than an hour of daylight left."

I pointed the way with my gun muzzle, shouldered my own bedroll, and listened to the musical timbre of his disgusted commentary as we headed down the gulch towards Antler Creek. He talked almost non-stop for the first half mile or so, sometimes sounding angry, sometimes tired and frustrated, and sometimes fearful. I cannot blame him for any of those emotions. I was confident, though, that given the proper time and place, I could make myself understood sufficiently to change his attitude.

Once we were on our way, I tried to keep the gun out of sight and walked level with him rather than behind his back, but if this disposed him in any way to feel more friendly and forgiving to me, he did not show it on his face. Still, with little to carry and level ground, we covered the distance in an hour. He was a good walker, in spite of his bad humour, and after a while his grumbling faded to an occasional grunt.

As we crossed the creek and the clearing beside Ned's cabin, it was becoming dark enough to make the irregularities of the ground indistinct, and I'm sure my fellow traveller was as happy as I was to be finished the day's journey. Although his frown did not disappear, there was a certain curiosity visible in his eyes as he entered the deep gloom of the cabin. I lit the lantern on the table and gestured invitingly to the chair, but he chose to exhibit his disdain and injured dignity by standing on the threshold with his bedroll still in his arms. I did not press the issue, but eased myself past him, collected kindling, birchbark, and a few blocks of wood, then started the fire in the stove. I hoped the warmth would help to thaw the man's emotions a bit, as well as his body. I wanted him to acclimatize himself – to feel a bit more at home in his new surroundings – before I began explanations and negotiations, and to that end I left him by himself within the house while I went back to the creek for a fresh pail of water, then lingered outside chopping up a few more rounds of birch and inspecting the mule, who seemed happy enough to see me, but none the worse for my absence.

I re-entered the building carefully, for I realized that I had forgotten to inspect the place for potential weapons before I left my captive unguarded, but there was no need for caution. He was seated in the chair now, with his blankets in his lap and the same dismal scowl on his face, watching a plume of acrid brown smoke rise from a cooking pot full of dried-out beans that I had inadvertently left on the heater. He was evidently not prone to violence, but neither was he about to be involved in anything against his will.

I took the smoking pot onto the porch and threw it as far as I could into the bush, then returned as if nothing untoward had happened.

"You'll like it here," I chimed cheerfully. "At least I strongly suggest to you, my black-eyed friend, that you make the best of things and enjoy it, because the alternative is pretty bleak, I'm afraid."

I was down now to a frying pan and one pot, which I filled with water and started heating. My speaking tone was, as I say, as cheerful and light as I could make it, but the meaning of my words was far from pleasant.

On the last leg of the road home I had reached the regrettable conclusion that if the Chinaman absolutely refused to consent to my working arrangement, or showed himself under close scrutiny to be unusable to me, I had no other option than to do away with him.

That I was capable of such a cold-blooded murder, I had some doubts, but logically I could not expect to kidnap the fellow, then set him free and hope that he would not bring some sort of attention and retribution my way.

Would it be easier to kill him because he was not a white man? I was unsure. I had killed Ned in self-defense, but even at that I had suffered a certain emotional turmoil. Would I be able to live with myself if I shot this Oriental in cold premeditation? I sincerely hoped that I would not need to find out.

Of the minimal number of things that I knew about the Chinese, only one fact seemed usable in the present situation, and that was that they were great tea lovers, and since Ned was well-supplied in that commodity, I was able to brew a potful in short order. Whether the resultant potation was comparable to any Oriental drink, I couldn't say, but the man was evidently thirsty, and he polished off two cupfuls quite eagerly.

He had relaxed enough, I thought, for me to make another attempt at communication, and the most obvious starting place was an exchange of names.

"Zach," I said, pointing at myself. "Call me Zach."

He smiled. I pointed at him and gave a questioning look. He shook his head negatively, and covered his cup with his hand. A person in a foreign country without any knowledge of the language should, I thought, be better at miming games. I wasted quite some time in repetition and gesticulation, trying to convey the idea that I wanted him to tell me his name, not drink more tea, or go outside. Finally, I was reduced to drawing little pictures of two men, giving one the name "Zach," and gazing at the other in bewilderment. He finally caught on, although I don't think he was much impressed by my artistry. I learned that his name was Rosh, as closely as I could imitate his pronunciation.

We both felt rather pleased, I think, at this successful exchange of information, and I was doubly happy that Rosh was forgetting his animosity and paying me polite attention.

"Rosh," I said.

"Rosh," he replied.

"Zach," I said, and again he covered his cup with his hand and signed that he had enough to drink. I considered the project to be successful enough, since at least I knew what to call him, and gave up trying to correct him. I didn't want to destroy the mood of the moment with pedantry.

After stoking the fire and waiting a few minutes for effect, I coaxed him over to the window and pointed out into the field.

"Mule," I said gravely.

He nodded his head with a questioning look and followed me back to the table. There I spread out a map of the territory from the Great Mountains to the Pacific, British Columbia, and south to California. He nodded his head and mumbled something affirmative when I pointed to our present location, signifying that he understood that position on the chart. Next, I leaned forward with a conspiratorial smile on my lips, pointed at the mule, myself and himself, and traced a line slowly down the Fraser River from Barkerville to the sea.

His response was delayed for a second as he ensured himself that he understood my meaning, then he spat out one loud negative exclamation. Pulling himself away from the map as if it were the devil's own contract, he ranted angrily at me in his native gibberish for a good five minutes.

I waited with a condescending patience until he was finished, then repeated my explanatory gestures and quietly spoke my case.

"You certainly will do it, old fellow — for me, or for yourself, or whomever, but resolve this quickly — you will do it! I give you the chance to choose for yourself, but I'm afraid I can be patient for only so long."

He was not about to be persuaded, or indeed to listen to any more of my discussions. He turned his chair to the wall, returned his bedroll to his lap, and muttered to himself.

My next step was to introduce the idea of reward, and here I thought I might again be able to use pen and ink, since I was of the impression that Orientals used the same notation for numbers as westerners. I wrote the figure, "$4000" in large characters on a sheet of paper and tried to call him over. He ignored me, stayed in his chair, so I took the paper to him and held it up for his perusal.

He closed his eyes. I attempted in my most imploring tones to get him to try to understand just a little more, but he refused. He could not have resisted me more if he had been Ulysses tied to the mast.

Perhaps I should have accepted his reluctance with grace and understanding. He was tired and confused, and no doubt still fearful for his personal safety, even though he now knew enough about me to allay his immediate fears. The problem was that I too was tired and confused. I had run pell-mell through a gauntlet of misadventures that lasted three days, with irregular food and sleep, and a constant mental tension that sooner or later had to show its effects.

The Chinaman stared at the wall, grumbling and thinking to himself, no doubt, that as soon as daylight arrived he must find a way to rid himself of my company.

Somehow, I was determined to bring this matter to a climax before I succumbed to the lure of sleep. I stood up, drew my gun out of my pocket, and took a step towards the door.

"Come on," I uttered gruffly, and drew back the hammer with my right thumb. The sound it made was as loud as a whip crack in the small room. The Chinaman flinched, but didn't turn or stand up. He probably reasoned that I was either bluffing with the pistol, and always had been, or had decided to shoot him. Either way, there was no sense cooperating with me.

I hadn't wanted to shoot, but there was no choice, it seemed. I aimed carefully, even though the range was only two feet, and fired.

Rosh let out a single shriek and crashed to the floor sideways, with his chair on top of him. I had shot a sizable chunk out of one of its legs, but it was mostly its occupant's momentum that sent it flying.

He was more angry than afraid, I think, but he followed me outside immediately, voicing easily recognized objections at great volume. I carried the lantern at first, but after we were on the trail I gave it to him and sent him ahead, and thus we walked into the darkness.

Even on a night well-lit by a half moon, walking along a forest pathway, navigating by the bouncing glow of a kerosene light, is a tedious task. It was a long trip. The trail was obvious enough, but at each branch in the route I had to direct Rosh with a tap from my gun barrel, and he issued a fresh expletive each time I touched him. He must have thought we would be walking forever, and I can't guess what he speculated our destination might be. I knew the route fairly well, yet I myself felt misgivings from time to time, thinking that we must have lost our way or had gone too far already. Then I would spot a familiar rock formation or obstruction in a gully, and recognize our position.

I bypassed the first drop-off altogether. There was no point in showing him my arsenal.

The time might have been nine o'clock or ten, or it may have been a small hour of the morning when we finally reached the second cache point and I took the lantern back from Rosh. He stood on the pathway while I stepped into the bushes, found the old keg, pushed aside the camouflage and removed its lid. I held the lantern high and called to him, and he picked his way daintily through the shadows to where I stood.

The lantern gleam needed only to tickle the surface of the gold bars at the bottom of the barrel for Rosh to recognize them. He was a miner. He could probably have smelled his way to the ingots without the aid of a lamp. Watching his expression, I was satisfied with the mixture of awe and new comprehension that showed in his face.

I could tell he was loath to leave the precious stuff behind, but I quickly popped the lid back in place and returned to the game trail. Looking again at his expression, I could see that there was a great deal going on behind his eyes. I gave him the lantern, and he turned to head back in the direction from which we had come, but I spoke to him and pointed the way farther along. There was no need to use my gun anymore.

He walked faster and needed less prompting at the forks and bends, and we reached the next cache quite quickly. Standing above the opened box, holding the light, I let him spend a long time on his knees, fingering and hefting the bags and boxes and jars of raw gold dust and nuggets. He murmured to himself softly — something that may have been quiet prayer, or may have been a steady, gentle stream of caustic Oriental oaths. I was satisfied that either way, he was voicing a very genuine appreciation of the stockpile.

I carried the lantern and led the way home. We did not stop to rest, but walked at a moderate pace in silence, and were both exhausted when we reached the cabin.

I went straight inside. Rosh stopped to bring in a few more blocks of wood. The room stank of gunpowder, but I did not care. I let the other man tend to the fire, threw my blanket over the bed, and crawled in. I was asleep before Rosh had got his mat and blankets laid out on the floor.

When he woke me it was full light, although it seemed that I had just closed my eyes. The cabin was warm, and Rosh pointed to the table, where oatmeal and tea steamed in their dishes. He had evidently already eaten, a necessary procedure since we possessed only one bowl. I ate hungrily, thinking, though, that he was better at cooking rice than oatmeal. He waited with a noticeable impatience.

As soon as I had finished the last spoonful, he took my bowl away and set it on the floor by the door. The table was now cleared except for our teacups, and as he pulled up a block of firewood for a seat, it became clear that we were about to begin another session of sign language.

First he made desultory gestures at the map, the mule, and the woods in the direction of the gold. I nodded that I understood so far. With that, he drew a handful of coins from his pocket — eight Chinese ones, brass, with square holes in the middle, and two English shillings. He laid the ten pieces in a row before us, pointed once again in the direction of the treasure, and carefully pushed five towards me, then drew five to himself.

He smiled graciously.

I smiled as well, but mine was a smile of amusement at his ingenuous attempt at graft, for such was what I judged it to be.

"Fifty-fifty you think, do you? Well, I must say you've got a lot of gall to even begin haggling with that. It'll take a fine sight more than a bowl of porridge and a cup of tea before I'll be that generous."

I reached across and retrieved four of his coins, shaking my head.

"I don't care to haggle, Chinaman."

He wailed as if he had been shot. His face contorted with anger and self-pity, collapsed into contrite sorrow, then sprang to righteous indignation. He pleaded his case in loquacious terms I could never grasp. He mimed to me our history of meeting, and himself being dragged off at gunpoint — terrified to the brink of apoplexy, if you were to believe him — then stabbed and stroked the map until even a dim-witted occidental ruffian like myself had to be impressed with the magnitude of the epic journey he was being asked to undertake, and the minuscule reward being offered.

Before I could react, his hand snaked out and swept away three more of the coins, giving him four to my six. He was still grimacing at the idea that I should demand so much for so little.

I took them back just as quickly.

"Look, my friend," I said patiently, hoping that the tone of my voice would somehow impress on him my logic. "With one-tenth of that stack of gold you can set yourself up for life — buy a little business, buy yourself a nice farm and some cattle, get yourself a house in the city. Whatever! You haven't even done anything to earn that stuff. You might have thought you were in danger, but I don't think your skin was ever really on the line. I risked my life and I've nearly lost it more than once just getting my hands on that gold. I don't intend to hand half or 40 percent to you just for helping me carry it away."

He summoned up another loud symphony of remonstrations, and before long had drawn back coins number two, three, and four. To finalize his statement he folded his arms and hardened his jaw, as if to say that enough was enough.

We sat that way and stared at each other for a long moment while I tried to think of an argument that he could comprehend.

"Stand up, Rosh," I said at last, scratching my chin contemplatively. He understood my meaning and did so.

The instant he was on his feet, I drove my fist into his stomach. When he bent over double, I smacked him solidly on the top of his head with my elbow, sending him backwards against the door, where he slid to the floor.

He kept his consciousness, but he squirmed quite a lot, trying to get his breath back. He groaned for some time. I helped him to his feet then, and led him back to the chair, dusted off his coat, fetched him a drink of cold water.

Then I took nine coins off the table and put them in my pocket.

"I'm afraid that that's the main reason why I get such a big share of the gold, Rosh. I can whip you any time I want. I'm giving you 10 percent because I think I like you, but if you'd expected to get more than that, your mother should have built you bigger."

At that point in my life, I considered mine to be an eminently fair and logical assessment of the situation.

CHAPTER ELEVEN

I KNEW WE WOULD need a full day to get our supplies organized and the final plans detailed. We had a long trip ahead of us, and we would not save time by rushing into it.

The prime item of business was to fetch the gold — a job that, for the main part, I planned to leave to my partner — but first I had to show him the way, since I couldn't expect him to remember by day where he had walked at night.

As I led him down the game trail I saw that he was marking each fork in the way with a stripped willow branch made into a hoop and hung in an obvious location. He should have been able to remember the route without this, but he was evidently a bit unsure of himself in the bush, and I thought it just as well that he took every precaution. I had no desire to find that my life's riches had wandered off into oblivion on the back of an over-confident fool.

My own packsack had been left with the mule outside the saloon in Barkerville, and if Rosh owned one, it was still at his claim, so between us we possessed only Ned's packboard. I gave this to my companion when we reached the third drop-off. He started loading up, with a broad smile still on his face, while I selected a single tin strongbox half filled with gold — about fifteen or twenty pounds. This seemed like a minimal load for a grown man, but by the time I reached the cabin I found my back was protesting and my convalescent shoulder was quite sore. I had expected it to heal much quicker, but I had only myself to blame for treating it without due consideration.

Rosh was sitting on the porch. He stood up to stretch when I arrived. He had evidently overburdened himself a bit as well, but I signed to him that time was short, and he should hurry back for another load. He nodded agreement, but before he left he stopped to inspect the mule — hooves, ears, mouth, and so on, quite carefully. It would have given me great pleasure to see the beast bite him the way Lord Nelson had me, but the Chinaman was noticeably more familiar with animals than I was.

Once he was gone, I went indoors and loaded the wood stove until it was hot enough to fry bannock. When I had that underway, I sorted out our foodstocks in the centre of the cabin floor. Ned was well-supplied for the winter, but apart from salt, sugar, and tea, all we could hope to carry was bannock, oats, beans, a few carrots, and some rice, which I thought my partner would appreciate. I didn't want to let my face be seen within three hundred miles of the goldfields, nor did I like the idea of sending someone who didn't speak our language to buy supplies. That too would attract attention.

Too much was at stake to take any risks. I estimated the total journey would take us three weeks, and for the first half of that, we should consider ourselves fugitives — from justice and injustice alike. If all went well we could purchase goods at some waystation or roadhouse near the midway point — Lillooet or Ashcroft.

To start with, I figured we could manage about two hundred and twenty pounds of goods, most of which would be gold. The mule should continuously be able to lug a hundred and fifty, the Chinaman forty-five, and myself twenty-five. At that, I would have to manufacture a special pack to carry all the weight on my good shoulder.

I was starting on this, ripping apart the canvas hammock that had been Ned's bed, and sewing shoulder straps and connectors to a crude sort of bag, when Rosh arrived back with his second load of gold. He dropped it wearily on the floor, squatted against one wall, and began devouring warm bannock from the pile I was accumulating.

I asked him if he thought one more trip would be enough, and he shrugged doubtfully.

When he had taken the edge off his hunger and fatigue, he began perusing the maps on the table. One was a large scale chart of the Cariboo, much of which was still blank, and the other a complete map of British Columbia. Both were furnished courtesy of our deceased host. On each I had scribed in red the route that I proposed to follow.

Still chewing on a handful of nuts he had discovered in a can on a high shelf, Rosh called me over from my sewing and pointed to the map of the Cariboo, specifically at a spot where my red line passed along Downey Pass and Martin's Creek to the Willow River. He evidently felt that this was a bad decision and spoke sagely in a very negative voice, stabbing and circling with his finger, indicating that a better route would be to add several miles to the distance, and to follow Nine Mile Creek to Cornish Creek, then the Willow River and Slough Creek.

I don't know whether proper etiquette actually forbids miming with one's mouth full, but I found his manner rather irritating.

"Enough of that," I growled and pushed him towards the door. "You go get the rest of the gold, and leave the map work and the planning to me. I don't know how things are done in whatever corner of the heathen world you come from, but in America the conscript does not offer advice to the captain. If

God had wanted you to examine my decisions, he would have made you with eyes that were all the way open."

He grabbed the packboard and exited, still jabbering away, and I returned to my needlework. I had just cut a new length of gut and sat down when I heard a horrible shriek from outside. I leaped to my feet, startled, but stopped even before I made it to the door. I knew what had happened without looking.

Rosh had found Ned.

He had gained control over himself by the time I reached him, but he was still obviously shaken and distraught. I didn't know why he had wandered over in that direction, but now that he had discovered my dangling accomplice, I thought I might as well explain as much as I could.

"Good afternoon, Ned. You're not looking any better today, I'd say, nor smelling much improved. You should be ashamed of yourself, you know — sneaking up on my new partner like that. You'll have him scared to death before I can get him out to where he's seriously risking his neck. You aren't jealous, are you, old man?"

It may not have been such a good idea to chat up the dead man like that in Rosh's presence. I don't know whether he was particularly superstitious, or just thought that my friendliness with the corpse was in bad taste, but it didn't improve his humour at all.

I knew it would be no easy task to try to explain the intricacies of my situation or even the history of recent events, so I thought carefully, and waited until we were back to the clearing beside the cabin before I began my presentation.

Not only was it difficult to mime out my story, it was a bit embarrassing. I felt like a child playing a parlour game, but it was a charade with rather serious forfeits, for if my companion didn't properly grasp our state of affairs, he might unwittingly betray us to the wrong person at the wrong time.

He was not a stupid man. I knew that even from our short acquaintance, so I felt that if I could explain the rough background to our current predicament, he might well be able to appreciate the ultimate implications.

Firstly, I had to introduce Ned. I acted out the scene where I came casually down the path, was ambushed by the evil man, but through heroic acrobatics and great marksmanship, defeated him. I allowed myself a generous and favourable amount of exaggeration, and it seemed to make the thing more enjoyable for Rosh, who was finally starting to relax.

The cabin belonged to Ned, I signed. The gold belonged to Ned. Then Ned was dead. The cabin and gold belonged to me.

I paused long enough for the story thus far to be secured in his thoughts, then added the next step.

In the inside chest pocket of my jacket were three papers which I carried with me more or less continually: a Royal Geographical Survey map of the Cariboo, a certificate of American citizenship, and the deed to my claim on Binder Creek. I drew this last document out, folded it so as to display the Colonial Governor's coat of arms and the Gold Commissioner's signature on the bottom of the back page, and set it on a stump of wood in front of my Chinese friend. It was my hope that it would be enough to act as a symbol for the legal authorities.

With slow histrionic motions, I put to him the all- important question: Should we take the gold and give it to the authorities?

It was not a difficult decision for him. He laughed, shook his head, folded up my deed for me and gave it back. We were in complete agreement.

As far as I could see, the matter should have been concluded, and I started back inside, but I was stopped for one more question. At least our method of dialogue was becoming more efficient. We now had several symbols to work with. A finger pointed in one direction signified the gold, another direction meant Ned, another still referred to our destination, and a tapping at the vest pocket area was the symbol for the forces of law and order.

Was the law looking for Ned, he wanted to know.

No, I replied. The law was looking for me. If the law saw me, they would hang me.

As I choked myself and rolled my head back, Rosh's eyes widened, and a confused look covered his features. He didn't understand this at all — how I would be known and wanted by the authorities. Without a patient interpreter, I had no hope of relating the twisted trail of events that had brought this about.

He accepted it all, though, checked the time by the blurred white disk of the sun, and started off into the bush for another load.

We were both quite tired by the end of the day and after a meal of fried potatoes, carrots, and a heel of salt pork, we were content to sit quietly in the feeble light of the kerosene lantern and speculate on what the morrow might bring. I also did the last of the packing.

The only things I took for myself from Ned's cabin were the book of Lamb's *Tales* and a new pocket watch — plain steel, this one, with no inscription. As a favour to Rosh, I picked out a watch for him as well — a gold one, with the name *Ball* on the dial.

He took it from me gratefully, wound it, listened to it, and compared it favourably with the other three still remaining in the tray on the rabbit skins.

I was pleased that he liked my choice, and a bit nonplussed a few moments later when, with a worried expression on his face, he replaced it with the others. He couldn't make himself completely understood, but he let me know that something about the fact that it had belonged to Ned disturbed him, and he no longer wanted the thing. I supposed he was superstitious, but his esoteric feelings evidently did not apply to the dead trapper's pipe and tobacco, which he commandeered and took onto the porch for a smoke in the night air.

Next morning, by the time it was light enough to see the ground at our feet, we had already watered and fed the mule, double checked our supplies, and gulped down a breakfast of bannock, nuts, and tea.

We carefully shut down the stove, brought axe and saw indoors, and barred the door before we finally took the first few steps of the six hundred miles to the sea. Then, at the creek, only a hundred yards from the cabin, I asked Rosh to wait, and turned back to attend to one more detail.

I needed to say goodbye to Ned.

Looking back from some distance in time and space, I must admit to the strangeness of this action, but at the time it seemed most natural, and indeed a case could be made for it being as normal as any other farewell, given a rather liberal attitude as to what constitutes friendship. One doesn't leave a friend without saying goodbye.

Granted — Ned and I had not had the smoothest sort of relationship. There were definite and obvious limits to our friendship, but I was not unaware of my imperfections, and I could see some things that we undeniably had in common. We were a matched pair of greedy, self-centred adventurers, and I could not quit the country in good conscience without looking in on the fellow one more time.

"Well, Ned, this is it, I guess," I began, sitting down on my usual stump. The faint breeze blew any unpleasant smell away from me. "It's me and the gold and the Chinaman on our way, and I suppose its fairly obvious that you aren't coming. Dreadfully sorry, old fellow, but I can't even pass along that money to your sweetheart. I don't suppose the authorities are likely to help me figure out your name unless I'm behind bars at the time, so I'll have to say goodbye without really being sure of who you are, but that's just the way life is sometimes.

"I'll try to be careful with your gold. I know you worked very hard in your own way for it. I've got to keep a sharp eye open for that Chinese runt. He's a greedy little beggar, but I don't think I'll have any trouble as long as I never trust him, and never let him forget who's boss and who's baggage. I know what your advice would be, but I'm not going to treat him badly unless I have to. We've made a deal, you know. We're partners, me and that Chinaman."

From the far side of the screen of trees, I could hear Rosh shouting, "Hello" — about the only word of English he seemed to know, although even there, the way he pronounced it made it sound Chinese. Suddenly I felt cold and irritable. My shoulder ached, and I was anxious to go.

"Got to go, Ned. Wouldn't want to hang around and let you be a bad influence, would I?"

Rosh had an impatient look on his face when I reappeared. I gave him my best voyageur's grin, pointed over the mountains to the southwest, and shouted "The Fraser River and the Pacific Ocean." He nodded, returned the smile and said "Ashcroft," or "Asscroft," really, which I took to be agreement in general.

I shouldered my pack with a brief grimace of pain, took hold of the mule's lead, and never looked back at the cabin.

The sun rose, pale and cool, first on our right, then behind us as we turned west towards Summit Creek. It was a cool, windy morning with high, wispy clouds lightening the lively blue of the clear skies.

Following the edge of the marshlands, we left Antler and took to the contours of Sliding Mountain around nine o'clock, by my watch. Since I had had no standard to initially set my timepiece by, this was a hypothetical hour, but when one travels through the wild country, the only times that have any real meaning are sunrise and sunset. I kept track only to satisfy my personal curiosity and sense of orderliness.

As we crossed the same clearing on the hillside where I had originally spied Rosh's campsite, we saw a thin column of smoke rising from that spot. My companion stopped and stared away in that direction for a moment, and I stopped as well, watching Rosh rather than the smoke. He had a distant, vacant expression, and when he heard the voice of one man shouting to another far below us, he winced, almost as if the sound was painful to his ear.

"They're looking for me," he signed, and for a moment I thought he might want to go down and talk to whoever was at his old camp, but instead, he turned and headed again in our original direction with quick, decisive strides.

I felt relieved, as if we had passed an important test — a first trial in our odyssey. It would be disquieting, no doubt, for him to vanish before his friends' eyes, as it were, and leave no explanation, but the fact that he was willing to do so and reasoned for himself the necessity of it, encouraged me greatly.

I could imagine the searchers behind us shouting for their friend, then looking for tracks, and examining his living area for any clue as to what might have become of him. They might wait for a day or two, then head into town to ask around, but they would never solve their mystery unless Rosh decided to return north after his trip with me. By that time, I wouldn't care who knew about me, let alone a bunch of Chinamen.

The Chinese in Barkerville were a large and very visible group — the most concentrated population of Orientals on the continent, apart from San Francisco, I would think — but they kept very much to themselves. They owned a good number of the local business and service establishments, and these catered to all segments of the populace, but when it came to private or social matters they remained politely aloof from the European community. They even had their own separate Masonic order, or so I was told.

We of the white-skinned majority probably had an exaggerated estimation of how ingrown and loyal this group of people was, but it was a comforting thought to me that by the time Rosh's brothers could mount an organized search for him, we would be far along the trail to anonymity.

We followed Summit Creek, uphill this time, around big granite pillars, then down through sheltered ravines, where it was surprisingly cold. I felt half worn out, and quite uncomfortable. My homemade pack was working reasonably well — spreading the weight of my share of the food and gold over my chest and one good shoulder, but my injury still gave me considerable discomfort.

Where the terrain opened out for a few hundred yards, and the sun reflected grey warmth off the rocks, I called a brief halt and we took some dry rations.

The days were getting shorter. The nights were getting colder. The sunshine's warmth was thinner and more restricted to the centre of the day. Oppressed by the shadows of the little canyon, I felt unreasonably chilled and tired, nearly unable to stand and lift my burden for the next stage of the journey, but I dismissed this as simply a poor attitude and forced myself to resume a brisk pace. The sun was past its zenith as we left Summit Creek and entered the alpine ravine of Downey Pass. I wanted to spend our first night on the far side of Beaver Pass, so whether I felt at my best or not, I had to keep going.

Rosh was once again protesting my choice of our route. He waved his arms, pointed at the rocky hillsides ahead, and jabbered an ongoing stream of negative opinion which I was fortunately, I thought, unable to understand and therefore not required to argue with. He seemed to know about a dozen words or phrases of English, and none of these were of much use in a logical disputation.

The entrance to the pass was a sharply-cut dry stream bed. Once past this, we found ourselves in a wide, shallow bowl covered with scrub pine, and bordered by talus slopes and slate cliffs. We descended for a short distance, then came to an area of wet marshland — boggy moss between fairly deep pools of standing water, twenty to fifty feet across.

As I stood on a raised clump of turf, trying to weigh our options, I became aware that the Chinaman was beside me performing a most amazing set of grotesque gyrations and bizarre faces, curling his lips back, grunting and gobbling with his back

---

153

hunched over. After a minute, he pointed insistently down the length of the pass. Eventually I realized that he was play-acting as a beaver, and that he meant to tell me that a dam had been built farther along, creating this great swamp. I had already reached the same conclusion myself, but I was not about to turn back yet. I was at that stage possessed by an obstinacy born of great fatigue, and an unwillingness to believe that a longer road must be followed.

I struck off to the left, ankle deep in cold water at times, hoping to find dry ground at the outskirts of the basin. Rosh followed with the mule, doing a good job, I must admit, of helping it to keep its composure. The animal was very unsettled by walking in water. I imagine its hooves cut right through the moss covering and sank into the slippery clay underneath, for it seemed nervous, and most anxious to pull each successive foot up as soon as it was down. Each time we reached a relatively solid hillock it was difficult to force the beast back down through the bog, but eventually we reached one side of the marshy bowl, where three inches of stagnant water slopped against the edge of a large talus cone.

There was not much point in trying to make the mule walk over this, but I scrambled up the loose gravel slope until I could see over and beyond — a perspective that finally made me revise my strategy. Ahead of us the pools became deeper and more continuous, the cliff faces rockier, and loose gravel slopes more daunting.

Rosh was behind me, asking awkward questions I could understand even in a foreign language.

There was no real indication that the going would be easier across the valley. I tried desperately, for the sake of both my body and my personal esteem, to see a free trail down the pass, and at one spot or another could imagine that a glimpse of such a thing was just visible, but there was truthfully nothing worth pursuing. It was a difficult moment for me. I was having a hard time seeing anything clearly — almost as if my eyes were not focussing properly. I thought perhaps a mist was rising off the swamp.

I climbed down off the talus slope and signalled an about-face. Our return route to the mouth of the pass was a little drier, or perhaps my feet were simply numb, but we struggled back to solid ground with Rosh mumbling invective behind my back. Again, I could understand "I told you so," even in Chinese.

I was exhausted, but possessed by a strange sort of determination. I knew that I had slowed the pace a certain amount, and granted, we were travelling by his directions, but I realized that it was vitally important that I should not let the Chinaman lead the way. I demanded that he walk behind, with the mule.

He was looking at me strangely — asking me questions I could not answer in a strange, piercing voice that hurt my head. More than before, I suspected that he was a dangerous, deceptive man. His language was changing, and now much of it was English, although I still could make no sense of it. Why had he pretended, thus far, to speak only Chinese?

My shoulder was on fire. I took off my pack, flopped it on top of the mule's bundles, and let Rosh figure out a way to keep it balanced there.

I had the sensation that my ears were full of heavy liquid. I was very hot, and sweated until my wet garments made me shiver with the cold. More than once I thought I saw furtive figures crouching at the edge of the forest shadows, or scurrying along at the periphery of my vision. Not only was I unable to get a clear look at them, I could not precisely recall who they were, although I suspected that they were communicating with Rosh.

I continued this way for quite some time before I admitted that I was sick. Even after I could no longer deny the fact that my body was nearing a stage of breakdown, I forced myself to keep walking, being obsessed for some reason with the thought that we must reach Beaver Pass before dark. My wicked companion suggested many times that we stop. I had no idea what he intended to do to me, should I agree. His coat looked unusually bulky, and I suspected he had a weapon hidden under it.

With me so feeble of both mind and body, it was surprising that we got as far as we did. I continued to place one foot in front of the other until I had lost all track of time and no longer had any idea of where we were. After a while, I realized that Rosh had now taken the lead, but I no longer had the strength to resist.

Even simple speech surpassed my abilities, but I felt that if the Chinaman was not totally devoid of merciful humanity, he must soon stop and allow me to rest, for the fire that had begun in my shoulder now raged across my back and licked down to the base of my spine.

When we reached Cornish Lake and Rosh began to unpack the mule, I flopped to the ground in relief and joy, deluded for the moment into the belief that we had somehow reached the sea. I was bothered, however, by the fact that I could see all the way across to the other side. Somehow, Rosh had led us to a place where the ocean was narrow enough for us to raft across to China. The idea worried me for a moment, then it slipped away.

I suppose I fainted, for I awoke to find my partner dragging me across the ground like a carcass. Miserably, I could do nothing much to help him, or to defend myself from the horrible pain he caused me by grasping me under the arms. He pulled me over to a bed he had made against a rock under a big spruce, and covered me with a blanket. He removed my boots, and the thought came to me that he was planning to abandon me, and didn't want me to be able to follow him. But if that were the case, I wondered, why was he making me such a wonderful bed?

I slept for a time, and awoke in full darkness, with a fire burning four or five feet from me. The Chinaman was watching me, and when he saw I was awake, he ladled a cup of water out of a pot and brought it to me. I wanted that water more than anything in the world, but I could not summon the strength to sit up for it – a fact that Rosh noticed easily enough. He placed his right hand under my bad shoulder, and attempted to lift me. The scream of agony that followed startled him into spilling the water, and eclipsed my own vision with showers of sparkling stars.

After he had found a better way to manoeuvre a cupful of water into my mouth, Rosh delicately unbuttoned my shirt and undershirt, and exposed the wound inflicted by the wolverine a couple of weeks earlier. The look of horror and revulsion on his face told me everything I needed to know. The chafing of the packstrap had stripped away the surface layer of skin and scab, and now the area was a pulpy mass of pus and blood. I was assaulted by an overpowering fear and panic.

I was a walking, breathing clump of infection. It had been three days since I had even examined my shoulder properly, let alone cleaned or cared for it. During that time, it had remained painful to touch – at times throbbing with heat – but I had developed ways of performing all my duties using only my good arm. I had had other things to occupy my mind, things I had considered more pressing. Besides, I thought the good, crusty scab that had formed was a favourable sign, and the residual pain was merely a nuisance. I could ignore the truth no longer. The poison had seeped inward from my wound and it now flowed through my body unrestricted. I was its plaything until it killed me.

I have not, either before or since, felt such a sensation of fear. Nothing is so frightening as sickness – the invisible demon warrior that comes from without and within, and can only be chased away, never defeated.

I don't know how I managed to return to sleep, but I must have done so very quickly. When my restless flurries of dreams and hallucinations next abated, the Chinaman was once again forcing me to drink. Why so much water? I thought. Why so much water? I was already soaked to the skin.

Again I slept, and again awoke. The fire was low, mostly coals laced with occasional flame. My companion was curled up under his own blanket at the edge of our pale circle of light. Shifting my position slightly, I could see shapes on the ground just past my feet — my boots, and my revolver.

I gauged the distance to my revolver, stretched out my arm, and wiggled my fingers towards it. If I could reach it, I would shoot the Chinaman before he could stir. It was a matter of self-defense, and revenge as well. First, though, I needed a bit more rest.

My eyes closed, and opened again to more water being pushed at me. He was up and had his boots on, although it was still dark. At first I thought I could see the beginnings of daylight, but the extra brightness came from the fire being more built up. The horror of night would never end. The water felt good on my throat, though, and when I slipped back below the surface of sleep, it felt more like I was relaxing, rather than returning to a great unconscious battle.

Although I had wandered in and out of wakefulness all night, when I next awoke I felt that it was the first time I had reached full consciousness. The day had dawned, the sky was bright blue above me, and I felt like I was neither burning nor freezing. My relief was great but short-lived.

Rosh was gone.

It was the first realization that my new-found clarity of mind brought to me, and I did not need to shout out or look around to confirm it, even if I had had the strength to do so. A person can somehow sense the difference between momentary separation and the emptiness of being absolutely alone. Stretching my neck a bit, I could see the spot where the mule had been tethered for the night, just past the boulder facing me. Rosh was gone, and he had taken my gold.

I thought for a moment. What would he do? If he were smart, and I had never doubted that, he would not return to Barkerville, for there he would find himself in the same predicament I had contemplated — the authorities might very well seize the booty, no matter how clearly and honestly he explained his righteous claims.

He would go down the same trail I had plotted — to Fort Victoria, or perhaps farther south to an American port to take passage home to his heathen land with my treasure in his baggage. He would never make it. I would catch him.

I looked down to see my boots and my Colt .45 still at my feet, and this time it was no feverish delusion, but a calm and logical assessment that made me say that I would blow the traitor's head right off his shoulders. He had a head start, but even if I laid up and recuperated for a full day or even two, I would make up the ground before he could reach the Thompson River canyon, because I would be travelling light and angry, while he struggled along under a greedy robber's double burden. He could have saved himself by taking my gun and boots, but he was complacent and in a hurry, which he would live to regret.

I am not sure if I slept at this point, and reawakened later, or whether I just lay there, fretting over my situation. Eventually, however, I could remain still no longer.

It took a great deal of time, and the pain was so intense that it made me nauseous and dizzy, but I eventually managed to get my boots onto my feet. There was no question of doing up the laces. I shoved my revolver under my belt, then hauled myself to my feet, and stood holding onto a spruce branch while I waited for the world to settle itself. Finally I started after Rosh.

A game trail led into the pines, down and away to my left, and I followed it without a second thought. I wasn't worried at all about getting lost, in spite of the fact that the world was blurred and quivering around me. The main thing was to catch Rosh. I would make him tell me where we were before I killed him.

The scrub bushes were thicker and thornier than usual. They grasped at me with sharp, crackly fingers as I tried to pass by, and when I stumbled into their midst, they clawed at my ankles and tried to drag me down. It was a bother, but I didn't let it stop me. It was just a matter of time until I was used to walking again. All I needed was persistence, and eventually my body would start to cooperate.

My senses of sight and hearing also caused me problems. The trail wound along a ridge, parallel to the lakeshore some distance below, but I had no idea where the best place was for a descent. My eyes would not focus properly for more than a few seconds at a time, and I couldn't tell how far it was to the edge of the cliff. It seemed important to know this, so I crept closer, a few steps at a time, pausing to regain my stability every few seconds. It was a long way down, I could tell. As I looked straight ahead, I was level with the tops of some pretty substantial trees. I thought perhaps I was doing something dangerous, but I dismissed the idea and crept farther forward, a few inches at a time, now. The loose pebbles scattered along the slate cliff top made the surface slippery.

During the moment that my vision cleared, I was able to ascertain that I was perched at the top of a forty- or fifty-foot precipice, with no hope for safe descent. A dizzy spell hit me, and I sat down heavily, only realizing afterwards how close I had just come to a calamitous fall. When I looked down, the distance seemed to expand to hundreds of yards. I was forced to close my eyes to stop my head from spinning, then creep away on hands and knees, back to the path.

I had spotted something of interest, though. About a hundred yards farther along the cliff top, I could see a spot where the sheer rock face went all the way down to the waters of the big lake. If I reached that spot, I might be able to dive off, saving myself the arduous labour of climbing down the steep slope. A quick plunge in the water might also be good to cool me off and wake me up. I was having no end of trouble concentrating. Should I take my boots off before I dove from the cliff? I couldn't decide.

I didn't go all the way back to the path. It would be wasted energy. I knew I couldn't get lost as long as I continued downhill and along the lake. For that matter, if I didn't catch the Chinaman and make him return my gold, it didn't matter much whether I was lost or found, alive or dead.

The cliff top was strangely difficult to locate at times. I stopped twice to get my bearings.

I began to hear strange and significant things. First, I simply heard someone coming through the bush behind me. Then I realized that it must be a great number of people. No matter how long I held my breath and listened, I couldn't tell whether it was simply the wind in the trees, or some band of travellers. Eventually I decided it must be the former, and continued in my search for the cliffs, but a moment later, I caught the sound of low, indistinct voices mixed with the rustling of leaves. Someone was moving through the trees, off to my right.

I crouched low, drew the revolver, and cocked it. It was extremely heavy, and I was terribly tired – too tired to carry it, so I stuck it back in my waistband. I knew it was dangerous to carry a cocked weapon like this, but I was forced to do so. I would move very carefully.

I realized that I was walking on the path again, and decided that it was a good thing. I would make better time if I stayed on the path. With luck, I could catch up to Rosh any time now. I was horribly tired. Time passed quickly. The sun had moved all the way across the sky, and it was starting to get dark. I walked with my right hand supporting my throbbing left arm.

I was only mildly surprised when I followed the path around an outcropping of rock, and found myself back at my camp. It was just the sort of trick that an evil person like Rosh would invent – in some way he had managed to lure me right back where I started.

It was dark when I regained consciousness. Somehow, I was going to have to care for myself for the next twelve hours or so, while my body destroyed the invading poison and my arm regained its strength. I would have to keep the fire alive, refill the water pot when it was empty and scrounge a bit of food from somewhere. Then I would find the best spot along the cliff, and jump down into that cool blue water. It would feel wonderful, and it would be good for my shoulder; it would clean it, heal it. With my right hand, I daintily lifted my shirt front to inspect my wound. It was developing a foul odour. I found my underwear to be solidly attached to the grey dried skin of the infection and knew that I would have to swim until the water soaked the material away.

I prepared to sit up, a move that required the use of both arms to some extent, but my left limb would no longer shift at my command. I touched it with my good hand but there was no feeling left at all. I might as well have been prodding at a chunk of pork. My arm was no longer my arm.

For the first time in my adult life, I wept bitterly — partly in fear, partly in frustration. I would not re-capture my gold. I would die here, alone in the wilderness. Probably the fever would burn me to death before I starved, but one way or the other, there was no question of recuperating and chasing after my turncoat partner.

My panic was so great that I was unable even to retreat into sleep. At times, I would try to reassure myself by saying that the great weight of my anger and hatred could accelerate the recuperative process and renew my strength, but one cold touch to the dead meat on my left side quickly deflated such postures. I was dying.

The Chinese were a despicable people as a race, I concluded. I visualized a scene that should have taken place many years previous. Judge Begbie had lined up every Oriental found living on the civilized side of the Pacific, and a gallows waited for every one of them. Once per Chinaman he banged his gavel until they were strung up all along Williams Creek Valley like Christmas ornaments.

Still awake, I became aware of the return of the fever in full force, and with the fever came my fear. At the periphery of my understanding was a knowledge that I could scarcely bear to face — that this night would be my last on earth.

It was a welcome release when blackness absorbed me.

It took a great deal of time and effort to decide whether what happened next was reality or painful dream, as Rosh propped me against his chest and levered my mouth open to make me swallow the most foul-smelling liquid I had ever encountered. If my metabolism had been more vital, I believe I would have vomited, but as it was, I let the horrible brew trickle down into my stomach and tried to make sense of this dream. Was he supposed to be helping me, or had he returned to torture me still further?

It was the centre of night. Sharp stars burned above me; a campfire crackled at my left. Rosh kept me leaning against his own chest and peeled away the clothing from my upper body, anointing me with another liquid which somehow managed to exude a stench even more disgusting than the stuff he had made me drink. Gazing past the cloth in his hand, I saw the flames flickering and dancing in the night blackness.

He had pursued me into hell.

He would not, it seemed, allow me to sleep in peace for any length of time that night. I was continually dragged from my rest to quaff more of his horrible potion, then subjected to repetitious ablutions in the other noxious liquid.

The disgusting odours and taste of Rosh's concoctions did not improve over the next couple of days, but by the time I had regained enough strength to resist their administration, I had been forced to admit their almost magical efficacy, and I accepted them willingly, albeit with revulsion. I cannot guess the nature of the components of those medicines, but I am living witness to their miraculous ability to carry a man from the brink of death to reasonably good health in three nights and two days.

To my great discredit, I did not, at that point in time, feel particularly grateful. My physical pain was accompanied by an overwhelming malaise, and even when I was able to rest more comfortably, with the alternating numbness and ache in my shoulder being replaced by an itchy tenderness, I felt a constant irritation. I was annoyed by the delay I had caused, and I was angry at Rosh.

I no longer harboured any delusions about his treachery or duplicity. Indeed, I recognized that I owed him my life. I was irritated, though, by his attitude, as I perceived it. I would have felt better if he had chastised me for holding up our expedition, but he did not. He tended to my needs with a bland patience. This is not to say that he showed any particular sympathy for me. He ignored me most of the time, whittling at sticks, or wandering around the clearing, humming discordantly to himself until it was time to fix my medicines. He treated me as he would have treated the mule if it had developed an ailment.

He was not angry; he was not sympathetic. I could only assume that he was gloating, and that bothered me a great deal. His face often seemed expressionless to me, and he did not exhibit his feelings in any way, but while I lay there, watching him and brooding over recent events, I became convinced that he was basking in the glow of his own success. He had every right to gloat. He had gone from cabin boy to captain almost overnight, and on top of it all, had proven his moral superiority by remaining faithful to me, even after I had showed him no consideration or respect.

Each time I awoke, I found him watching me. He would greet me with a word that I initially took to be Chinese, but later realized was his simulation of "hello." Presumably, he was also able to say "goodbye," but the occasion did not arise for him to make use of it. To pass the time, I made an attempt to teach him a few more words of English, but he brushed it aside, revealing that he was not always as patient as I had thought. He was satisfied with a six-word English vocabulary, and preferred to whittle, juggle pebbles, and mumble to himself.

At sunrise on the morning of our fifth day at the Cornish Lake camp, I arbitrarily reset my watch, which had completely unwound. At first, I called it seven o'clock, then, decided that was a little late and changed it to six. I then wound it. Taking the map from the side pocket of my pack, I spent some time examining it. The line I had drawn for our projected course was already obsolete — a fact I found unreasonably distressing. Resisting the temptation to call Rosh and have him point out our position, I finally guessed where we must be, and the route we would now have to take. I couldn't find pen and ink to mark it down, though, which also irritated me.

My partner watched me carefully while I did my share of the packing-up, and as we sat in the morning sunshine, each chewing on a slab of bannock, he evidently concluded that I was well enough to do some walking.

Only when he came forward to return them did I realize that he had taken from my pocket the nine coins that symbolized my share of the gold. I was still eating, seated on a rock, while he carefully counted them into my hand, from one to eight. The ninth coin he held up for me to see, then dropped it into his own pocket, and smiled.

I scowled briefly, then shrugged and stood up to leave.

On the one hand, I had paid him — for three days' doctor's wages — enough money to build a hospital. Then again, I reasoned, I had bought back my own life with only a tenth part of my fortune. It wasn't a bad bargain. I would have conceded four times as much without argument. I began to feel some of the gratitude that I knew I owed my travelling companion.

We could not hope to cover much territory on my first day, but we knew we needed to reach the Willow River and make lower ground as soon as possible. The snow on the Cariboo Mountains behind us crept lower each day.

CHAPTER TWELVE

W E TRAVELLED SIXTEEN or eighteen miles that first day – an excellent distance for a convalescent. It was fairly easy ground, down the Willow River to a main junction with a tributary not named on my maps, then up this stream to the opening of Beaver Pass. The descent was gentle, the valley fairly wide compared to the gullies and crevasses higher up, and the trail, while occasionally rocky and occasionally wet, made for easy walking. We stopped three or four times, and Rosh always waited for my signal before standing up to move again. He momentarily showed his disappointment when I signalled that I had had enough although there were still a couple of hours of daylight, but he quickly set to work making camp and would accept none of my help. He knew as well as I that our rate of progress would be established by how much my battered body could endure. In spite of the feelings I had experienced on my sickbed, there was now no sense of competition between us. For my part, I was too tired to attempt to regain any of the status I had lost.

I was able to make myself a very comfortable spruce-needle

bed, and I felt one step closer to rejuvenation when we started off next morning.

Up to that point, we had not met up with anyone, although in several spots we saw or heard evidence that mining was taking place close by. Beaver Pass was populated to some extent, and several active claims were strung along its five-mile length, but since it was also a fairly well-travelled route of passage to the main road south, I thought we could slip past anyone we found there without raising suspicion by being unsociable.

The closer we were to Barkerville, the more dangerous it would be for me to be seen. My notoriety may or may not have seeped from town into the hills, but here it would be disastrous if someone was to recognize me and note my passage, especially in the company of a Chinaman — an unusual enough thing to make me easily followed, should the law choose to do so. Once I was south of Quesnelle Mouth, I would achieve the anonymity of the highway traveller, but until then, I would avoid speaking to any man, and I would keep my face in the shadows.

Where the pass met with Lightning Creek and the main road south, there stood a roadhouse which sold meals and provisions. I would have paid a hundred dollars to wash up in a basin of hot water there and eat a plate of potatoes and eggs, but it was out of the question. We thought it best to leave the path a quarter mile before this, so we cut across the hillside and avoided coming within sight of the place. It might have been the hardest mile of travel on the whole journey, for we did not follow even the faintest game trail, but simply burrowed through bush as dense and tangled as spiders' webs. We had to fight with the mule every step as well, so it was not surprising that we were less than alert when we stumbled out onto the main road. Crashing and cursing, we blundered out about twenty feet away from a man on horseback who had paused to see what the commotion was about.

As had been my habit of late, I chose the worst possible course of action, and ignored the fellow completely. I could have bettered the situation by nodding to the man and handing him even the flimsiest lie, but instead I adjusted my hat, scrambled out of the ditch and kept walking, while he stared at us in bemused fascination. He was going north, so I didn't need to speak to him or see him again, but I had a terrible apprehension that our brief meeting would be elaborately described to anyone the man met.

The road from Barkerville to Quesnelle Mouth was a poor one, but any road at all was an improvement over the rough trails and creek beds we had followed to that point, and the countryside was pleasant — solid forest of pine and spruce, with enough birch and poplar to bring variety and give scattered tokens of autumn colour. The weather in the afternoon was cool but not cold, with solid high, dark cloud cover threatening rain but never delivering more than an occasional spatter. My mood brightened, and I soon forgot the man on horseback.

We had travelled for fifteen uneventful miles past Beaver Mouth, hurrying past Wingdam and the workings there along Lightning Creek, when just before sunset, as the prospect of stopping for the day was already beginning to appeal to me, I spotted three deer grazing where the forest met the road. I saw them before Rosh did, and stopped him with a raised arm. For a moment we stared at them, and they returned our gaze, wondering if we were something to be feared. I pondered how long it had been since I last ate real meat, then motioned to my partner to come around to my side of the mule and take the .30-.30 and shoot. I did not think it wise to use my tender arm any more than absolutely necessary, but Rosh frowned and shook his head. I wanted to persuade him, but he stubbornly refused to look at me and I couldn't count on the game to stay put much longer, so I slowly unslung the rifle and pumped a shell into the chamber.

Still looking behind them, the three whitetails started into a quick stroll away from us, and I shot the smallest one just behind the shoulder. I wondered whether Rosh was uncomfortable with guns, or was he perhaps squeamish about the business of killing animals? As if to answer my question, even before the echoes had died away he was on one knee beside the young doe, slitting her throat neatly, then dragging her by her hind legs farther into the bush, where he began to gut her. He wasn't squeamish, but he evidently could not or would not use a rifle.

I led the mule and carted the backpack up the hillside into the trees until all was well out of sight of the road. Then I found tinder and kindling, started a fire, and flopped exhausted onto the ground. Rosh arrived, carrying the animal's heart in one hand and a good part of a hind quarter under his other arm. I drifted off to sleep. When I awoke, I was presented with a birchbark platter covered with two or three pounds of meat, all of which I ate. I knew I would probably feel ill and develop the trots, but I thought it was worth the discomfort and I noticed that my travelling companion took a portion nearly as large as my own.

We slept well, but began the next day in haste. The smell of snow was unmistakable in the cool breeze, and the grey wool clouds above us veritably bulged. We hadn't travelled more than a mile before the first wet flakes began to fall. Soon the air around us was thick with floating, swirling snow, and within ten minutes the ground began to whiten. I tried to remember what the date was, and guessed that it must still be only in the first half of October, but in the mountain country, high above the plateau, any month can bring a blizzard.

I had hoped to make it down from the mountains and past the river junction and the settlement at Quesnelle Mouth, but it soon became obvious that it would be a short day and poor passage. It was small comfort to know that the snowfall would disappear, probably within a day, for the chilling wetness soaked our clothes and blanketed the trail with an inch of slop that made the track difficult and treacherous. Even the mule looked miserable — head back, ears down, trudging along at half his usual pace.

Once we were completely soaked, mind you, we didn't feel any inclination to stop and rest, so we carried on almost without a break through the morning and early afternoon.

We saw no one else on the road that day. As we passed Cottonwood House we kept to the far side of the clearing and were chased briefly by a trio of loudly barking dogs, but I was little afraid that anyone would brave that weather just to see what had stirred up the obnoxious beasts.

At about two o'clock the weather cleared, or at least the snow stopped falling for a few hours, and I thought we might have a chance at making it down from the higher elevation before night-fall, but just when the contours of the land began to suggest that we were starting our long last descent to the plateau, the sky opened again, this time with a steady downpour of freezing rain.

Darkness fell early, so we were delighted when around five o'clock we saw, at the edge of a field, perhaps fifty yards from the road, a sort of hay barn or large open-walled shed. It was only a feed station for range cattle, but to us it resembled a grand hotel.

The sheltered area was about twenty feet by twenty, but three-quarters of this was covered by hay — loose and in bundles. The unused space was liberally spotted with droppings — from both pack animals and deer — so our mule was definitely not the first four-footed creature to gorge himself at the unknown rancher's expense. I would have been quite content to squirrel down into the hay until I was warm enough to sleep, but Rosh had sufficient energy left to make a clear spot on the shed floor and pull to-gether the makings of a fire.

Being officially still in the process of recuperation, I was per-mitted to stretch out on the hay and watch while he did all this, then cropped together a pot full of slush from the grass outside to heat for tea. The only drawback was that Rosh therefore felt it expedient that I should continue being dosed with his vile elix-irs. I believe he derived some sort of perverted pleasure from forcing these noxious liquids on me, for he brewed them even before he cooked supper. The odour that lingered on my body made my rice and venison taste like rotting weeds.

We had finished our meal and were just scrubbing pot, bowl and cup, when I heard voices from out in the evening gloom. Someone else was arriving at our crude hostel. There was no chance to hide. We could only hope that whoever had found us would not cause us trouble.

Down from the high hills and in from the darkness and the sleet strode a group of Indians – three adults and a baby. They seemed to carry little in the line of baggage, although I got the impression that they were some distance from home. The woman carried the child in a sort of sling against her stomach. The old man had a single light bag over one shoulder; the younger man who walked in the lead and sat closest to our fire carried an old army-issue carbine.

This fellow, obviously their leader, gave us a friendly smile as he dragged a hay bundle closer to the circle of warmth, but gave no other greeting or sign of deference. He was tall, dressed like any miner or trail hand, with long black hair and a broad-brimmed hat, bedraggled now with the rain and snow. He had about half his teeth.

Two Indians had travelled part of the way in the company with which I had come north eight months previously, and I knew enough about those people to be unsurprised at the casual way he made himself at home.

There had been some hostilities between white men and these Indians in the past few years. A few of the early gold seekers had lost their lives, in fact, but that was farther south and some time ago, when the Indians were still confused and worried by the unknown pale-skinned invaders. As a culture, the Indians of the interior were gentle and easy-going. Far from considering their land a harsh one, they were almost lulled into lazy indifference by the ease with which they could survive. They seemed to be basically nomadic, but wherever they tethered their pony and propped up their tepee, they knew that ample fish and game would be at hand, so they lived a leisurely, undemanding life, with the men doing the hunting and the women covering all other forms of work.

The little group had been seated for some time, with the younger man close to the fire, and the others back in the shadows in what seemed to me a subservient pose, when the first words were finally spoken.

"I'm Red Antoine." It was said with another ingratiating toothless grin.

"Pleased to meet you. I'm Beddoes. He's Rosh." I realized after I said it that I probably shouldn't have supplied my real name, but I thought it wouldn't matter in this case anyway.

The conversation ended there for another half hour. The Chinaman and I watched the fire, dozed and let our clothes dry, and the three Indians did much the same.

They are a great people for sitting still without a word, those inland natives. They seem to be able to squat down and pass any amount of time, punctuating the wait only with a shuffle of the feet and a chuckle at some unspoken thought. Orientals are generally considered difficult to understand; the red men are nearly impossible.

"I suppose you wonder why I speak such good English."

Since our new friend Red Antoine had not actually spoken more than his name, that question had not, in fact, been troubling me, but he offered an explanation anyway.

"I did a lot of guiding for the Englishmen." He whispered it as if it should really be kept secret. "Englishmen are kind of funny, you know. They get lost real easy, but they can always find an Indian. Then they try to get the Indian lost. They usually want you to take them to places that aren't really there, and then, when they don't get there, they get mad as dogs." He shrugged. "Anyway, they taught me the language plenty good."

I couldn't think of any way to respond to that line of conversation, and in reality I felt much too tired to try.

We returned to silence for a few minutes, then I went to the mule and got the bottle – Ned's Scotch Whisky. I knew it was unwise, perhaps even illegal, to give liquor to an Indian, but I had been looking forward to that draught of internal warmth for the past four hours or more and if Antoine decided to ask for a turn at the spout, I was not ready to refuse him. He was a big fellow and I hoped he would not take offense one way or the other.

I took a good mouthful and passed the mug to Rosh, who accepted a swallow appreciatively and smiled thanks. Sure enough, Antoine reached for the cup, took it, and drank thoughtfully. He offered none to his friends, but drained the cup, reached past me for the bottle, and refilled it to the brim. I glared at him, which I don't think he noticed, and removed the container to the pile of packing beside the mule. The big Indian drank down another few inches and passed the mug back to Rosh.

"That's very good whisky," he judged. "You must be quite rich."

That startled me. As usual, I could not read his expression at all. When the mug reached me, I kept it until I finished it, and again we sat in silence. It wasn't yet eight o'clock but I felt exhausted, and I moved outside the building to relieve myself preparatory to sleep. When I returned, Rosh had his eyes closed and was singing quietly. I grimaced, thinking that he sounded like a goose trying to imitate a robin, but Red Antoine looked at me and said, "It always makes me and my old brother happy to hear music. At first we only stopped just to be friendly. My brother always says we have to be friendly. I'm glad we stopped though, because of the music, you know."

I shrugged and yawned – almost, but not quite sure that he was joking. As he continued speaking, I concluded that he was quite serious, and was enjoying our company in his own way.

"Weather like this makes people happy to see each other, no

matter what. Life is good when one person builds a fire and five people get warm. I don't know who made this fine wood building either, but I think I like him too. Maybe he was an Englishman, but that's all right. You aren't an Englishman I don't think, but I can't always tell with you white men."

I was dreadfully tired, and just about to inform him that I had had enough of his frivolous meanderings, when he said something that demanded more of my attention.

"You're either English or Yankee, I know, and I know that your friend is an Indian. I can tell that. It's a good thing too, because some people might think he was a Chinaman, and everyone is supposed to be on the lookout for a Yankee and a Chinaman. Some sort of crooks. That's what my old brother heard back at Wingdam."

I didn't know what to say. I stood with my mouth wide open until eventually old Antoine looked at me and said, "You're pretty tired, aren't you? You go to bed if you want. I'm going to stay up and listen to the music."

For the moment, I responded with only a silent nod and crawled into the hay to consider what had been said, leaving the Indians to savour Rosh's bleating songs to their hearts' content. An unruly variety of questions presented themselves for my analysis. Was this Indian something other than he seemed? Were the sheriff's agents already close behind me? Evidently the man we had stumbled past at Beaver Pass had heard about Zachary Beddoes and discussed his suspicions with others when he had a chance, but who had he told, and how much did they care about a mysterious pair of travellers? Would a troop of Royal Engineers descend on us immediately, or would the authorities choose to ignore us? These weren't questions I could easily dismiss.

By now Rosh had stopped singing and it was Antoine and his brother who were droning painful monotones into the night. As if he knew of my mental distress and wanted to reassure me, the big Indian stopped for a moment and said loudly, "I know the difference between a Chinaman and an Indian real good, but it's too bad I don't remember names like other people."

I appreciated the implications of his statement, but I still found it hard to sleep.

I had decided to ask some direct questions of the Indian in the morning, but when I roused myself just as the sky was hinting at daybreak, the little group of natives was gone.

We walked quickly, without taking time to eat. Rosh knew I was worried about something, but of course he had no idea what that might be. The weather had cleared a little, although the road was still muddy. After travelling seven or eight miles, we saw the first twisted strands of smoke rising from the settlement at the river junction, and I decided I should explain. With our usual miming language, I described Red Antoine as "tall man, floppy hat, back there," and said that he had seen me and knew me. Legal authorities were looking for me. I was worried. Rosh understood. Did Red Antoine know about the gold? No, only about me. He knew the authorities were looking for me.

We both understood the implications of a stray Indian knowing me, particularly since I had made the unforgivable mistake of giving him my name.

At mid-morning we were standing on a well-situated bluff, overlooking the townsite of Quesnelle Mouth, trying to decide on a route. We wanted a road or track that would lead us around the inhabited area without actually ploughing through the bush surrounding the river forks. We would have to come close to the town to cross the Quesnelle River, since I knew of no other ferry or fording place, but I had no desire to pass through the populated area itself. So far that day, we had passed several houses set back from the road, and waved to a settler who seemed to be working on a wagon, but had yet to come into real contact with any of the locals.

I had the feeling that the sheriff, or whoever was in charge of apprehending me for questioning, would probably focus the main part of his attention on the stretch of road ending at this point. Logically, the two ferries — both the larger Soda Creek Ferry and the smaller, locally operated one where the road crosses the river — would be good places to keep watch. I didn't know whether those searching for me were sufficiently informed and organized, or sufficient in numbers to be doing this by now, but I had to take the chance. Once beyond Quesnelle Mouth, the land would be so vast, and traffic so scarce, that finding a single man there would be like hoping to snatch a particular flea off a dog's back.

From our viewpoint, we couldn't see any route that skirted the town, so we returned to the main road and started our descent following it, but kept our eyes open for a promising side track.

With still a mile to go, we passed numerous houses and buildings, some with people coming and going, and I grew extremely nervous.

A wagon track split off to the left a half mile or so from the townsite proper, and we followed this. It snaked left and right for a hundred yards and seemed to be going roughly the proper direction, when we suddenly found ourselves in the yard of a log house on the edge of a meadow. A dog barked angrily from the porch. Before we could consider whether to turn around or cut across the meadow, a woman, large and of middle age, dressed in trousers like a man, stepped out of the front door of the house.

"Good morning, ma'am. I wonder if you could help us," I began, but she interrupted me with a most unladylike curse and shouted instead:

"I can help you off my land, you miserable vagrant. I'll help you with a shotgun, if you like. You stinking gold grubbers just keep moving wherever you like, but get off my property before you find yourself here for permanent. You start digging around my land and you'll be digging your own graves, by gosh! Get moving!"

We struck out across the meadow, while behind us, the lady of the house continued to rant and scold.

"If you were any kind of a decent dog," she decried to the animal, "you'd have gone after those two and took a chunk out of somewhere."

Past a screen of trees at the edge of the meadow we found the river bank and followed this downstream to the crossing. One man was panning the river gravel, but he didn't even look up as we passed above him.

Near the ferry we paused and waited, watching both banks of the river from a place of concealment in the short poplars. We saw a child with a dog cross over into town, then a farmer with a small wagon. Finally we emerged from the bush and tramped across the pebbled flats to the river crossing. We could see no one watching, but both of us felt the glare of a hundred eyes upon us, and expected shouts and gunfire momentarily.

The crossing was accomplished without incident.

Travelling south all that day, we covered the first twenty miles of the route along the Fraser under cloudy skies that gave no rain. The next day was also successful for us. My strength seemed to have totally returned, although I saw no need to change the status quo, and left the carrying of the gold to the Chinaman and the mule. If I had judged that such a weight of supplies and precious metal could be carried by one man and one animal, I would probably not have thought it necessary to include a partner in my plans. In that case, however, I would presumably have died from the fever before I ever made it out of the mountains, so everything seemed to be working out for the best.

Towards the end of that second day, as the sun slipped out between the cloud layer and the hilltops, we approached the Soda Creek area, and the geography changed somewhat. The trees were mostly pine now, scattered in clumps across rolling open country, or forming light, easily-travelled forests along the hillsides. The ground was, in fact, so nicely passable that the road was often not clearly delineated. One simply followed the general direction of the mighty brown Fraser River, which carved its great canyon through sand and sandstone alike.

We had not seen a single soul since leaving the Quesnelle Mouth region, so our guard may have been a bit low, and it took us by surprise when we topped a rise and found a company of range hands making camp in the little valley below us.

We paused and looked at each other, then again at the scene before us. A half-dozen men were spread out there, some setting up camp, some tending to horses, while one pair headed in the direction of the river. They may have been workers on some ranch nearby, for a few people had already set up homesteads or ranches in the vicinity, or they may have been driving the herd of animals on the hill behind them towards Barkerville, for auction at the goldfields. One way or the other, they presented a problem.

Two men working with a pile of packs and saddles were looking towards us, screening their eyes from the setting sun with their hands. It would have been suspicious for us to make a long circle around the valley to avoid passing through their midst, but I did not wish to spend an entire evening being polite to a group of curious cowboys.

I have never feared unlikely schemes, and I had one at the back of my mind that seemed to fit the situation. I just had to communicate to Rosh what his part in it was. Once I had convinced him to start singing, we started down the hillside directly towards the trail hands.

I wore a long grey wool scarf that Rosh had given me. It appeared to have been made out of a blanket at some time, and it kept my neck and shoulders warm, but now I pulled it up over my head and around my cheeks, leaving only the space around my eyes visible. Walking bent over like this, in the deepening evening shadows, I should, I thought, be able to pass for a Chinaman — especially once I began to sing along with Rosh.

He stopped his own song when I began to wail away with what I thought was a fair rendition of a Chinese ballad, and I had to coax him to start again. I gather he eventually figured out the gist of my plan, for we sang out a most unpleasant harmony all the way through the cowboy camp and up the other side of the draw. Rosh paused long enough to chatter some Chinese greeting, and I kept my head bowed, and hung close to the mule's flank.

It was dark when we made our own camp a mile or two farther along, but even in the blackness of night I could sense that I had offended my partner with my use of his music in our little scheme. He avoided me that evening, and I never heard the man sing again.

We had been late in choosing the site for our camp that night, and because of darkness we had set up in a little grove of pines that offered minimal protection. Before full morning light we were thus up and on our feet, hastily loading packs and mule when a steady rain began to soak both our clothes and bedding. It is a depressing thing indeed to find your socks are wringing wet even before you put them in your boots.

We trudged along without fluctuation as the downpour continued. Like a mountain stream in flood, it neither slowed nor increased from daylight to noon.

Two normal travellers would probably have agreed to hide out under a tree until the worst was past, regardless of the danger behind them, but our communication was not good enough for us to justify it to each other. Because of this we made ten or twelve miles before we were mercifully delivered.

Somewhere around midday we walked along the base of a section of stark rock cliffs — basalt, or some type of slate — when we saw, more or less simultaneously, a cave. Perhaps it might better be described as an angular cleft in the rocks, but it was a protected spot big enough for two men and their gear, and it was so naturally inviting that we both headed for it without hesitation.

We spread our packs and baggage around the back of the little enclosure, although they could hardly have gotten any wetter if we had left them outside. The mule was tethered on his long rope fifty feet away, under the pines.

It was hard to say which was worse — plodding through the fog and the cold rain, or the deadly boredom of waiting in a cramped little stone prison. Such tedium compounds when one is impatient to accomplish something, and while we looked in vain for a break in the clouds, we were conscious that the cashing in of our riches was not getting any closer, but a group of pursuing law officers might very well be.

Rosh passed the time by whittling little pieces of wood into rectangular pieces the size of poker chips. If anything, I became even more irritated to see that he had found a way to distract himself. Then I remembered the single diary and the few letters from Ned's booty that I still possessed and had brought along.

The little red volume was wet around the edges, but the pages were only slightly wrinkled and none of the ink had run. The entries began a year and a half previously when the writer, who never gave his own name, arrived at the goldfields and staked a claim somewhere on Lightning Creek. After a description of what he did to set up, his notes were mostly brief accountings of his gold findings to date. I skipped over much of this, to the longer, more interesting journals written during the winter months, when he turned his pen to more philosophical jottings. He hated the north country, it seemed, with the ten and twelve feet of snow and the freezing winds, but he resolved throughout his writings to last another full season for the sake of a woman named Andrea.

Reading this, I felt a sense of disquiet, for I knew that the fellow did not in fact last the season, and I now carried Andrea's inheritance somewhere on my mule.

If I had turned the gold over to the government to distribute as they saw proper, would Andrea have received any share? I doubted that very much. For that matter, did she have a valid claim to the murdered man's gold? Even I had worked for it more than she.

I closed the book and pushed it back into its place in the baggage. I had never intended Andrea or her gentleman any harm, and there was now no way to offer either of them redress. It made no sense to unsettle myself further.

Rosh called for my attention, and drew something in the soft sand of the cave floor — a sort of grid of lines with a box around it. He had manufactured a game. He gave me a pile of sticks six inches or so in length, then took the same number of shorter twigs in a pile before him. The little chips that I had seen him making were inscribed with a single slash on one side and these were thrown, five at a time, like dice. The object of the game seemed to be to get one's pegs spotted on the board before one's opponent could do so. After my turn at throwing the chips, Rosh would indicate how many pegs I could place, and which ones I was allowed to move around. It had something to do with the number of slashed sides and the number of blank sides that showed up.

After ten minutes or so, it appeared that I was winning. I had more pegs on the grid, nicely aligned along one edge, and my opponent wore an expression of amused concern. Then he took his turn at throwing the chips, laughed gleefully, plucked three of my markers off the board and threw them back on my pile. When I next took my turn to throw, he simply shook his head to state that I was not entitled to place any pegs at all. He threw again, laughed loudly, and placed four markers on the grid, rattling off some incomprehensible Chinese maxim as he did so. He now had more pegs in place than I.

It was my turn, and I shook the little chips for quite a while before I dropped them on the cave floor. Four blanks and one slash. I was entitled, Rosh said, to one peg, and reached for the chips. I waved him back, though, and shook my head. Then I

181

placed five of my pegs on the board, picked off four of his, broke them in half, and threw them out into the rain.

He shuffled away and sulked, while I leaned against the baggage and pretended to sleep.

For three or four days after this, we travelled across undulating ranges of forest and rough meadow, skirting boggy lowlands and wearing our feet raw on rocky highlands. Both of us suffered from severe chafing and blisters, for it rained sporadically every day and we were never completely dry. It is on sore feet and numbing monotony that I blame the stupidity I exhibited when we next came near the company of other men.

While we did not dare to travel on the road itself any more than necessary, it was necessary for us to stay relatively close to it for a source of direction, and we came within sight of it more than once each day. It was somewhat unexpected, though, when we trekked over a sage-speckled bluff and found ourselves looking down onto the yard of a roadhouse. It may have been the 150 Mile House, or we may at that point have been a little farther south. Initially we did as common prudence dictated and diverted our passage out of sight and away. As we walked, however, my spirit and resolve drained quickly away.

We had been travelling a miserably long time. Moved by a sudden rush of self-pity, I was overcome by the temptation of a proper meal, a glass of ale perhaps, and a hot stove by which I might dry my socks and boots.

It would take only an hour, I thought. We were a long way from Barkerville, and there was no reason that anyone should consider me anything other than a simple travelling miner, even if the description of Mr. Beddoes had already been circulated. I would further minimize the risk by employing subterfuge, and profess to speak no English. As a dockhand in San Francisco I had once worked with a Russian, come down from the north coast settlements, and I had picked up a bit of his language. In truth, my knowledge consisted of only four words, but I thought that if I repeated them in varying order and invented a few more plausible phoneticisms, it should pass for a language of its own. I didn't worry that I might run into another Russian in that neck of the wilderness.

Rosh paced and muttered nervously as he watched me preparing myself – trimming my beard shorter than it had ever been and pomading my hair back with boot grease. He did his best to make his objections clear, but I exercised my prerogative of understanding nothing. Backtracking to join the road and enter the compound from the south, I trudged up to the roadhouse feeling invigorated by my own nervousness.

The main room of the place was large, warm and dark, as are all log buildings. It took a moment or two for my eyes to adjust. Coats and baggage were on the right, and I dropped my pack there, as one of four men stood up from the big central table and came to face me. He appeared to be the owner, so I addressed my best Russian greeting to him. Once the other three heard the jangle of my foreign speech they returned to their own discussion, and I prepared to mime out a request for the biggest platter of hot food available.

Before I could do so, I recognized the voice of the speaker holding forth at the table two steps away from me, and I became immobilized with shock. Hec Simmonds, sometime deputy of Sheriff John Stevenson, looked me full in the face. It was only a single glance, after which he turned his back to me, but I was quite sure that if he looked again, he would have no trouble recognizing me, particularly since I was the reason that he was now installed at the roadhouse. I stared silently at the trio for a long second. A tall, thin man across the table stared back. The innkeeper likewise waited for me to express myself. Hec Simmonds droned on about nothing.

The fact that he was a fool was beside the point. Hec Simmonds was no doubt employed in hunting for Zachary Beddoes.

183

He had guns, friends, and some level of official authority, and he was six feet away from me in an enclosed space.

"Bah!"

I tried to say it in a tone of voice that implied that for some reason or other I was deeply offended, then I sounded a sort of low growl, simply because my Russian acquaintance had been wont to do so, and headed for the door. The proprietor, bewildered by my actions, called for me to wait, but I stomped on out as if I had been unforgivably insulted.

"Would you hang on a minute there, brother — give me a chance. I don't understand what you're saying," he protested. I never slowed my pace. Swinging my pack angrily at my side and muttering variations on my three Russian words, I strode up the dirt bank to the level of the roadway and turned right, out the north end of the clearing. All the way I could feel the burning sensation of eyes on my back. I expected to be shouted at, or even fired upon at any moment by Simmonds and his cohorts, but I was giving them credit for too much alertness. Perhaps sometime later they realized just how strange my appearance and disappearance had been — I cannot say. I was satisfied to escape with my skin intact, and when once again I reached the spot where I had left Rosh, we were gathered and gone within two minutes. Our poor communication was most convenient for me at that point, for although I could easily convey the need for speed and caution, I was not forced to describe what had happened at the roadhouse.

We made camp that night after dark, without a fire. I crawled into my bed hungry, but I could stomach no cold rations.

Next morning we wasted a certain amount of time regaining our bearings. Travelling quickly through the previous twilight, we had wandered a bit too far from the road, and it took us until nearly noon to ascertain exactly where it was. My map, now so badly worn that it fell into two pieces, had once again proved to be unreliable. When we finally came upon the twin wagon ruts of the main road, we rested, for the last quarter mile had been across steep ground. Rosh inspected the mule and cleaned its hooves, while I spread out some of our foodstuffs to take inventory. In those few moments we were approached unawares.

We had not moved far enough off the track, and when the stocky little man with the long rifle came over the rise he could hardly miss us. Unfortunately, he did not have the good grace to walk on by with only a nod and a greeting; he had to stop for a chat.

I was immediately uncomfortable with the man. He reminded me in both his physical appearance and mannerisms of a man I had tracked down and turned over to the police in a town west of Chicago when I worked for Pinkerton's, and I should have trusted my instincts more.

He was older than I was, round in the belly and dirty — even by the standards of long distance travellers — with hair and beard somewhere between blond and brown. He had the habit of glancing around continually, even while he spoke, and he didn't seem to accept our unwillingness to respond to his chatter as any reason to continue on his own way.

"Sore feet, so it is, eh? My oh my, that's bad. Nothing worse for a traveller than sore feet. My oh my. Don't you look sad, all barefoot and hobbling. Wet boots, that's it, isn't it? Dry those boots, man. Dry those boots. New socks, do you have new socks?"

"No."

"Too bad. Nothing more important for a traveller than dry boots, good socks. Chinaman don't talk, eh? Don't talk English? That's strange. My oh my. Beautiful day though. You're going north? 'Course not — you're going south, just like everyone else. Quittin' Barkerville for the winter. I'm going north, but not far, not far. I could take a rest myself, though. Man like me can always take a rest on a beautiful day."

"We're about ready to get moving again," I said. "Have to move when the weather favours you, of course."

I was trying to bundle up the food and tie the blanket around it as quickly as I could without revealing my nervousness and impatience, and I had my back to the stranger. Rosh likewise was turned away, lacing up his boots.

Suddenly the Chinaman shouted, and a commotion ensued behind me. Rosh had stood up to find the stranger casually undoing one of the strings on our main baggage bundle to peek into our belongings. By the time I had fully stood up, the brief altercation had begun and ended. Rosh slapped the man across the side of the head, and the stranger swung clumsily back. His momentum caused him to stagger forward when his punch came nowhere near the target, and Rosh took advantage of this, grabbing him by the collar and launching him onto his belly. The fellow cursed loudly as he tried to scramble to his feet, but the words were knocked out of his mouth by a carefully placed kick to the side of his jaw. He had the bad sense to stand up again, and Rosh again flicked a heavy foot out, as quick and graceful as a French dancer, and sent the man sprawling.

I had not moved. Our hapless visitor gasped and crawled around with a most surprised look on his face. Rosh stood over him, showering him with streams of Chinese verbal abuse.

I tried my best to cool the situation and placate the battered wanderer. I gave him a good swallow from our bottle of Scotch, explained that all Chinese are subject to unpredictable fits of irrational rage, and sent him on his way with my apologies. I considered holding onto his rifle, in case he decided he deserved vengeance, but decided against it. He seemed more confused than angry.

I was annoyed with Rosh. I thought he had overreacted terribly, and endangered us by doing so. I should have known better. The man always controlled his temper very well, and I should have trusted his judgement. After all, he saw clearly what the stranger was doing, and he knew more exactly than I what the fellow had seen.

I had the opportunity to ensure the man's silence, and to keep him from causing us any trouble at all, but instead I sent him on his way with an apology I would regret having issued.

CHAPTER THIRTEEN

O
UR SPIRITS WERE low as we limped along beside the mule over the rolling meadows of the southern end of the great Cariboo Plateau. We bypassed the 100 Mile House, and could now sense the downwards trend of the land as we began our long, gentle descent to the level of the Thompson and Fraser Rivers. This knowledge should have been exhilarating, but was not in fact strong enough to buoy our emotions.

We were close to exhaustion. We needed a day of rest.

Around three o'clock we reached a spot where a brook crossed the wagon road and meandered from thence down a fairly open little side valley. It looked a promising place to find a decent day camp, and I led the mule downstream, beckoning Rosh to follow. He caught up to me, protesting eloquently in Chinese that Ashcroft was just around the corner — only one or two days away. I shrugged off his entreaties and led on. Ashcroft was just another roadhouse that we dared not visit. Our goal still lay two hundred miles distant and more.

We could greatly improve our chances of making a speedy trip to the coast if we took the time now to revive our spirits and dry our boots. I could not translate this argument, of course, but the idea must have been obvious enough, for the Chinaman soon lapsed into a sulky but cooperative silence.

The campsite we found for our layover could not have been more perfect. The little brook flowed into a small lake only a quarter mile from the wagon road, and here we tethered the mule, laid out to dry those of our goods and clothing that remained damp, and stripped down to bathe in the ebbing warmth of the afternoon sun.

As I saw him without his clothes, scrawny and hairless as a young boy, I once again thought of my companion that if I had had a better chance to examine him originally, I would never have chosen him to help me carry my great burden on this arduous journey. As if he knew my thoughts, Rosh waded into the lake, swam effortlessly into the middle and circled about out there for a half hour or more. I had to admire his strength and ability. I myself can only paddle and flounder.

The little lake was about two hundred yards across and pushed up against the trees along one side. I found a small, deep pocket of a bay where a windfallen tree projected out over the water, and put my fishing gear to use for the first time in many weeks.

I lay there lazily on my log, twitching the thread coiled through my fingers for most of an hour, enjoying the peaceful forest sounds and watching with one eye as Rosh built a fire half-way round the shore. The green waters grew darker, and I was about ready to give up when I felt the faint tugging of a nibble at my hook. Cautiously, I applied a bit of counter pressure, and was nearly pulled off my perch into the water with the result. For a moment, I thought I had lost him, then a second later, I thought my fingers might be sliced off by the pull of the line.

Ten minutes after that, I strolled into our camp with a trout that must have weighed close to three pounds. Rosh was eloquent in his praise, and I was graceful in my nonchalance.

Our first afternoon of leisure had been profitably passed.

189

❖

Somewhere in the middle of the night I was brought to full wakefulness by the realization that the campfire was crackling bright, when normally it should have burned to embers by that late hour. I sat up on my bedroll and found Rosh, who had retired before me, sitting up with his blanket draped over his shoulders. He pointed back towards my pillow.

"Are you all right there, man?" I asked.

He mumbled something of a dismissal, and gestured once again that I should go back to sleep.

"So you can't sleep. Are you all right? Are you hurt?" I held my head to try to designate the idea of pain, and he understood well enough, shaking his head negatively. When I continued to watch him sitting there in the firelight, he began to talk in his native language — a long speech with a melancholy flavour, or so I fancied. I thought I heard him mention Ashcroft, but again I could not be sure in the continuous flow of foreign words. At last I lay down again and slept until morning.

I had intended that we should spend the entire next day at rest — a Sabbath rest it could be, although I had long since lost track of the days of the week — but before midday I changed my mind. Our clothes and gear were dry, we were well-fed, and we had soaked and rested away any minor aches and pains that had bothered us. Physically and spiritually we felt reconstructed; our good humour and attention were back to their peak, and further delay would only increase our gnawing impatience. We began to pack up.

Feeling relaxed and expansive, I was in the mood for a bit of conversation — something that my companion and I still could not manage. In that spirit, though, I tried my hand at teaching Rosh another word or two of English. It was still not too late in our relationship to facilitate our daily routine with an improved mutual vocabulary. I pointed to the big canvas pack and said, "packsack."

He caught on to what I was doing, and without enthusiasm repeated the word – "packsack." He didn't do badly. The word was recognizable.

"We will go," I said, miming the action of walking, "and you will take the packsack. Go."

"Go," he said, nodding comprehension.

"We will go. You will take the packsack. I will lead the mule. Mule."

He had a little trouble with that word. He pronounced it "mooah." The letter "l" seemed to be in the wrong place, so I tried a substitute, not worried about technical accuracy.

"Donkey. You can say donkey. I will lead the donkey."

Rosh was not enjoying our session, which irritated me a bit, because it seemed so appropriate to me at the moment. Still, he patiently repeated the lesson thus far.

"Packsack," he said, and pointed to the bundle.

"Mooah," he slurred, gesturing to the mule.

"Donkey," he chirped brightly, and pointed at me.

"No! No, I am not a donkey. If anyone is a donkey, it's you, my friend. You're as stubborn as a mule and you have that talent at kicking people, so don't blame me if the similarity becomes well-known. Just grab the packsack and let's go."

It was obviously the end of my attempt to tutor him in the language of his new homeland.

"Packsack. Go."

"Shut up."

We returned to the trail and travelled ten or fifteen miles before making camp on the edge of a bluff giving view to several benches of the descent to the Thompson River Valley.

In spite of my recent near-disaster running into Hec Simmonds, we were now so far from Barkerville that it seemed reasonable to risk travelling full time on the main road. We had already been forced by the terrain to do so from time to time, and we had been able to use a few simple techniques to avoid confrontation with passers-by and the few other sojourners on the route. We kept to one side of the road as we walked, and as another person came into sight or within speaking distance we would contrive to be busy with our bootlaces, or some segment of the mule's baggage. People on horseback or in wagons were past in a moment, and pedestrians such as ourselves were usually in too much of a hurry to be gregarious. Apart from the Indians, there were few permanent residents in that country, and no one had much reason to loiter along the way.

Thus it was that my attention was so closely drawn to the strangers we passed on the next afternoon. Two men and a horse stood fifteen paces from the verge of the road on the uphill side. They were not camped, but neither did they seem to be on the move. Both men were tall, one clean-shaven, one with a dark beard, and when they exchanged nods with us as we passed I felt as if they were watching us in a way that was more than casual. Observing them, though, I saw nothing out of the ordinary, apart from the saddle on the sway-backed grey, which was a homemade affair with stirrups of braided rope. I did not want to seem overly curious, and had returned my gaze to the path in front of us, when I caught a glimpse of the third man as he stood up in the dark shadows, deeper in the trees.

It was the slippery little fellow that Rosh had kicked around two days previously.

That section of road is rough and rocky, up and down over gullies and ridges as it switches back and forth, moving down a fairly steep slope. It also weaves in and out of stands of pine and spruce, and once we were out of sight of the three watchers, I made for the nearest patch of forest, telling my partner to wait there with the mule at the meadow's edge.

I don't believe he had seen, let alone recognized the third man, but he had picked up my nervousness. I would have liked to explain the situation to him, but could not, of course. Since the day was sunny and warm, my coat was draped across the packs on the mule. I reached into the pocket and took out my handgun. My thought was to circle back and above the others to watch their movements, but I was no more than twenty yards uphill into the bush when they hallooed and called for us to wait.

I squatted down and peered through the branches to the spot where the trail ran up in front of Rosh and the mule. Four or five minutes later I saw them walking up the approach — the short man and the bearded man, along with the horse. They kept up a flow of jovial greetings, but now that they could see my companion, their eyes moved quickly from place to place.

"Where's your partner, Chinaman?" the little fellow asked. "Where's your friend?"

From my hiding spot I was thinking the same question — where was their partner?

The pine trees were fairly well-spaced, with little underbrush. It was better country to hunt than be hunted in, and I scurried farther up into the trees, bent over almost onto all fours. A hundred yards up, I emerged cautiously into the open and slid behind a great grey lump of rock, puffing like a broken boiler.

Far away I could hear voices calling, but could not make out the words. The run through the woods had left me almost too tired to think. I was safe for the moment, but I needed to come up with a plan, and I couldn't conjure up a thing. The only clear thought that I had was that if I didn't act quickly, I would lose everything.

After checking to make sure that the Colt was fully loaded, I crept down in the direction from which I had come.

Once I felt sure that no one was going to come up behind me, my fear was assuaged, and I slipped as lightly as a ghost from tree to tree over the bed of moss and needles, crossing the slope systematically but quickly. As I have said, there was little underbrush and visibility was good, so it almost startled me when I found myself immediately behind my quarry, no more than ten feet away. He was moving parallel to me, and like me was slightly hunched over, squinting into the gloom.

"Looking for me?" I whispered.

He held his rifle at the level as he spun around, but when he fired, the shot went off somewhere into the tree tops. I gripped the Colt firmly in both hands, and my first bullet hit him directly in the chest. He rolled some distance when he fell.

I had no time to pause and consider what I had done. I ran as silently as I could in a great semi-circle through the forested area, wanting to come out of the trees close to the other three men, but from a different direction than they might have expected from the sound of the gunfire. I misjudged both the exact layout of the trees and meadow and my own stamina, though. I ran too far across the hillside and had to backtrack. It must have been ten minutes later when — plodding, panting, and covered in sweat — I stumbled into the clearing where I had left Rosh.

Everyone was gone.

I must have made a strange sight then, hurrying laboriously up the wagon road with no hat or coat, swinging the oversized revolver at my side and mumbling a stream of foul threats. My emotions were a poisonous mixture of anger, impatience, and fear. They boiled around in my head, clouding my vision for the better part of an hour. Only then would I admit to myself that I was going in the wrong direction.

I had rushed off northwards without examining the ground — assuming without thought that since the slimy little bandit of our previous acquaintance had come from that direction, that would be the route of his flight. Without even glancing at foot and hoofprints, I had scurried on like a winded beetle for most of a mile as the road climbed the hillside, intent only on speed and my own vituperative imaginations of revenge.

When I finally took the time to look over the trail, and discovered my folly, I was well up the ascending folds of land, on a bench of meadow growing in high yellow grass spotted with sagebrush. I am more than a decent tracker — that being the one lesson I properly learned in the long boring months I was employed by Mr. Pinkerton, and there was no mistaking the situation here. All prints pointed south.

Loquacious musings on my own stupidity gave me no satisfaction at all. By way of self-punishment, the only thing I could do was plot a course back down the hillside that was steep and straight. More than once, I stumbled and tumbled as I clambered over rocks and down scree slopes. It would have been a fitting end if I had shot myself in one of those falls. I had given the blackguards a ninety-minute head start at the least, and I would be hard-pressed to catch them up before dark, if indeed I caught them at all.

Once I had worked my way back to my starting point I found their trail painfully easy to follow. For the first stretch, at least, it followed the main road, and since they had two animals in tow I knew it wouldn't be hard to spot any divergence. Thinking of my partner, I guessed that he would be doing his best to slow their progress as much as possible, but I hoped that he would temper his efforts enough to maintain his own safety. Logically, there was no reason why the brutes shouldn't dispose of him immediately, but so far as I could see from signs on the trail, they were leading him along as a prisoner thus far. Perhaps they were curious about the immensity of our riches, and wanted to interrogate him further once they had the time. When they reached the stage of dividing up their loot and separating, though, I had to believe that Rosh would be in serious trouble.

I was determined to do whatever was necessary to make up the time I had wasted, so I continued my hazardous and difficult course straight down the hillsides, in and out of windfalls and gullies, sliding half the time on my backside and hands, rather than following the roadway proper. The wagon road descended in great loops back and forth down this section, and whenever I crossed it I would check briefly to ensure that my quarry was still keeping to the track.

This steepest section of the route took me an hour and a half

---

195

to descend, and it was after four o'clock when the country levelled out for a while and the highway met up with a creek. I am not sure of its name, but even at that time of the year it was twenty feet across and looked to be deeper than a man's waist at many points.

Accordingly, the road wound away upstream towards some ford or bridge, which I took as an opportunity, since I could see it emerge again some ways down the valley. I didn't know how long the detour was, but I saw that I could bypass it by wading directly across, and I did so. The next half mile was a tangle of willow bushes, but it was level at least, and I slogged through it without any trouble.

I was scuffed up a bit on hands and knees, and my trousers were torn, but I was not particularly tired or hungry. I was not really afraid anymore, either — not of danger, nor of losing my fortune. I was driven by anger. I wanted to rescue my partner, and of course I wanted to save my gold, but at that moment I wanted more than anything to teach two wicked fools their due lesson.

I scrambled up an embankment of gravel to get back to road level, and stood for a moment with my gun tucked into my belt, picking slivers of sagebrush out of my hands, and glancing around for animal tracks. I found none.

I looked back and forth closely. The ground was easily read, and there was no sign of mule or horse having been through in the last few hours. As soon as I realized that I had overtaken and passed the Chinaman and his captors I ran for the shelter of the cottonwoods and willow trees along the road's verge, and tried to stay hidden in their midst as I hurried back, parallel to the main route.

I trotted along on the north edge of the main path, expecting at each turn to see the object of my chase ahead of me, so that I almost overran the tracks when they crossed unexpectedly beneath my feet. A few leaves had been kicked up, and some rough signs could be seen going up a little dry gully, perpendicular to the main thoroughfare. Down to the road I went to check the tracks there.

I was right. The characteristic hoof markings I had come to know quite well had followed the main route to that point, then left it to move up the draw on the left. There on the bare dirt between the two wagon wheel ruts, something else caught my eye — a spray of gold dust catching the late afternoon sun.

That puzzled me for a moment, then brought a grim smile to my lips, for I could come up with only one explanation. Rosh hoped that I would follow, and he had dropped a signal to indicate the junction in their path, using the only thing he had at hand. It showed cleverness and courage, but if I had a chance, I thought, I would reprimand him for it. After all, he should show a bit more confidence in my abilities as a tracker and a little more respect for the value of pure gold.

I had wondered why the two ruffians so quickly abandoned their compatriot back at the scene of the ambush. Now I guessed that an arrangement had been made to rendezvous later at a predetermined spot. This was evidently the spot, though how far down the gully they were was impossible to say.

My first plan was to move up through the pine and scrub to the top of the ridge, then slowly down the length of the ravine, keeping watch below me as I went, but this proved easier said than done. The ridge top, when I got there, was thickly treed and hard to follow. After a few hundred feet of crawling and winding through the bushes I realized that I was unsure even of where I was in relation to the main line of the gully. In that cover, with the rustling breeze confusing even the sounds nearest me, I could skirt past a herd of buffalo and be none the wiser.

I was catching my breath, leaning up against a pine tree, when I heard the mule bray a short distance below me and to my right. This was followed by a loud argument, carried on in two languages. As I reached the edge of a clearing next to a high rock face that formed one border of the gully, the tired bellow of the mule rang out once again, followed by the angry voice of the character I now thought of as Squealer.

"Stop that! You just cut that out!" he shouted. "There's nothing wrong with her feet. Leave her alone, you yellow devil!"

Rosh responded with loud protestations and explanations while the other man declaimed with foul curses and coarse insults that spanned several generations.

From my initial vantage point, I could not see Rosh or the mule, but Squealer stood not ten feet away with his back to me, holding a rifle by the barrel like a walking stick. When there was a break in their colourful conversation, I spoke in a voice just loud enough for him to hear.

"Don't move one muscle, friend, or you'll be dead before you can say 'God help me'," I said. "Now let the rifle drop, and step backwards. Don't turn around. Don't speak a word. Just step straight back."

He went straight as a stick, and the gun clattered to the ground. He was smart enough to follow my orders on the whole, but he took it on his own initiative to stick his hands high in the air.

With my revolver clasped in both fists, I nosed forward through the last screen of bushes, trying to see in three directions at once. Straight ahead of me, the old grey horse munched at the tall grass on the far side of the clearing. To my left, Rosh knelt beside the mule, who was tethered to a pine tree. To my right, the path headed back to the main road. I couldn't see the other villain anywhere.

I slid up behind Squealer, grabbed the back of his collar, poked the gun barrel into the vicinity of his kidneys, and pulled him close.

"Where's the other fella?" I demanded. My captive made a noise like someone stepping on a frog, but Rosh stood up and pointed down the trail. His easy smile told me that we were alone, at least for the present, and I gave Squealer enough of a push to land him on his stomach in the dirt.

My partner was happy to see me, of course, but he looked a little the worse for wear. His first steps forward betrayed a bit of a limp, and a cut along one cheek had swollen his eye half shut.

I looked at our captive — face down now on the ground before me.

"Where's your pal?" I asked him, and when he hesitated a second before replying, I kicked him in the ribs about as hard as I could without losing my own balance.

When I looked at Rosh it was hard to read his expression, his face was so badly puffed up. I guessed that it had taken him some time to convince the two bushwhackers that he spoke no English.

Squealer was all twisted up, gasping for breath, but when I repeated my question, he managed to blurt out an answer very quickly, before I had a chance to use my boot again.

"Bill's gone after Percy," he choked. "Looking for you and Percy."

I presumed that I knew who Percy was, and that Bill would be disappointed when he eventually found him.

"When's Bill supposed to be back?"

The little hoodlum was resting on his hands and knees now, with his head down.

"I don't know," he grumbled.

That may have been the truth, but I knocked him over with another kick in the ribs, and turned to Rosh.

I pulled my pocket watch out and let it dangle by the chain against my leg, then pointed in the direction that Bill had gone and asked whether it was a short time or a long time. He responded by holding his hands a fair distance apart and nodding. The other crook had been gone for a fair while. I was lucky I hadn't run into him on the way.

Looking closer at the Chinaman's face, I saw that the cut was more ugly than serious. The eye was not endangered. I reached out and touched his left side and he winced and drew back, but in answer to my gesture of concern, he shook his head and waved one hand in dismissal.

———

"We're all right then," I said, but I knew that the statement was a bit of an oversimplification. I spoke again to our captive — "You're a lucky fellow," I stated. "You're a snivelling skunk, but you're alive, and if you play your cards right you have a decent chance of staying that way."

He cursed under his breath, but since it was a general sort of curse and not specifically directed at me, I let it go. Finally he rolled into a seated position and looked up at me.

"What'd you do with Percy?" he asked.

"He's waiting for you at the gates of hell, and it's all the same to me if you want to join him now and keep him company until Bill's ready for the trip, but I'm going to give you a chance to hang around here for a few more years, if you act nice for us."

The scruffy little man put his head between his knees and rocked and moaned. I had the impression that his sadness was at least partially on behalf of the departed Percy. It appeared that these characters held some concern for each other, if for no one else.

Particularly in this modern age, when steam trains roar across the prairie faster than the fastest horse, and messages fly through wires, connecting town to town almost instantaneously, there is a strata of mankind that does not even pause to consider their sins as they pursue a life of greed and violence. Neither fearsome threats nor sweet persuasion can teach this sort of person the meaning of compassion, and I regret to say that they exist everywhere I have ever been. Most especially they congregate where money is loose and liquid.

Percy, Bill, and Squealer were good examples, but there was at least a shadow of empathy between them, which was a good thing, for it was possible we would need to use Squealer as a hostage later on, if Bill didn't fall too easily into our hands. I wasn't sure exactly what we would end up doing, but I hoped that we could avoid killing the two in cold blood, so to speak. The sense of having killed someone — even a murdering scoundrel — is a foul thing to have at the back of your mind.

The first step was to capture Bill, and I thought I should begin the watch for him right away. The little cliffs behind us could be climbed fairly easily by a roundabout route, and they looked like they would give a good view in the direction of the wagon road.

Firstly, I went to the mule and got a length of rope from the packs. While doing so, I released the rest of the ropes, dropped the baggage to the ground and relieved the poor pack animal. I used the rope to tie our prisoner's hands, then looped it over a high limb so that he was standing rather uncomfortably, with his arms above him. He commented unfavourably on the position with his usual tasteless colloquy, but as I informed him, his comfort was not my concern.

I motioned Rosh to sit on a nearby log, cocked the .45 revolver, and handed it to him. I explained to him both verbally and in signs, partly for Squealer's benefit, that if the prisoner made noise or talked too much, he should be shot dead.

The Winchester was gone from our baggage, possibly now in the possession of the third robber, so I took the big Sharp's buffalo rifle and moved down the ravine to the steep slope at the edge of the cliff. I scrambled up there like a water bug, sending showers of gravel and rocks into the trees below, stopping to rest every dozen yards or so. The fatigue of the day was beginning to catch up with me.

Finally I reached the level of the cliff top and scrambled over until I was next to a single stunted pine tree on a little patch of ground overlooking the ravine. I leaned the rifle against one great grey rock and sat down on another. I would be inconspicuous enough up there, I thought, but I could see the far half of the clearing beneath me, including both animals, and more or less the entirety of the trail to the wagon road.

I knew that Bill might return from his scouting expedition at any time. If I climbed up the little pine tree, I might be able to see all the way down to the last turn of the wagon road, which would give me enough advance warning to return to the clearing and meet the fellow on level ground.

While I was still considering this, I heard the sound of gunfire. I was too startled to be sure of the exact order, but there were several shots, some from a rifle, and more than one from the Colt handgun. My mind went into a spin, and I couldn't decide what to do, not knowing what had happened. If Squealer had somehow escaped, I should go back down by a different route, or he would be waiting for me at the cliff base. Then again, by the time I made it down to the clearing, would everyone have disappeared, just as at the last ambush?

During the short time I was thinking this and peering down from my perch, the shooting stopped and two men ran across the clearing into my field of vision. Bill hadn't come down the path, but he was back. He ran directly for the horse and mule, while Squealer, still trailing rope from one wrist, dodged over to pick up his rifle where it lay on the ground. He scooped it up, worked the bolt, and turned around to where I had left Rosh. He hadn't time to finish aiming before I pulled the trigger on the buffalo gun and knocked him a full six feet backwards.

In the time it took me to realize that a second shot at Squealer wasn't necessary, Bill had decided that it was no use for him to try to help the man, and he danced past the frightened mule and into the trees. I fired one more shot at his shadow as he hurried through the bushes, but there wasn't much chance at a clear angle through the timber.

I watched him all the way back to the main road, where he made the mistake of stopping and peering back like Lot's wife. Maybe he wanted to see if he were being pursued, or maybe he was having a hard time leaving all that gold behind. It should have been a mortal mistake, for the Sharp's rifle is engineered to kill at distances up to a mile. I had no practise with the thing, though, and merely kicked up a good handful of dust a few paces from his feet. My only satisfaction was to see him disappear like a scared rabbit. He looked like a man who was heading for home — not simply running for cover.

It was just beginning to get dark. The sky was still clear, but the wind was building into strong, chill gusts.

When I made it down to the clearing, I found I was shivering, although I was not really cold. All my movements seemed stiff, and my mind likewise would not move swiftly or willingly.

Rosh lay half under a scrub alder bush, against the log where he had been seated when I left him. Blood flowed from his left side and his hip. He was in great pain and obviously frightened, but he was alive.

CHAPTER FOURTEEN

M Y PARTNER'S INJURIES effectively destroyed all my plans just as I had begun to relax in the belief that they might actually be successful. My plans were ruined beyond retrieval; I could only hope that the same was not true of my partner. I was no doctor, and could not even measure his chance for survival, but his condition was definitely serious. I managed to stop the bleeding from his wound, and once I had made his bed as comfortable as possible, his breathing steadied and he lapsed into a deep sleep.

Whether he lived or died, he would not be ready to carry a burden before winter, and I certainly could not manage transporting him as well as the gold. I had recovered completely from my shoulder wound and my bout with fever, but one man can manage only so much. For that matter, even though we were far from Barkerville and could relax our secrecy to some extent, carrying such a huge quantity of precious goods made it necessary to remain as inconspicuous as possible.

Watching Rosh sleeping at the edge of the campfire light,

these ideas settled on me like blizzarding snow, and my mood sank steadily. I knew I should keep a better watch, for Bill the Badman might yet return under cover of darkness, but I didn't have the energy to try to outthink him. I merely hoped that he had either given up on the project entirely, or that it would take him some time to round up new accomplices.

Like a child escaping from unpleasant reality by hiding in fantasy, I spent much of that sleepless night dreaming of what I might do with the small mountain of raw gold sitting behind me in the dark.

I would buy myself a steamship, I thought – big enough to carry a profitable cargo up and down the coast of California to Mexico. It would have staterooms enough for a couple of dozen affluent guests, and a fine restaurant with room for them to dance in the sea breeze under the warm stars. I would busy myself with the details of international trade, and perhaps meet some elegant young lady who was accompanying her father on a cruise. There would be much to occupy my time, but no danger.

I thought of Percy, stiff-twisted and silent, miles away in the forest, and Squealer, just out of sight where I had dragged him. They had paid the price for gambling beyond their means. My mind balked at estimating my own odds.

I roused Rosh when he began to squirm in his sleep, and gave him the last of our water to drink. I would have given him some whisky as well, but the bushwhackers had finished that off before I caught up to them. When it appeared that Rosh had returned to a restful unconsciousness, I left him there and found my way in the moonlight over the half mile of path and roadway to the big creek, where I refilled our water containers. The night hours in that desert place were absolutely majestic and my mood changed from bleak depression to a sort of melancholy.

It was a state of mind that had its own dangers. As I walked, I thought, for instance, how unusual it was that during that entire afternoon and the course of my confrontation with our ambushers, not a soul had come within sight or hearing. In my sad and fatalistic atmosphere of thought, I half wished that some congregation of on-lookers had arrived to bring my long struggle to a halt.

In the small hours of the morning, in the heaviness of pre-dawn, my patient awoke. He was in great pain, for which I could do nothing, but I did have two bowls of warm liquid prepared – the oriental medicines that had done so much good for me. I presumed that such medicaments would do roughly the same good for gunshot wounds as they had for gangrenous fever. Since I was not overly anxious to undertake the removal of his band-ages to clean his wounds, I began by giving him the bowl of the other brew to drink. At first he refused it, and I let him know that I would not allow him to deny me the pleasure of adminis-tering the atrocious stuff. Eventually he made it clear that I was giving him the wrong potion to be taken internally, which brought about a lengthy disagreement. The two elixirs had equally nauseating but quite distinct odours, and I felt certain that the one he chose to drink was the one that he had regularly used to cleanse my infected shoulder. I didn't want to worsen his condition with a prolonged argument, however, so I allowed him to gulp down his chosen bowlful while I gingerly removed the strips of torn shirt which sufficed for bandages and bathed the entry and exit wounds the bullet had gouged in his lower left abdomen. Not much new blood flowed, and after rinsing the dressings in warm water, I reapplied them as well as I could. I lectured the man severely, telling him that I knew very well by sense of taste that he had just convinced me to wash him with oral medication, but he was by that time asleep.

When proper daylight arrived I was no closer to deciding on our long-term plan of action, but I knew what was immediately necessary, and I forced myself from under my blanket just when I was starting to feel like sleep might finally be possible. Once I had the bundles of gold loaded on the mule – (I discarded most of the rest of our supplies except for some bannock and dried venison) – I returned to the fireside to find Rosh awake, and I explained our situation to him.

Someone might come looking for us at any time. We had no choice but to move out, and try to find a hiding place as far from our present location as he could physically manage.

I gave him more water and another dose of his medicinal tea, and he stoically limped, with my help, to where I could lift him onto the ancient grey horse we had obtained from our attackers. He assured me that he was fit enough to ride, and I led the procession towards the wagon road, the horse on a short rope, the mule on a long one.

I toured the animals in a roundabout path, across the roadway, among the trees, and towards the creek, along whatever strips of gravel or hard pack I could find. When I reached the creek's banks I left the animals tethered to a snag, broke off a willow broom, and ran back the way we had come, erasing as many signs of our passage as I could see. If I had learned to recognize a track when I worked for Pinkerton's, I had also learned a trick or two for disguising one.

Back at the creek, I checked again on Rosh, who could still manage to affect a smile, then moved off downstream, walking either in the shallow skirts of the water or on the cobblestone of the flat banks. We travelled a weaving route, going east or southeast, but at that stage, one direction was as good as another as long as our footprints weren't easily seen and Rosh was able to stay on the horse's back. Periodically I asked him if he needed to stop and rest, but each time he shook his head in casual refusal. It seemed that he might actually be able to relax as he stretched over the animal's back, and I gradually lapsed into a sort of hypnotized plodding, watching my boots and concentrating on my own fatigue.

When we arrived at the little island in the stream, some three or four miles from our starting point, it was for my own benefit that I felt we must call a halt, but when I turned to speak to my partner, I found him gritting his teeth like a death's head, sweat mixed with tears covering his face. He did not respond to my voice, and once I had waded the pack animals over to our new landing, he almost caused the placid grey to bolt by refusing to release his iron grip on its mane and hair.

Seeing him in such a state made me suddenly alert and animated, but I knew that fatigue would soon recapture me, so I busied myself making the invalid a soft bed of reeds and rushes. Then I unloaded the animals, tethered them to graze on the far bank of the creek, and gathered a stock of firewood. While walking along the north bank, picking up dry branches, I was surprised to see an ox cart at the far edge of the meadow, only a quarter mile or so distant. The watercourse ran parallel to the wagon road through here, it seemed, so we had not actually put much space between ourselves and the main thoroughfare, which bothered me at first. We had done the best we could, though, and anyone looking for us had no reason to carry their search down this route. I was confident that our tracks were discreet, and neither Bad Bill nor Hec Simmonds would find us without a bit of luck. Our hiding place itself and the grazing ground for our animals were well out of the line of sight, and our campfire smoke would be nicely dissipated by the breeze that skimmed along the water.

When I returned to the island, I gathered tinder and twigs and started a small fire. It was not cold; in fact, it was pleasantly warm in the sunshine, but I hooked a cooking pot full of water onto its stand and fetched the little bags of powder and herbs in preparation for another batch of Chinese medicine. Rosh was still sleeping, but his breath came in hurried little puffs, and his forehead was hot.

Now that the immediate need for physical action had passed, the melancholy depression of the previous night returned, and I closed my eyes, trying again to envisage a trim white steamboat cutting a clean line across blue waters under a tropical sun.

When I awoke, the sun had changed sides of the sky. The fire was out, the water cold, and the cottonwoods cast shadows from one creek bank to the other.

There seemed to be no change in my partner's condition, although he had rolled from his back to his side, where he lay slightly curled, with one arm over his head. I covered him with a second blanket and set to work finding fresh tinder.

When the new bowls of Chinese liquid were at last prepared, I attempted to change his bandages and wash his wound without actually rousing him. He awakened gradually as I did this, mumbling to himself and shaking his head. I left the injury open to the air while I washed the strips of cloth and dried them by the fire, then I helped Rosh to sit up, and enticed him to swallow the other draught of medicine.

He was aware of my presence, but I am not sure that he knew who I was. In a desultory monotone he spoke quietly to me in Chinese, not inviting conversation, but rather as if to recite some sad story. I hurried the bowl to his lips at every pause. His lengthy speech worried me. We sometimes spoke briefly to each other in our respective languages, heedless of the lost meaning, but this rambling monologue implied to me that he was becoming increasingly detached from reality. I wondered how much damage had been done by the morning's travel down the creek.

The clear sky and the breeze brought cooler weather that night, and protection from the elements was not an advantage that our island campsite afforded. I left both blankets covering the invalid, and lay as close as I could to the fire, covered by my coat and an oilcloth normally used for packaging the baggage. I was physically exhausted enough to manage a few stretches of sleep, but my rocky mattress stopped me from letting the last embers die away.

I'm not sure which of us was the first to open his eyes, but before dawn was all the way down into the valley, I became aware that Rosh and I were watching one another across the fire's glow. He didn't move or speak, but I felt somehow that there was a bit more clarity to his aspect, and I was able to drift back to a more peaceful sleep.

When full daylight arrived, I found the change less substantial than I had thought. Rosh was awake and aware while I boiled water for tea and medicine and washed myself in the creek, but he made no attempt to communicate, and showed no sign of vitality whatever. His fever was evidently not so consuming as it had been at its peak, but speckles of sweat still stood out like pox on his face. He stared sullenly at the ground beside him. After the usual twin bowls of ministrations had been dispensed, I boiled tea and a broth made from the venison hardtack. Rosh would have none of it. Granted, the stuff would not have got a great reception in any fine restaurant, but there was health and strength in it, and I tried valiantly to induce him to take a few sips. I am not sure whether it was intentional when he spilled the whole cupful, but I didn't press the issue.

He stretched out again on the reed bed and closed his eyes. For my part, I ate a slab of bannock and realized that our food supplies were almost totally depleted. The countryside around our little hideaway was mostly rolling desert — painted in bleak pastels with clay and sagebrush, and I was not too optimistic about what kind of game I might be able to hunt. There were probably deer in the pine forests farther up the hillsides, but I didn't want to travel that distance. Rabbits and gophers were around, no doubt, but it was quite doubtful that I would get close enough to shoot one with a handgun, and if I used the buffalo rifle, I might never find the fragments. I could put a couple of fishing lines in the creek, I thought, and check them from time to time while I kept watch over my sick companion.

I had cut my line into two lengths and was in the process of attaching them to a dead branch long enough to cross one arm of the creek, when Rosh's eyes opened. He shifted himself so one arm was behind his head and spoke to me in our usual blend of words and gestures.

His voice was low and his movements awkward, so it took me a few moments to grasp his basic meaning. Ashcroft was not far away, he said, and he was very sick. I must leave him, and go on alone.

I growled my refusal.

He tried to further argue its rationality but I found the words as repugnant as they were incomprehensible, and I walked away dragging my tree branch to set my fishing lines.

The layout of my equipment was poor. There were probably fish in the creek, but I saw no reason that they should be attracted to a pair of hooks so close to the surface in a quick-flowing channel. I could find no better arrangement or location within walking distance, however, and returned to the camp to keep the fire alive. I had passed an hour on my angling outing, but Rosh was still awake when I returned. He gestured for me to come closer, which I did, bringing a cup of water for him. He drank peremptorily, let the tin cup fall to the ground, and grasped my hand in his. His eyes seemed unfocussed, but his grip was strong. With one hand, he held me by the wrist, then reached across with the other and carefully placed the two coins symbolizing his share of the gold in the centre of my palm.

I didn't know what to say or do. Was it a sign of gratitude, or one of fatalistic surrender? In the end, I said nothing at all — just stepped across to the water pot and busied myself with making tea. My hands shook, and I spilled half the water into the fire.

Once I was seated again with my cup of mud-brown tea, Rosh began to speak. He wanted, I could tell, to say something persuasive in a simple and concise manner, but it sounded much like a tolerant parent lecturing a difficult infant, and I found it painful to sit quietly while he rambled incoherently on.

"Ashcroft," he said at one point, and held thumb and forefinger just an inch apart. "Go. Go. Go," he told me in impeccable

English, then lapsed back into Chinese. Quite irrationally, I found myself leaning forward, clinging to the rise and fall of his tone.

I was to carry on alone. That was the upshot of it all. I told him to forget the idea, adding a rather crude epithet that I trusted he would not be able to translate. I was staying here, I said. I would look after him. He would be fine.

We sat in silence for a few moments, until he interrupted my thoughts to add further argument.

I must go. Ashcroft was just over there. I should leave him my revolver.

Why did he want my revolver? I threw the dregs of my tea on the ground and went to check the fishing lines. They were empty and badly tangled, which was no surprise to me. The freezing water chilled my fingers, so it took me a long time to right them, but I kept stubbornly at it, trying not to visualize Rosh making a gun out of his thumb and forefinger.

Finally I left the fishing apparatus and walked the hundred feet to the downstream tip of the little islet, where I crouched on the gravel, throwing pebbles into the current.

After a half hour I returned to build up the fire and heat more water. Rosh tried again to get my attention, and I knew from the tone of his voice what he wanted to say. When he wouldn't let me ignore him I shouted angrily that he should be quiet.

"There's nothing to talk about, man! I'm staying here with you. Do you understand? I'm staying here!"

His morose silence indicated his comprehension, and I went about preparing another batch of the fever tonic. I had no idea how often the stuff needed to be administered, but I trusted that I couldn't overdose him, and planned on having him drink it every few hours. The cleansing agent could be used twice daily.

I figured I had pacified the man with my final blast, so it took me by surprise when, as I knelt beside him, he gripped me tightly, and burst into a pleading monologue.

Ashcroft. I must go. Then he muttered fervently at some

length in his own language, with the words "go," "Ashcroft," and something that sounded like "mang sang," which he repeated several times.

I managed to keep my composure as I stood, setting the cup down on the ground within his reach.

"No," I said quietly. "Drink up. Drink your stuff like a good fellow."

He flopped back onto his bed and began to weep feverish, frustrated tears. I took my gun and started walking.

I was hunting, I suppose, or that is how I would have rationalized my lengthy wanderings down the stream bed, then up to high ground, travelling with my eyes fixed blankly on the ground before me. I passed an hour at this, or perhaps more.

When I arrived back at camp the fire was out, but Rosh was asleep, his breathing deep and even. His cup was empty, so presumably he had consented to swallow his medicine, but when I straightened the blankets over him I saw fresh blood on them, as well as on the tattered side and front of his shirt.

I didn't eat any supper, but it was about that time of day — nearly dark and rather chilly, when he awoke and spoke to me again. He spoke quietly this time, with less emotion.

"You go?"

"No," I said. "I'm staying."

Over our time together we had accepted a hand signal tracing the arc of the sun as symbolizing a day's time, and he made this sign to me.

One day. Two days, and you'll go?

"No. I stay. I don't know when, but you and I will go together."

He drifted back to sleep, muttering to himself. He didn't seem to find much comfort in my assurance that he and I would go on together. Perhaps he could detect the note of insincerity creeping into my voice.

I had to be thankful that the weather was remaining clear,

although it was very cold once the sun had set. It would snow now, rather than rain, when the weather turned. I didn't think I could stand a wind-blown desert blizzard. I knew that Rosh could not. We had pretty much run out of time.

I felt very much alone in the starry black emptiness of the desert night. I tried to sleep, but that was impossible. Even in fantasy there was no escape. My picture of a steamship on a sparkling sea was two-dimensional and unattractive. Other people danced across the decks, but there was no place there for me.

Would I be lucky enough to find someone along the way who I could send to Rosh's rescue? Chances were slim, and even if everything went well, Rosh would be alive and abandoned, probably penniless, two hundred miles or more from Barkerville. I would be gone, never able to explain myself, or to find out if he died a natural death or was hung for the murder of Percy and Squealer.

I didn't sleep, but neither do I remember the arrival of dawn — only a stage of the early morning when I reluctantly recognized that it was time to load the mule. The baggage sat close to the water's edge. Rather than bring the animal across to the island, I carted the bundles one by one across to him, so as not to awaken Rosh.

I was in no hurry to speak to him because I had no idea what to say. Should I show him how sad I was to go? Should I thank him, or wish him well, or hide my feelings like some family secret?

As it was, I led the two animals around the camp and left them at the brink of the other channel of water while I went back to say goodbye to my partner. He was awake, and smiled wanly when I strode up and calmly added a few more sticks to the fire. I placed the cooking pot full of hot water along with a cup where he could reach them, and set the two bags of dried medicine by his pillow. I also fetched him a piece of venison and some of the last of my bannock.

"Well, I'm going then," I said. The expression on his face was tired and dreamy. I had watched him all night, and I knew his sleep had been hot and fitful.

"Ashcroft," he answered and signalled that it wasn't very far. "You go. Go." I could tell that there was more he wished to say, but could not translate into hand gestures. He spoke again in Chinese — tantalizingly futile to my ear. At the end, almost as an afterthought, he pointed two fingers and cocked his thumb, with an enquiring look on his face.

I took the Colt .45 from my coat pocket, checked that all chambers were full, and laid it carefully on the ground beside his bed. Next to it I put a cloth pouch of small nuggets — fifty dollars or so.

Without looking at him again, I turned and headed south and east across the pale grey prairie, winding between the rocks and the great clumps of sagebrush. The night breeze had blown in a blanket of low cloud, and it felt like I was riding across a great low-ceilinged hall towards the roadhouse at Ashcroft.

I wondered why that little featureless stopover had held such a special significance for Rosh. From the start of our journey, he had referred to it whenever he needed a name for our destination, although by my recollection it had nothing of interest to recommend it.

I travelled rather aimlessly, halfway between the creek and the wagon road, and made good time, although it was more or less by accident. My mind was not on the business of travelling at all. It jumped from sour events of the past to sour possibilities in the future.

I considered several events that could have changed everything if I had handled them differently. I thought of how I had once come to the aid of the little fellow I later knew as Squealer, and wished I had given his neck a good twist when I first had the chance. I resolved in future to take ruthlessness as my byword, and never again to risk on the side of mercy.

As the long-suffering beasts clambered across the rolling hills of hard-packed clay, always in sight of the road but just out of hailing distance, my mind travelled a repetitive circuit of speculation and regret.

It came as a surprise to me when, at one o'clock, I plodded over the crest of a shoulder of high ground, and I saw Ashcroft Station below me in the valley centre. In that spacious, barren country there are few places that offer enough water and shelter for a decent camp, and briefly I was tempted to risk a night's respite in the comfort of civilization, but I immediately discarded the idea as a bad risk.

Neither was this the right place to tell someone about Rosh. There would probably be a dozen people around, and I would surely be detained for an explanation — something that I could not, of course, give. At the very least, someone would be delegated to follow and find me later, when the nature of Rosh's injury was ascertained. Once I was held and questioned we were both doomed.

I did decide, though, to cross the compound of the roadhouse and inspect the place, partly in sentimental deference to my partner. Also, it was the most direct route to the lowlands. I wasn't sure, but I thought I might be able to make the Thompson River before dark.

I continued along the top of the ridge for a short distance, then turned the animals down a dry gulch towards the handful of buildings perched on the scratchy lines of the wagon road.

At the foot of the gulch I turned again and cut across to the roadway, past a little square of split rail fencing. On first glance it looked like a small, grassy corral, until I spotted the row of crosses near the back. It was a sad testament to this harsh country that a cemetery should be established before a church, a saloon, or a proper store.

The sensation of walking openly into a populated place unsettled me, but I tried to maintain my composure. The roadhouse itself was a two-story log structure on the south side of the road — quite large, with smoke rising from two stone chimneys. There were frame outbuildings beside and behind it, as well as a large fenced corral. A stout woman in a grey dress hung clothes on a line in the back yard. She waved as I came to a stop, and I returned the gesture. The main barns were on the other side of the road, along with more corrals and a smith's shop, from which came the sounds of someone hammering iron.

The central well and pump were close to the barn doors. I pumped fresh water into the troughs, let my animals drink at their leisure, and took a lingering look at the country and the settlement. Whatever it was that had made this place memorable to Rosh, I thought, it was neither the scenic beauty nor the excitement of the metropolis.

There was one other house in town, on the same side of the road as the barn. It was a small, white frame building, and as I stood there with the smell of the forge and the stable acrid in my nostrils, the door blew open and one small boy of eight years or so ran out and across the clearing to the main yard with the loud cries of his companion ringing out behind him. I was relieved to find that no one paid me any attention, and I washed my face and hair in cold well-water before I started leading the way south.

Ashcroft was behind me. Ahead lay the barren solitude of the river canyons.

I was just past the way station proper when the big woman at the clothesline shouted towards someone inside the house.

"May Sang!" she called. I heard her clearly enough, but it was only when she shouted the second time that I spun around and stared with wide eyes. "May Sang!"

A tiny Chinese woman in a green dress and a white jacket emerged from a side door and scurried towards the back yard.

As if to let me hear the name once more, the big woman said it loudly again — "May Sang," and led her out of my sight, around the corner.

I didn't need to know any more. Someone was guilty of some poor pronunciation, but I was perfectly confident that "May Sang" was what Rosh had repeated more than once to me from his sickbed beside the creek.

CHAPTER FIFTEEN

*T*HE COUNTRY AROUND Ashcroft was so bleak and blank that I was forced to follow the road for quite some distance before I could be sure I was out of sight of the little settlement. Then I cut back into the undulating folds of terrain that led up from the distant, unseen river basin to the sparsely treed hilltops and chose a place to stop.

I was exhausted from leading the animals up the long climb, but when I finally paused to catch my breath I was almost too excited to sit down. I knew I had to wait and think carefully, for any precipitous action could still bring disaster. The last time I had abducted a foreigner, it had been a much simpler proposition — far from the risk of interruption. I would have to think this operation through carefully.

Even if I had had an interpreter, it would have been a chancy situation to explain to Miss May Sang: "Madam, I have just travelled some distance to speak to you on behalf of a sick friend of mine whose full name I do not really know. He is a countryman of yours, and seems to know you, so would you please sneak away with me, and not mention a thing about anything to anyone."

If the good woman had her wits about her, she would hold up her sharpest kitchen knife and scream for help.

Still, my optimism and my enthusiasm were back, and I already had the seed of a plan in mind. I knew I would have to act fairly soon, though. The telltale heaviness of my hands and feet reminded me that I had not slept in thirty-six hours, but I could allow myself no rest while my invalid partner lay in the freezing dark. I grimaced to think of the poor beggar's frustration when I kept walking away while he tried to explain himself. I pulled the bundles from the mule's back and stacked them on the ground, then slouched against them and closed my eyes as I considered the situation.

I was awakened by the grind and snort of the horse chewing up a bunch of grassy weeds next to my ear. It was almost dark and I still had much to do, so I was on the run the minute I was up.

After I had disposed of the horses, I set up the markers I would need if I hoped to find my way in the dark once the last threads of light had disappeared. Then I crept up to a woodpile close to the roadhouse and peered through a window at the dinner-time comings and goings. In these minutes I should have had ample time to rehearse my words and actions, but in fact, when I entered the front dining hall, I was still nervous and uncertain.

No one seemed particularly surprised at my late and unannounced arrival, and I was greeted most politely as I leaned my rifle in the corner of the room next to the door and hung my coat on one of the wooden pegs.

The fellow who stood up and shook my hand was tall, broad, and robust in appearance, although he was nearly bald and squinted even in the well-lit front room.

"Cox," he said. "James Andrew Cox."

"Jack Baxter," I replied. "I'm camped just down the way and I wondered if I was too late to purchase a hot meal."

"Not at all. Not at all." He looked around as he directed me to the big plank table that dominated the room, and called out in the clear firm voice of someone accustomed to giving orders. "Mavis!"

The big woman appeared in a doorway across from us and smiled broadly.

"Mavis, have May Sang prepare a plate of victuals for Mr. Baxter, would you please," said Cox, and she disappeared without a word.

I was alone at the big dining table, except for the master of the house, who sat quietly at one end seat while I devoured a huge platter of beef, bread, potatoes, gravy, onions, and carrots. I immediately liked this man. I liked the way he maintained authority in his establishment, while at the same time making me feel very much his honoured guest. I liked his inn, as well — spacious and clean, with papered walls and bearskins on the floor. Six lanterns lit the room and rows of fancy china plates sat along a rail at eye level. Two men played cards on the hearth of a great stone fireplace at one end of the hall, and two others spoke in low voices at a sofa in the opposite corner. Some of the roadhouses along the Cariboo trail were nothing more than barns for human livestock, but the station at Ashcroft displayed a civilized warmth.

Mr. Cox waited graciously until I was working on a great slab of pie with a mug of coffee at hand before he spoke again.

"You're camped nearby, you say, Mr. Baxter. I should mention that we have plenty of room if you wish to spend the night. If this were April or May we would have men sleeping on both sofas, under the table — even out in the barns — but right now we could give you a room of your own upstairs."

"Thank you, but I've already set up my camp and I enjoy sleeping in the fresh air when the weather is good. It'll be fine tonight. Mind you, after a wonderful meal like this I could probably sleep peacefully through a hailstorm and wake with a smile. Your wife does the cooking?" "No, no. Mavis does the baking. That's her pie, of course, but we have a cook." Cox's smile was one of relaxed pride. "Chinese girl. You'd scarcely believe it, but when she came to us a year ago she wanted to chop everything into little pieces and fry it. Now — well, you've tasted the result . . ."

"Chinese? I don't believe I've ever seen a Chinese female this far north," I said. It was quite true. All of the numerous Orientals I had seen in Barkerville had been men.

"There's not many," Cox agreed, "but May Sang can look after herself, and she'll learn anything you show her better than any white gal I've had work for me. Your dinner was satisfactory?"

"Maybe the best roast beef I've ever eaten," I replied with all sincerity. "You're lucky to have such a talented employee this far from any centre of civilization. She lives in the house just across the road there?"

I managed to slip the question into conversation casually enough to avoid suspicion in my host.

"No. My wife and I live there with our boys. . . . " His voice trailed away as he squinted towards the front window.

From the doorway behind me and to my right came the Chinese servant, gathering up empty plates and silently filling our coffee cups. She appeared so small and fragile and moved so quickly that I felt as if I should stand well aside. As she disappeared into the kitchen, Cox finally offered me the information I needed.

"No, I've always felt it best to have a home for my family separate from the guest house, even if we spend most of our time here anyway," he laughed. "May Sang has a room just off the kitchen."

Now that I knew where to target my attention, I began to look for an opportune moment to withdraw. Although I enjoyed the warmth, the pleasant torpor of overeating, and the company of the good James Andrew Cox, I wanted to leave before the conversation could turn to such matters of current interest as the search for Zachary Beddoes, suspected murderer, or the strange disappearance of Bill's friends, Percy and Squealer. We chatted a while about insubstantials — the weather and the condition of the road through the canyon — before I stood and stretched.

"No problem, I hope, about paying for my meal in gold dust?" I asked.

He assured me that it would be fine, and sent his wife to the office to bring a set of scales. I dropped a small cloth gold poke on the table, then fetched my rifle from the corner. Cox's squinting eyes brightened suddenly.

"Now that's a gun!" he stated admiringly. "Sharp's. That's the gun a man wants to have in this kind of country. You shoot your deer when you see it — a mile away. Or wolves — one bullet a wolf, and no trouble trying to chase them."

I agreed that it was a fine weapon. "It's a bit big and clumsy for my purpose right now, though. I had a handgun, which was good for the trail, and a .30-.30, but I lost them. Crossing a river, you understand. I lost quite a bit of stuff. Both guns."

The man's wife faithfully brought his gold scales and set them on the table, but we never got around to using them. Instead, I gave Cox the Sharp's buffalo rifle, and in return got the meal and a matched pair of .44 calibre revolvers — Union Army issue, and a leather holster. They had been accepted in trade for supplies from a deserter on his way north, but I was quite obviously not much worried about the previous owners of my firearms.

Cox and I seemed equally pleased with the fruits of our bartering, and we shook hands goodnight like old friends. As I walked away into the darkness, I realized that my new freedom of movement might prove invaluable in successfully enacting my plan that evening. The holsters flopped about when I walked, the guns fit into them very loosely, and the box of bullets in my pocket pulled my coat awkwardly to one side, but at least I had both hands and arms free, and that was important.

Once I was past the last peripheral shed and the night had closed around me, I returned in a wide circle to the roadhouse and found a comfortable place of concealment where I could squat and watch the kitchen window. From time to time I glimpsed the Chinese girl as she carried out her evening chores. I seated myself on a block of cordwood and leaned against the wall of the woodshed as comfortably as I could, for I didn't know how long I would have to wait. I saw the shadowy path towards both the water pump and the latrines, and I hoped I might intercept her out-of-doors, but I had to consider the possibility that I would have to go inside after her if necessary.

Sitting there in the dark, I reflected regretfully that I should have tried to learn some Chinese words from Rosh. Almost anything could have been used to some effect in my forthcoming confrontation, if only to establish a moment of unguarded contact with her before I had her within arms' reach.

During the next hour and a half, I continued my intermittent battle with fatigue. My lavish meal might have given me a supply of strength for the long term, but it did nothing towards keeping me awake while I sat in the dark. From time to time it became necessary for me to stand up and wave my arms over my head, or even to go for little promenades along the length of the shed wall. I was back in my position, though, with the rags and ropes I had prepared in a pile at my feet, when the back door to the building – the kitchen door – opened and May Sang struggled out carrying a large basin of water.

By the time she had thrown the water onto the ground next to the little path and was shaking the drips from the basin, I was behind her. I covered her mouth from nose to chin with one hand, while the other laid a cold gun barrel against her temple. She dropped the metal basin on her own foot and gave a little involuntary jump, then stood stock still.

I have always considered crimes against women to be despicable. My only hope was that the young lady and I would both live long enough to have the situation explained.

In that awkward position we did a peculiar sideways sort of

dance to the deeper shadows of the place around the corner of the outbuilding, where I had laid out my equipment. Sufficient moonlight filtered through the clouds to make our faces visible to each other at a distance of a foot or two, and as I slowly removed my hand from her mouth I held her eyes with mine and tried to communicate with the same sign language I might use with Rosh. I touched her lips, made a talking sign with my hand, then drew one finger like a knife across her throat.

The fear I could see in her eyes, even in that inky gloom, was repulsive to me, but necessary under the circumstances. At my signal, she quite readily accepted one rag into her mouth and allowed me to run another one around her head to hold the first. Likewise she turned passively around and stood stolidly at attention while I tied her ankles together with a section of rope. Once again I had her turn to face me, and was in the process of tying her hands when the kitchen door swung open and slammed noisily shut again.

I swung flat against the wall of the shed, pistol in my right hand, with my left arm wrapped ignobly around my prisoner.

We were as silent there as intense fear can make two people — stiff as pokers, breathing lightly. Into our line of sight walked a small boy of eight or nine years, swaggering and whispering to himself. If he hadn't been so intent on his own fantasies, he might easily have spotted us, for the darkness was incomplete and the little fellow was so close to us that when he unbuttoned the front of his trousers, he peed on the ground not four feet from us. Having done his duty, though, he refastened his pants, climbed onto an imaginary horse and ran back into the night around the corner of the main building.

I relaxed slowly, feeling the girl do the same, and wondered briefly what I would have done if the child had seen us and raised an alarm. There was no time, though, for idle thoughts. I quickly tied my captive's wrists, signalled an order for silence, and hoisted her onto my shoulder, with her legs against my chest and her arms dangling down my back.

A human being is always an awkward bundle to carry, but May Sang was so compact and light that I thought I might be able to trot all the way back to the horses. When I broke into a run, though, my shoulder bounced into her belly, and she groaned in pain. I slowed again to a fast walk, but still made good time. Circling the buildings until I was across the road and behind the blacksmith's shop, I headed towards the little graveyard, trying to walk smoothly and not punish her too badly with my shoulder. As we passed the last of the buildings, she grabbed at my coat with her tightly wrapped hands, presumably to control the bouncing movement.

Then she cocked the hammer of the revolver from my right hand holster. I jerked to a stop just as she fired, which evidently ruined her aim. The bullet kicked up the dirt between my heels, but did no damage. In one motion I threw her backwards over my shoulder and sprang ahead, tripping over my own feet and landing on my face.

I scrambled to my knees, my other pistol in hand. May Sang writhed on the ground and emitted a sort of squealing groan through the folds of her gag. My thought was that she had somehow shot herself, but she had only had the wind knocked out of her, and in a second or two she had rolled into a sitting position with the revolver gripped between her nicely bound hands. While I stared stupidly at her, kneeling eight feet away, she cocked and fired again, but she was no marksman. I ran quickly to my right, and before she could shoot again I was behind her. With her hands and feet trussed up, she couldn't turn around, but she tried gamely to point the gun at me backwards, over her shoulder. One more flash and bang erupted through the night air before I could disarm her. Behind me I heard voices shouting, and I looked back to the roadhouse to see James Cox standing in the roadway holding a lantern and squinting in my direction. One man stood beside him, and another ran towards the veranda to get another storm lantern.

225

I tried to pick up May Sang, but she was through with being cooperative. She kicked and squirmed like a wounded snake, and all I got for my efforts was an amalgam of rope and fists that nearly broke my nose.

As I have said, I despise the very thought of assaulting a woman, but that night had to be declared an extraordinary instance, and I knew of only one way to quickly sedate an uncooperative companion. Even once I had recognized the necessity of striking the lady — as I heard the men of Ashcroft advancing like hounds on a fox — I wavered momentarily, not knowing quite how hard to hit her. In Chicago once, I had knocked out an Irishman with a single blow — my only notable pugilistic success. I figured that a woman would require a little less force than an Irishman, and accordingly popped May Sang with about two-thirds of my weight. She went as limp as an uncooked Christmas goose, and I scooped her up once more over my shoulder.

For the next few minutes I concentrated on silence rather than speed, as I could hear Cox and associates rummaging around the barn looking for the root of all the noise.

It was tricky walking across the uneven ground without a light, but I had set up markers earlier on, and I hadn't left myself too far to go. A quarter mile from the buildings, I followed a small path that led up a gully, where the shadows were deeper and footing was even harder to find, until I made it to the crest of the ridge. As we got to the animals, I was puffing and wheezing until I thought my heart might burst, and May Sang had come to her senses enough to whimper quietly.

All in all, my kidnapping expedition had succeeded, albeit clumsily. Everyone had heard our departure, but it would be a while before they sorted out the confusion enough to guess what might have happened, and they wouldn't likely pursue us in the dark. Even in the morning, my trail on foot over the hard-packed clay would be nearly invisible, and with any luck they would decide to start their search to the south.

I stopped long enough to catch my breath, but there was no point in trying to take a real rest. I needed at least twelve hours of sleep, and anything less would only serve to stiffen up my joints.

The poor little Chinese woman was as polite as a bag of flour as I set her into the saddle of the old grey horse, who was probably as tired and confused as his master. I watched her closely for the first few steps as I led the procession out, but she was now fully conscious and evidently had no illusions about leaping to freedom, even though I had had to remove the bindings from her legs.

Before sunset, when I had brought the animals to this section of the plateau's edge, I had sighted my route towards a distant wedge-shaped indentation in the horizon, and to my great relief I now found that I could still see it quite clearly against the night sky.

I needed to put some distance between myself and Ashcroft before morning. "If the animals can do it," I thought, "then so can I." We started off.

The physical exertion soon ceased to bother me, especially after we were down from the little clutch of hills and onto the level desert plain. My eyes adjusted to the dimness well enough to make out the contours of most of the holes and boulders, and I trudged evenly along, with the mule's long line tied to the back of my belt, and the horse's reins tied to my wrist. The Chinese woman might have been another bundle of gold and blankets. She didn't make a sound, apart from a single sigh when I removed her gags, and hardly shifted her position.

Physically, I was competent enough, but once the excitement of the kidnapping episode had passed, I sank into a most distasteful and morose mental state, which I was unable to shake. I wondered what I would do if Rosh were dead when we arrived — overcome by a rush of the fever's poison, or ripped apart by wild animals. How could I use signs and symbols to persuade May Sang that the man had been my friend and not my victim?

These were cruel thoughts, and it did me no good to dwell on them, but my weariness made them hard to dispel, even to the stage that I would find myself deep in my foul postulations, staring at my boot tops until I suddenly realized that we had strayed far off our course, and I had once more to sight a line between the hills behind us and the wedge cut out of the hills in front.

We were some three hours along in our nocturnal journey, not having stopped to rest for a minute, when I looked up from one of my periods of trance and realized that I could not spot the wedge at all. I seemed to be in some hollow of foothills, and my single guiding landmark was nowhere to be seen.

My confusion nearly led to panic before I realized that the indentation in the horizon was directly above us. We had simply arrived so close to it that its appearance was not immediately recognizable. We would turn to our right here and follow the base of the slopes until we met with the creek.

With a deep breath and a smile of relief, I started the animals forward, and immediately heard a great thumping noise behind me. Turning around, I perceived that May Sang must have been about three-quarters of the way descended from the saddle when I pulled the horse forward, more or less out from beneath her. She sat there on the ground rubbing her legs with her hands, which were still bound, and moaned rather pitiably.

I tethered the animals to sagebrush, got the big canteen and my cup from the mule's baggage, and walked back to kneel beside May Sang.

Before I tried to communicate with her I gave her a cup of water, which she accepted and drained in one gulp. She seemed nervous when I crouched close to her, but I needed to be close enough for her to make out my gestures, and she watched me willingly enough, still with a confused expression on her face.

With my hands, I pointed at her and the horse and made a tumbling motion to symbolize her fall, then held my head and scowled in concern. I wanted to express to her that I was sorry she fell down. Next I tapped myself on the chest, smiled broadly, and held out both hands to her, palms up.

"Friend," I said, and repeated, "friend."

She narrowed her eyes and tightened her lips to a sneer as she stared at my hands before her.

"If you ever touch me with your filthy hands," she said in a low but clear voice, "I will tear your eyes out. Also I will rip your heart out and leave it sitting before you, and I shall be gone before you wake up."

She spoke with an unusual way of clipping each word short, but her tone and her accent might have been the Queen of England's, although her vocabulary proved less than regal.

I was shocked, and for a second just stared open-mouthed.

"You speak English," I said finally.

"Don't you?" she replied.

"Why didn't you tell me?" I demanded.

"You did not ask me, you swine. You gave me not one chance, you unclean dog," she spat back. "I never said I did not speak English."

"I could have explained myself a long time ago — saved us both a lot of trouble, you know. Why did you think I was using all that sign language nonsense?"

"You stuck a filthy rag in my mouth, you disgusting, cowardly blackguard. You gave me no chance. I thought you were some deaf-mute idiot."

"Nonsense," I protested. "You heard me talking back at the roadhouse."

"Well then, I should have thought you were just a fool. Give me some more water."

I gave her another cupful and waited for her to drink it. "Please try to calm yourself. I can explain my actions back there," I began, but I was immediately forestalled.

"I can explain your actions very well, thank you. I am not a child. I do not need such matters of life explained. You are a heartless, mindless dog. You are a coward running around in the dark. You are a hopeless, continual liar, consumed by your pride and boastfulness. Like a cowardly dog you grab me and tie me and stick rags in my mouth to take me away and ravish me in some solitary place. When I defend myself, you box me on the chin, and when I wake up with my head throbbing and pounding like poison, I find myself on the back of a horse, off into the perilous darkness. You think you can explain. Shut up! In dear heaven's name, shut up! I know that you are an animal without conscience, and you probably do this sort of thing each and every day to poor girls who are far from their homes, but if you touch me with your filthy hands, I will tear your belly open for the birds to eat."

After this lengthy tirade she burst into tears, and sobbed and wailed into the lap of her dress for several minutes. I was not altogether convinced of the genuineness of this display, but if its purpose was to hold me at bay, it succeeded. I couldn't hope to make myself heard, and if I had felt any impulse to try and comfort her in any other way, it would have been stilled by her eloquent description of what would result should I attempt to touch her. Finally her volume subsided, and I tried to interrupt.

"Please, miss. Please — I have something I must ask you. I can tell you . . . "

"Monster! You are a stupid beast with stupid questions! It is you who should be told a great deal. What could you possibly tell me? You are a creature sent from hell. You are sent to torment poor girls, but for what reason these things happen to innocent souls is the question of the ages. If you want to explain something, then explain that. But no, you should just shut up, you vicious dog."

It was amazing to me that someone could for several hours be so quiet that I was unaware of her ability to speak my language, and immediately thereafter could launch into such an endless vituperative onslaught that it was impossible for me to interject two sentences. Any gaps in her haranguing were filled with over-dramatized sobs and loud moaning. She insulted me with every caustic noun and derogatory adjective she knew, then used some others whose meaning she clearly did not understand. When she ran out of English slurs, she lapsed into Chinese, but her basic meaning could not be misunderstood.

I was too tired to fight the verbal battle any longer. Stepping behind her, I swept up the little woman with one arm and dumped her unceremoniously onto the horse. We walked along the line of low hills, May Sang still muttering low derogations.

When at last she quieted, no sound disturbed the stillness of night except the endless shuffling of eight hooves and two feet. I had decided to let the objectionable young lady stew in her own juice until her countryman could set her straight. My sense of the passing of time disappeared completely — supplanted by the ache in the small of my back.

Only once did the woman distract me from my somnambulant self-pity with a question.

"What is your name, sir?" she asked politely.

"Beddoes. Zachary Beddoes."

It was mildly pleasing to me to be allowed simple honesty in such an elementary matter as my name. Soon enough this young woman would hear my entire story.

CHAPTER SIXTEEN

O NCE WE REACHED the creek and began to follow its banks, not much of my attention was required to keep our course, and I focused more on the dimensions of my own exhaustion than on the details of the countryside around us. Thus it was not altogether surprising that our little company wandered several hundred yards past our objective. Even when I raised my bowed head and found that I recognized the little quarry-like basin we were crossing, it took a long minute for me to figure out that we must turn around.

Going back downstream, I also realized that the outlines of objects around me were becoming more visible. Day was dawning.

I had missed the island on our first pass because I irrationally expected to see a fire burning there, and of course we found no such thing. I waded the animals across the little channel and left them drinking from the shallows for a moment, while I helped May Sang from the saddle, removed the bindings from her hands, and walked over towards the little campsite.

"Come on this way," I told her. "Someone over here that I think you know."

She hesitated for a moment, then stepped tentatively forward.

"Are you there, partner?" I spoke quietly into the shadows at the base of the big cottonwood trees. "Are you all right, Rosh?"

I stumbled over the cold remnants of the campfire. My heart chilled with dread for a moment before a slight movement caught my eye. Then I was able to discern the outlines of his bed, and saw the pale circle of my companion's face as he turned towards us.

The girl stood immediately behind me. One last wave of uncertainty assailed me as I prayed that I had done the right thing, and was not about to bear the brunt of a horrible misunderstanding.

"I brought someone to see you, Rosh. I brought May Sang."

"May Sang?" Rosh's response came as a shout.

She started upright as if she had been stabbed with a needle. "Who is there? Who is it?" she demanded.

A short burst of two-directional Chinese ensued, and the girl threw herself at the figure beneath the blankets. A momentary whirlpool of questions and answers was replaced by embraces, endearments, and a torrent of tears. I left them and plodded back to bed down the animals.

Our long-suffering animals had behaved heroically. Never again would I permit anyone to use the mule as a symbol for a lack of cooperation. They had blandly traversed every step that I had, but with heavy loads on their backs, and had never balked once. If I had been a better man I would have put aside my fatigue long enough to curry and towel them both.

As it was I let the saddle and baggage fall to the ground on the far side of the creek and stumbled back to the island.

It was light enough now to see the smile on Rosh's face and the trails of tears down May Sang's cheeks as she sat beside him on the ground, stroking the hair off his forehead. As I returned, I saw her shifting her posture a bit — straightening and half turning to me.

"You called this man your partner, I believe?"

"Yes I did," I said. "I tried to explain that to you earlier."

She turned to the invalid lying before her and spoke briefly. In response, he grinned and nodded positively.

Before either one of us had the chance to move a muscle, May Sang pulled her left arm back in a roundhouse windup and gave Rosh an openhanded belt to the side of the head. He howled like a coyote. By the time I had shaken my astonishment enough to come to his defense, she had gripped one of his sideburns in each fist and was shaking his head like someone trying to shake the last drips from a slop bucket. As I sprang towards them, she paused long enough to jab her elbow solidly into my solar plexus. It was a lucky shot, but it knocked the wind out of me.

When the stars had faded from my vision, she was once again stroking the skin on the man's bruised cheek and cooing at him like a fretful dove. I presumed he was in no more need of help, so I sat where I was, listening with a mixture of relief and disgust to the gentle tones of their singsong exchange.

As I stood up to depart and give them their privacy, May Sang spoke to me once more.

"I have heard about you, Zachary Beddoes. I have heard you are a wild and murderous animal with no conscience or respect for God or man. How you made my poor love to be your helper, I don't know. Even if I forgive him, it is because I should not have let him go so far off away from his home, and I might still rip you to pieces. You know you should have kept your evil to yourself and left my poor, poor love out of this."

I was much too tired to argue. I swept the rocks and sticks away from a patch of moss near one end of the little islet, pulled my coat over me, and fell asleep.

I didn't sleep for long. I felt like the corpse of someone long drowned, being hauled slowly to the surface of a deep tropical pool, and it required almost a supernatural effort to make my eyes focus on the face before me.

———

"Wake up. Wake up now, Mr. Beddoes. You are always so difficult, and here I am trying to be nice to you. I know you are awake. Please open your eyes."

May Sang crouched directly in front of me, at the centre of my blurred vision, with her elbows resting on her knees and a short stick in her hand, tapping on my shoulder. When she judged that my eyes were stuck open, she gave me a thin smile. At least, from the context of her words, I would assume that such was meant to be her expression.

"It seems I have misunderstood you, Mr. Beddoes. I have judged you badly perhaps, and I should apologize."

The greatest token of her remorse and esteem would have been to allow me to return to my slumber, but my lips would not move quickly enough to interrupt her with this suggestion.

"I spoke a little harshly in the night, I think, but you must realize that I was very confused. You should remember, Mr. Beddoes, that it is extremely discourteous to spirit away young ladies in the dark, and what was a poor girl such as me to think? And if you absolutely must kidnap a girl, you should at least be gentle, you know. Here I am with bruises all over, and a cut on the knee. Yes, and all night I was thinking that in the twinkle of an eye I might be killed."

She managed to make the apology seem more like a lecture than any statement of remorse.

"Still," she said turning her head to a profile, "I was hasty in my thinking perhaps, although what can I hope to know, except what has been told to me about such things, and about you in particular? Now, of course, Leung has told me the full story, and I appreciate the predicament more fully."

The peculiarities of her speech and her train of thought made it difficult for a half-awake man to follow her.

"Who's Leung?" I asked.

"What a question!" she chirped. "Leung is Leung!"

"You mean Rosh?"

"Ah, here is this Rosh business again. What is 'Rosh' supposed to mean?"

"That's his name, girl. His name is Rosh. He told me so when we met."

"Oh no. Oh no. He thought your name was Rosh, and it was very hard for me to convince him that no, it was Beddoes."

I was confused and frustrated, and I couldn't begin to figure what I was doing awake.

"I've been calling the man Rosh for three hundred miles, for heaven's sake," I insisted, but her reply was equally as confident.

"Leung says you have called yourself Rosh ever since he discovered you."

I was tempted to demand to know what was meant by him discovering me, but I was too impatient to pursue it.

"I have called him Rosh for too long now," I shouted, "and I will continue to call him Rosh. I am Beddoes and he is Rosh and I am going back to sleep now."

That, of course, was not about to happen. No sooner had my eyes closed, than the tapping resumed on my shoulder. My first impulse was to lunge forward and bite the stick in half, but instead I merely glared at my tormentor without lifting my head.

"You are once again being most impolite," she informed me. "Here I am, being most humble and apologetic, and you shout back at me. I am forgetting the demands of my station, and trying to be friendly with you. Whatever Leung may say about your good attributes, I am suspicious still that you may be a villain, I am not such a precious, naive young girl as you think, and I heard about you before you ever came to Ashcroft station. Still I am trying to be friendly, and you insist on shouting."

She was waiting for a response to her last outburst, so I apologized for shouting.

"Now I really must get some sleep," I mumbled.

"Oh no!" she exclaimed, and jumped to her feet as if she had just discovered that she was sitting on a rattlesnake. "Get up! Look around! Feel the sky!"

I had no idea what she was talking about, but I wasn't about to leap to my feet for the sole purpose of indulging my senses.

"Poor Leung is very sick. He's been shot, you know — shot and beaten very badly. Then, I'm ashamed to say, he was left all alone by you to shiver and gnash his teeth in the dark while you went off travelling. You should have come and got me much sooner. Now we have to look after the poor soul. It might rain any time. It might snow. You can feel it. Get up now, and we'll all go where we can get under cover. Come along."

I concluded that I had made a grave mistake in travelling fifteen miles or more across naked wasteland to bring this black-haired demoness to our camp. I have never been a man to ignore or escape my problems, but in this case, every fibre of my being demanded that I pull my coat over my head and retreat once more into unconsciousness. May Sang, unfortunately, was not the sort of problem who would allow herself to be avoided. She disappeared for only a moment, then returned once again to chide and chatter like an angry squirrel, and tap her little stick on my coat. Finally it seemed easier to submit than to resist, and I climbed unsteadily to my feet and followed her.

When my head cleared, enough of my sensibility returned for me to object to the plan at hand.

"Listen, young lady, we are not on some city street corner here. The nearest place of shelter is the place we just travelled from, and Rosh is in no shape to make that kind of trip. Besides, I don't know how much of our situation he explained to you, but it would be a bad idea for either of us to be seen in public. I at least have some things that I couldn't explain to a magistrate."

She dismissed my protests with a shrug.

"I know all about your troubles. Don't you worry, Mr. Beddoes — I know all sorts of things of which you are ignorant. Come along. Three miles up this very creek is the Farrell homestead, and we can move Leung into their old cabin. No one will suspect a thing. Mr. and Mrs. Farrell built their new house over the hill by the road because the cabin was dark and ugly and small, but we will be quite happy there. It will be dry, and we can make it warm. Look here — I've already loaded the mule and saddled the horse. You must help Leung up now."

May Sang may have been a woman of great ability and much knowledge, but she didn't know how to load a mule. I undid everything and retied the baggage, which prompted her to sulk a bit. Then I helped Rosh onto the horse. He seemed to be much improved since I had last nursed him — partly, I suppose, because the return of May Sang had lifted his spirits. I resolved to find out later whether she was wife, sweetheart, or sister, but at that moment I was intent only on the job at hand. Eventually I would be allowed to sleep. I wasn't particularly curious about the abandoned cabin, so long as it was functional, but she volunteered the background information with a tone of pedantic pride.

"I know every place and every person around here," she explained. "They all buy their supplies from Mr. Cox, you see, and I am what he calls his 'right-hand girl.' When there is important mail for these far away farms, it is me he sends, because he knows I ride horses very well, and have no fear of calamities. Mr. Cox has also commented that when I work I never seem to get tired, which I am afraid could not be said about you, Mr. Beddoes. Don't you think we should hurry along before some stranger on the road catches sight of us? Laziness is all right for crooks who have already escaped from the clutches of the law, Mr. Beddoes, but we certainly must not be seen."

Without a pause, she shifted languages, and showered Rosh with what sounded like a mixture of encouragement and admonition. The poor fellow saw my dour expression as I tightened the belly straps of his saddle and gave me a helpless half-smile. He pointed at May Sang apologetically and made signs to me, but his explanation would not translate into our form of communication, and he ended by shaking his head and patting me once on the shoulder.

The aching in my legs behind and below my knees bothered me at first, but disappeared once we had started walking, and the dreamy, monotonous plodding reflex took control. The day was once again cloudy and cool, and the world looked wide and flat to me. The rocky creek bed we travelled seemed expanded from its actual width of fifteen or twenty feet to being an immense, badly cobblestoned highway. On the other hand, I felt that if I could manage the energy to straighten up, I might scratch the fluff of the low clouds with my extended arm.

Rosh was silent, as always. The one time I glanced at him, he seemed to be as comfortable as could be hoped. May Sang, on the other hand, was rarely silent. She spoke to either of us whenever she could think of something to say, and to herself much of the time when she could not. She annoyed me in any number of ways. When she was not speaking, she hummed the same tuneless oriental melodies that I had recently heard from my partner's lips. Worst of all, she affected the most unladylike habit of whistling. When she walked, she kept a position to the fore, which was natural enough since she was the one who knew our exact destination, but even her manner of walking disturbed my tranquility. She never moved in a straight line. Like a water beetle, she dodged and wound her way around the slightest obstacle in the path. I suppose her small stature and her long skirts may have had something to do with this, and I grumbled to myself that no man should be forced to walk any distance with a woman.

In this sunken attitude of mind and heart, I kept no track of the hour, but it must have been some time around midday when we arrived at Farrell's cabin.

May Sang informed me that the cabin was abandoned because Mrs. Farrell had finally refused to sleep with her husband until he had built her a new house, and she offered me her personal opinion that the man should not have wanted to sleep with the old turtle at all, but he had built her a new home anyway, just over the ridge and a half mile towards town across the meadows.

I had to agree with Mrs. Farrell. The cabin looked grim within and without, with much more deterioration than one year of vacancy should have caused. It had been built of cottonwood logs, poorly sorted as to size, with only one window and a plank door with cracks in it big enough to slide a slice of bread through. The weight of the sod on the roof had started to collapse one corner of the building, but it was dry and stopped the wind, and there was still a hope that I would be allowed to sleep once we were settled there, so I accepted it readily as my temporary castle.

The animals were unloaded once more and left to graze at the edge of the pine forest that encircled the clearing. I gathered sticks and started a small fire on the dirt floor close to the window while May Sang made as comfortable a bed as she could from boughs and moss.

Some of the smoke from the fire escaped through the window opening and some drifted up through the old chimney hole. I was satisfied that if we kept it low, it would not be enough to draw attention to us from any distance, but I had yet to consider the opinion of the woman of our party.

May Sang wished to pile on enough brushwood to heat the breezy little room to kitchen temperature, and I refused her this luxury.

"Please be reasonable, Mr. Beddoes," she declaimed, "and think for once of others. Poor Leung has been grievously injured by villains, and he must be kept warm."

"Keep him close to the fire and under his blankets. He'll be just fine, " I suggested.

"Oh no, no! He was not born in this cold land, you see. Persons from China and such countries need to be very good and warm when they become sick. Not freezing. He has a fever already, you see, and these things worsen if disregarded by thoughtless people."

"He'll have more trouble than fever if we get all the neighbours poking in to see who's made camp in this cabin. Your poor Leung could very easily end up at the end of a hangman's rope if he gets caught with me."

I had her at a loss for words for a few minutes and she just glared at me. While she primped and adjusted Rosh's bed and wiped his forehead with a wet cloth, I made my own nest on a corner of the floor and let my throbbing muscles uncoil. She mumbled, to herself but for my benefit, that her poor, poor love should never have allowed himself to be seduced into aiding in my vicious schemes. I ignored her and had almost dozed off when I realized that bit by bit the size of our campfire was subtly increasing until it approached bonfire proportions. Finally I roused myself enough to carry the stock of dry wood from its place near at hand, and stacked it in the farthest corner of the room.

"You say you know this country, do you?" I asked her with a sneer. "Well, you should know better than to heat up an empty building in winter, then. Right about now there's rattlesnakes hibernating down in the cracks between the logs at the bottom of old walls. If you get this place good and warm, you'll have them all awake and crawling in here to get comfortable."

I flopped back down in my corner and once again she was silent. I don't know if she really believed me, but after that, the fire stayed at a respectable size. It was the only time I had reason to think I might have won an argument with May Sang.

She must have allowed me several hours of sleep, although it seemed to amount to only a protracted blink, for when she shook my shoulder, I awoke to the long shadows of late afternoon.

"That will have to be enough slumbering now, for we are in desperate need, Mr. Beddoes. We don't have any food, you see."

I was afraid she might be right.

"Nothing?" I asked. "You checked both the white bags on the mule?"

"Nothing. Leung has told me that you fed him only dry deer's meat and fried wheat paste. Now there is none of that."

I believed her, although I objected to hearing my good bannock referred to as "fried paste."

"Tomorrow," I promised. "It's no use starting to hunt at this time of day, especially with a pistol. This country is too blamed open. I'll have to go all the way to the hills before I'm likely to find any game I can shoot. It might be a day or two hungry for us, I'm afraid, but that's the best I can do. Maybe you could scout around the trees for some late mushrooms or something."

"You just wake up, please. I am totally aware of all these things you have to say. Here I am again, doing the thinking while you sleep and make rude noises. Wake up, please, and come with me. I will show you."

I followed her outside and she pulled the old door tight behind us.

"Follow you where? What are you going to show me?"

"Never mind. I shall show you the path over the ridge, and you can go over to Mr. Farrell's new place. It's almost dark, you see. You will not have long to wait. Do you have a knife with you? Good."

I thought I knew what she meant for me to do, and I stopped her.

"Let's stop right here, May Sang," I said. "I won't have any part of rustling livestock. We're trying to lay low here, and that'd be the best way I know to get a bunch of angry ranchers on our tracks. I hate to say this, my friend, but I could run off with all the servant girls in British Columbia and probably get away with it, but if I tried to run off with a calf or a sheep I'd get someone seriously upset and they'd come looking in earnest."

She didn't slow down — just kept heading up the slope into the trees.

"I do not speak of cows or sheep, Mr. Beddoes. I know all the people in this region, you see — from the roadhouse, from the mail. I know their households, and everything they own. Mr. and Mrs. Farrell have a dog named King — very big, but fortunately very old and friendly as well. He doesn't bark much and he will come straight to you if you call to him from the edge of the woods. Probably he will follow you all the way back here, or he need only come part way if you want. Too bad for him, I agree, but we need meat for Leung, and best not to go shooting off guns while we are this close. The Farrells will think he has run away for a while. Dogs do this, you know. Look here. This trail should go all the way to the hollow over there where the house is."

I protested briefly, but I could not argue with the woman's logic.

It was not an afternoon of which I am proud, and I shall not describe the events in detail. The dog was, as May Sang had intimated, completely guileless and trusting, and I rewarded him with the sort of treatment that is commonly afforded to those who trust strangers. When the deed was done I cleaned and flayed the poor fellow, trying to view him as simply one more species of game.

It is perhaps even more embarrassing to admit that a couple of hours later I was comfortably leaning against a cabin wall, having sated my hunger as happily on May Sang's meat soup as I once had on her roast of beef. She herself had wolfed down a large bowlful and now exhibited some signs of the fatigue that had for so long been seated on my shoulders. Even Rosh had managed to eat a bit, and slept now beside her on the outskirts of the campfire's pale circle of light.

Finally I broke the peaceful silence.

"You loaded up the mule this morning, May Sang. You must have taken notice of the gold."

She nodded once and continued to stare at the orange embers at the base of the flames.

"Come on now, woman — didn't that do anything for you? Didn't it make you just a little bit excited? There's more gold there than most people will see in a whole life, let alone hold it and have it to own."

"It is not mine."

"It's partly Rosh's. Leung's, that is."

She shook her head.

"He has told me that he felt compelled to relinquish his part."

I laughed. "There's still a good part of it that belongs to him."

"Well," she said, and shrugged. "That will be good for us. Good enough, I am sure."

When I had wanted peace and quiet, she had prattled on without a pause; now that I was inclined to talk, she was suddenly uncommunicative. She wouldn't volunteer a thing that I did not ask directly.

"It's too bad he and I can't talk things over properly."

"Yes."

"Your English is certainly good enough."

"Thank you. I have spent considerable amounts of time and read a multitude of books."

"But Rosh?"

"Stubborn. Leung is very stubborn."

"He's smart enough. Even without trying, he should have made better progress with it than he has by now."

She hesitated a second, then spoke without looking at me. "He is of the opinion that it is dangerous to become too involved in the life of this uncivilized place. If one speaks like a wild person, one might become too much like a wild person. That is his idea."

"He thinks the white man might be a bad influence, does he? There's a laugh!"

She returned my sneer. "And what is it that you have taught my poor Leung? Wild living and lawlessness!"

She did have an arguable point at that. I didn't want to antagonize her any more than I already had, so I took it philosophically, and changed the subject.

"So then, you're his sweetheart?"

"He is my husband." She said it with a touch of defiance.

"Husband?" I pursued. "What was he doing up in the gold-fields then, and you down here?"

"That is no place for a Chinese lady," she informed me. "I am too proper, and too sensitive. He wished me to be sheltered from the wickedness of wild mining men."

"Not much better down here, is it?"

"At least we are farmers here — not highwaymen, shooting each other for gold."

"Well, I can see why you'd be angry at him for leaving you behind."

I hadn't meant to offend her, but she seemed suddenly rather angry. When she spoke, it was in a low, controlled tone.

"And what do you know about such matters, Mr. Beddoes? Are you out here in the wild country protecting some wife that I cannot see? Will you teach us about honour and duty before you run off with your gold?"

I began to regret that I had initiated this conversation. Her assessment held the sting of truth.

"I meant no offense. You're quite right. I don't know the slightest thing about women. Never had a sweetheart — not even a girl who knew me from any other beard and trousers passing by on the street. I know a bit about gold and guns, and all about how to get myself into a proper pickle without even trying — that's what I know."

It was her turn to placate me then, and after a moment or two of silence, she spoke in a soft voice.

"Leung tells me that you are strong and brave. He says you captured this great mountain of gold from a gang of very fierce bandits. As he understands it, certain corrupt magistrates and sheriffs wish to steal it back from you, and you have been forced to flee from one battle to the next. This is correct?"

I shrugged, choosing not to contradict my friend on matters

245

of detail. I could tell there was something else she wanted to say, and in a few seconds she blurted it out.

"A man named William Atherton has been to Ashcroft and all across the country telling lies about you. He shamelessly bore false witness to the effect that you shot two of his friends and stole his gold."

I recognized the reference to the scoundrel who had tried to bushwhack us, and I couldn't help but half admire the way he had turned his failed criminal enterprise into a chance for personal profit. May Sang did not feel such appreciation for his subterfuge.

"Mr. Cox already knew your name from a Barkerville newspaper, and he said 'Oh yes, this must be true,' and now the whole country believes these lies."

"Don't worry about it," I advised her, then had a disturbing thought. "Did this Bill Atherton say anything about Rosh? Did he say I had a partner? Did he say anything to anybody about a Chinaman? This Atherton was the fellow that shot your husband, you know."

Her eyes flickered with a mixture of anger and fear while she thought back.

"No," she said finally. "He said nothing of that."

I gave her my advice as specifically, as carefully, and as adamantly as I could. She must return to Ashcroft, claiming to have escaped from me. She should say that I was on my way down the canyon towards Fort Hope. Rosh could stay at the cabin alone for a while. In three or four days, she should pretend to have received a message that her husband was on the way back from Barkerville, quite sick. If she let everyone think he had been hurt in a mining accident, not shot, then Bill Atherton was unlikely to make any connection and she could come and collect her husband in safety.

She considered all this carefully.

"What will you do, Mr. Beddoes?"

I laughed, trying my best to be nonchalant.

"I always knew this was going to be a bit of a long shot," I told her. "I still have a decent chance of getting myself and my goods across the border, but I'll have to try a different route, I think. They'll be watching for me in the canyon, so I'll try going across to Fort Kamloops and south from there. There's a big lake I can follow, and a lot of desert country to stay lost in."

She didn't offer an opinion of my plan, but she looked worried. I suppose she realized as well as I that after the excitement of the last few days, it would be difficult for me to escape.

By the time we let the fire die out, I felt as if we had achieved something a little better than a truce, although I still didn't know if she genuinely cared about my fate any farther than it affected the future for her and her man. Still, she gave me one of the blankets before she wrapped herself around her husband under the other. We all slept soundly until dawn.

CHAPTER SEVENTEEN

I ROSE FIRST IN the morning, while the young couple still lay bundled in their own parcel of warmth. I collected my towel from the stack of supplies and personal goods next to the door and stepped out into the fresh, cool sunlight of the first hour of day.

After washing up, I draped the towel over my head and sat on a rock by the creek-side to watch the sun peer over the horizon, as I tried to think of a better way out of my predicament.

Travelling south via the Fraser canyon route was out of the question – too many bottlenecks and too few places to hide where the road hung on to vertical cliff faces for miles on end. Going south from Fort Kamloops would allow me plenty of room to manoeuvre, but it also admitted the distinct possibility of getting lost and starving to death in those broad, unknown spaces. The odds would be even worse if I attempted to cross the mountains and reach the great plains. The only other way out of the Cariboo was the Lillooet to Fort Douglas route. This required distances of travel by steamboat along the lakes, and I would be too conspicuous for the authorities to miss. It is an amazing phenomenon that in this country of great distances and sparse population, news sometimes travels even faster than in a metropolis.

Waiting would not improve my prospects, however, so I made up my mind to head south, then east that same day. I could be of no further assistance to Rosh and May Sang. Indeed they were constantly at risk as long as I remained in their presence.

They were awake, with a fire going and a pot of water heating, when I returned to the cabin. We had no tea to add to it, but we sat together and drank the hot water in silence. The mood among the three of us was sombre — we all recognized somehow that I was about to leave, and the uncertainty we felt was mixed with sadness.

There was only one thing to do before I took my leave, and to that end, once I had emptied my mug, I picked up one of the short iron bars we used to make a cooking tripod and went outside. I selected a large, gnarled pine tree with a great grey boulder at its base, and I used the bar to dig a shallow hole between the roots. It didn't need to be big — just inconspicuous at present, and easily found at some date in the future.

May Sang watched me from the doorway and followed me inside when I returned. She sat down beside her husband, and the two of them looked on as I rummaged through our baggage, separating for myself one of the blankets, one towel, one bowl, and so on. Finally, I divided the gold.

There was no question of being exact, but I assumed that the two gold bars totalled sixty pounds. The loose dust and nuggets weighed in at perhaps a hundred and forty.

I carried the rest of my kit outside and set it in the sunshine. May Sang took one armload out for me and tried to speak to me, but I asked her to wait until I had all my gear assembled in one spot. When this much was accomplished, I turned to her, expecting some sort of farewell.

"I have contemplated and speculated, Mr. Beddoes, and in due time I have assembled a sort of plan — something that you may wish to consider before you proceed on your expeditions."

I raised my eyebrows. I would hear her out in time, but there was one thing I wanted to finish while my mind was still on it. I asked her to hold her suggestion for just a moment and follow me.

I made three trips, staggering down the path to the hole I had dug under the pine tree. I carried with me both gold bricks and a good-sized canvas sack full of rough nuggets. May Sang watched with a concerned expression as I dropped the three packages into the little pit and stamped a layer of earth over them.

"You just leave that where it is for now," I advised her, "but it belongs to you and your man when you need it. There's a stamp on each of the bricks from the place that originally owned it, so be sure to scratch that off or pound it out. Maybe you shouldn't dig it up for a year or so — until you're ready to leave the area, and people have had a chance to forget some things — but that's up to you."

She shook her head. "I don't know. This is entirely too much, I think. Leung said only a small share belonged to him. I should speak to Leung."

"Speak to him after I'm gone. He's not strong enough to argue with me, and I don't want a big fight when I'm trying to leave. Even shares — that's fair."

"He did not earn this, though."

"He just about got himself killed."

"But this is a huge fortune, and he has only been with you for a few days."

We were already walking back towards the cabin.

"If time and sweat are the measure, then I didn't earn it either," I said. "For that matter, neither did the Ne'er Do Well Company. They dug that much up in less than a week — robbed it out of a hole in the ground. I've got enough gold to set me up for life. As it is, I just might break that poor mule's back."

"Don't take the mule," she blurted out.

"What?"

"You don't need the mule. I have an idea, or rather Leung and I have discussed this problem, and together we have formed a proposal."

It was a plan with two halves, and by the time she explained it to me, I had added enough of my own thoughts to claim a share in it myself. As she saw my interest growing, her eyes shone even more brightly, and we became so animated in our conversation that Rosh called out to us and May Sang felt obligated to go inside and tell him what all the babble signified. I walked down to the creek, then up and down the bank, trying to foresee problems or inconsistencies in the scheme.

There was more than one place where the plot could be ruined, more than one step that would have to be planned as it arrived, but I had never expected security or predictability in this project. All in all, May Sang's devious strategy was a definite improvement on my own.

Once the decision had been made, I was anxious to proceed, so I hurriedly strung my bundles of goods across the mule's back and saddled the horse. It was a good day for starting out — the confused weather patterns of the past few days having given way to a perfectly blue sky and cool, cleansing sunshine. Even those monotonous hills of sand, sage, and scrub pine had a beauty about them.

At last I turned to the cabin. I had no great practice at saying goodbye to friends, but I recognized the solemnity and the importance of it, so I couldn't disappear without formalities. When I entered the room May Sang helped Rosh to his feet, then took a step or two backwards.

I reached out to shake his hand, and with a stern, dignified look on his face, he took both of mine in his.

To some extent I had rehearsed what I meant to say, but now the words came out differently than I had planned.

"I'm leaving now, then. Goodbye, Rosh. I thank you for your work, your assistance in my endeavours. I couldn't have asked for a better partner, and I couldn't have made it anywhere near this far without you. I think maybe I should apologize, really, because I know that I haven't always treated you with due respect. I always meant to act squarely with you, I think, but sometimes I become impatient and I fail to be kind. I trust you'll forget those things. Maybe you didn't even understand some of my harsh words, and that's all the better. Anyway, I'm off to the coast, and then back to my home in California. I wish you could come along the rest of the way, but that's impossible, of course. Still, I think I might make it. I've lightened my load, and I'm over the worst part of the journey, so I have a pretty good chance. One thing you should know: If anybody catches me, sheriff or outlaw, they'll never hear about you from my lips. I've still got some running to do, but you should be fine now. If you can keep away from drinking and bragging, you're free and clear."

The moment I finished speaking, Rosh began his own speech. He was long-winded and probably eloquent, although the only words I could pick out were the names "Rosh," and "Barkerville." Nonetheless, a good deal of meaning can be discerned from a squeeze of the hand and an intonation of voice, and I was deeply affected. His stern expression remained, but as I watched, several tears ran down the man's cheeks. One landed on the back of my hand.

When he was done with his farewell address he nodded, and I helped him to sit down again on his bed.

"Goodbye, Rosh," I said.

"Goodbye, Rosh," he replied in his best attempt at English.

I turned and walked outside, with May Sang following behind. She touched me on the shoulder as we reached the animals.

"Do you wish to know what Leung said to you?" she asked.

"Not really," I answered.

The first part of the plan involved stealing Mr. Farrell's horses — not just one or two, but all of them. May Sang thought that would total four or five. By the time Farrell made it on foot to the road and from there to Ashcroft, I would be well clear of the resultant activity.

The initial idea had been to bring the horses over the ridge trail and load my gear onto them there at the cabin, but I pointed out that that would bring the first trackers right up to their hideaway. My Chinese accomplices were clever enough, but they hadn't as much experience with devious theories as I, and they had missed a few elementary flaws such as this one.

May Sang and I led our animals down the creek, parallel to the road going east, then circled back to a spot we judged to be just below the main farm buildings. There we tethered them and unloaded their burdens, then headed off over the wooded rise. It was easy terrain for travelling cross-country, and within a few minutes we were at the edge of the clearing, trying to see signs of activity.

Smoke came from the chimney of the main house two hundred yards away, but no one was visible there or at the big barn half that distance in front of us.

After a minute we took a deep breath and ran across the clearing like frightened coyotes until we were behind the barn, out of sight from the house. The building had two wide double doors, facing each other on the north and south walls. When we stepped through one of these, we found ourselves in a central work area, with feed and storage rooms to the right and animal stalls to the left. I turned to inspect these, and four horses — three dark, one mostly white — returned my gaze expectantly. They hadn't yet been fed.

I walked from gate to gate, wondering where to begin, when a voice boomed out behind me.

"What's all this then? Who are you?"

I spun around to face a stout, red-headed man with a feedbag at his feet and a rifle in his hands. I couldn't speak. I felt the rush of blood up my neck and into my face and thought, "This is it. I've been caught."

My next jolt was when May Sang scampered three or four steps forward and pressed her back against my chest so suddenly it almost knocked me over.

"Stand back, Mr. Farrell!" she shouted, "or this villainous highwayman will surely shoot me."

I quickly pulled out a revolver and pointed it at her side.

"Oh misery and woe!" the girl wailed, "This is an evil man that has me in his power."

Farrell held his rifle across his chest. He now appeared to be as confused and unsure of himself as I was, but I managed to re-gather my wits first.

"Just stay calm and move slowly, Farrell. Put that rifle on the ground. I have no wish to harm the girl or you." I tried to sound as conciliatory as a priest. In reality, I was far from calm, for I had neglected to ask May Sang how many farmhands, sons, or brothers I might have to face in an emergency.

He paused for a moment, then answered me thoughtfully.

"I suppose you must be Beddoes, the gunman from the gold-fields."

It was easier to confuse one of these homesteaders than to frighten him. Farrell stood still and peered at me closely, but he showed no inclination to put down his gun.

"My, oh my," he said "you certainly have created one mighty big ruckus around here. And now it's come home to me. My oh my!"

I listened for approaching footsteps and strained my eyes, try-ing to look at both the big double doors at once. I wished madly that May Sang would give me some indication of how many oth-ers I should look out for. I could surely have shot this single potbellied farmer before he could point the rifle at me, but for all I knew, there could be an army behind him in the dry stor-age bins.

"Put the gun down," I whispered acidly.

He seemed to remember all of a sudden that he was holding it, and leaned it gingerly against a rough wood half-wall.

"May Sang, are you all right, my girl?"

He took a step forward to see her better in the gloomy half-light, and both she and I said "stay back!" simultaneously.

"I am fine," she continued. "He has not harmed me thus far."

Farrell returned his gaze to me.

"And now you're here to prey on a poor old man and his wife, are you? Well, well. That's just fine, Mr. Beddoes. What do you want? I have no money. Horses, I suppose. Take whichever you like. Someone will bring it back to me when they've hanged you. Yes, indeed. Don't expect to get far, though. There's a good group of men not far behind you. You might do well to turn yourself in before you get yourself in any deeper. Plead for mercy. There's a magistrate or two that might show you some, if you gave up of your own free will."

But I had begun to feel considerably more cocky once he admitted that he and his wife were alone there.

"Thanks for the advice. Now I know what you will do if you're ever in my situation," I chirped. The old man showed neither amusement nor anger at my derisive comment, and I immediately began to feel slightly embarrassed at my own coarseness. I am not, I think, as hard a man as some things in my past might lead a person to believe, and I found it difficult over the next few minutes to maintain a cold-blooded facade, especially to order May Sang about rudely enough to keep up the image of her as my hostage. "Get over there, woman. Get those ropes," I snarled. "You, Farrell — move the horses outside. All of them!" I kept one revolver pointed at each of them, stabbing directions with the barrels. "Put the rope there. Now come back and get that bag of oats. Farrell, tie the oats on the back of that one there."

With a mixture of obedience and inner defiance, he followed my orders. When all the horses were properly lined up on their rope leads and the girl and I were mounted, I asked the old farmer for one more thing.

"Whisky. I want a full bottle – unopened."

He shook his head.

"No such thing. Don't drink the stuff."

Momentarily I was worried that May Sang had misinformed me. I would need that liquor soon.

"Whisky or gin," I insisted. "Either you go down to the house and get it, or I go inside looking for it. Maybe I'll have to talk your wife into getting it for me."

I had struck the right chord, and he walked beside us down to the house, his jaw set and his eyes narrowed. When he went indoors I kept the rifle and one revolver pointed very deliberately at my supposed hostage and watched every window and corner of the building for a surprise attack. All I saw was a brief glimpse of a middle-aged woman – pleasant looking but very fat – as she peeked past a curtain.

Farrell returned in less than a minute, and passed me a full bottle of spirits – the paper seal unbroken.

Without a word, May Sang and I rode across the field towards a double-rutted track that led to the road.

We followed the horse path down to the main road, then doubled back to where we had left our own pack animals in the shelter of the trees. There we quickly transferred all the baggage onto one of Farrell's horses, then rode out of the trees, across the road and due south over the open desert hills. With five horses and a mule, we left a trail that a blind idiot could follow, but such was our intention. I knew that I would be pursued sooner or later, but if my followers travelled along the route I laid out for them, and if they did not catch me up too soon, I might still survive the week.

I felt badly about the way I had treated the old couple, for I knew that their life's task of trying to raise a few cattle and vegetables on a barren hinterland was difficult enough as it was, without the intrusion of malicious strangers. Gold seekers and gold robbers will come and go, but if a country is to be made fit for humanity, it will be up to folks like the Farrells to make it so. The loss of the horses must have been a great inconvenience to them, although I had left behind a glass jar with enough gold in it to buy the four best animals in the colony. I had left it sitting on a fence post, for the old man wouldn't deign to touch it in my presence.

I was not in high spirits as we rode – the encounter with the Farrells having left me feeling dirty and depressed. I suppose May Sang must have sensed this, for she proceeded to thank me at great length for bringing her husband safely back to her from the wild Cariboo regions, and to compliment me repeatedly for the kindness and generosity I had exhibited in dividing up the gold. Like any other man, I admire the observant wisdom of anyone who wishes to compliment me, and I listened carefully to her speech.

Unfortunately, May Sang did not stop talking once I had lost my gloomy demeanour, but went on and on, telling how the gold I had deposited with her and Rosh would benefit each individual friend and family member both at home and abroad. She was indeed a strange sort of conversationalist – alternating between wistful silence and unrestrained ramblings.

Finally I interrupted, as much to stop the monologue of genealogies as to ask a question.

"This Evans fellow – how do you come to know him, if he lives so far into the back and beyond?"

"Jack Evans? Well, he is a man of a most colourful reputation – very wild, you understand, and prone to drink and all sorts of foolish excess. Mr. Cox assures me that he is harmless, although he has been imprisoned for lawless behaviour more than once. There was a time, for instance, that he used blasting powder to explode the toilets behind the government agent's office, for no reason at all. I believe he simply enjoys the noise and the flying smoke. Very frightening to the government agent. For this reason Mr. Evans is often known as 'Blasted Jack.' He comes to Ashcroft House about once a month for beans and coffee and such, and the rest of the time he's out at his ranch. He calls it a ranch, but I think he has three, or maybe four, cows."

"He just goes down there for supplies?"

"And to drink." She wrinkled her nose, as if she had detected a foul odour. "Drinking is definitely what Jack Evans does best, but he will suit your plans quite nicely. He is not as stupid as people think. Also he hates the sheriff and spits on Governor Douglas — very bitter and mean, and very sneaky. You and he should work well together."

She carried on to tell me about how Evans had arrived in the area after being tricked into buying worthless land by a confidence man in New Westminster. The accepted story was that he was the youngest son in a wealthy family and that money was sent to him regularly by messenger, on the condition that he did not show his face among his relations.

I did not pay close attention to her narrative. I cared about the man only as far as he could assist me in my plan, and if he could ride a horse and hide when someone shot at him, then he was capable enough. Being thus deep in my own thoughts, I was surprised when May Sang informed me that it was time for us to part company.

"That is the way you must go," she said. "Through that gap, and keep to your left where the trail is on the dry creek. When the trail separates from the creek, you follow the creek, not the trail. It will take you up a sort of canyon, maybe a half mile or perhaps a bit more. I was there only once with Mr. Cox when we took Jack home to sober up."

She had said before that Evans' place was very remote, so it surprised me that we did not travel far that morning. In reality, of course, our starting place at the Farrell homestead was already ten miles from nowhere. We were a long way from any landmarks, but I thought I could follow her directions easily enough.

"I will follow this ridge down past those round hills," she said "and ride back in a circle, so I come to Ashcroft from the south. The men chasing you will hear about me soon enough, and I will say you let me go when you reached the Fraser, some distance to the south. They should ride off and begin the chase down there. Goodbye, Mr. Beddoes."

I was not prepared this time to say goodbye, and for a moment I just stared down at the leather horn of Mr. Farrell's best saddle. When I looked up, she had already started to ride away, leading two more horses and the mule.

"Goodbye," I said to her back.

I watched her ride out of sight until my own horses started to get restless. They hadn't been fed or allowed to graze at all that day, but I didn't wish to stop until I found Blasted Jack Evans.

I couldn't find a good piece of ground to disguise my tracks when I turned north across the fields towards the gap May Sang had pointed out. I trusted that when the trackers reached that spot, they would follow the trail of four animals going southeast, rather than two going north.

An hour later, I reached the dry creek bed; another half hour brought me through sharp gullies and wind-blown clay cliffs to a depression like a giant's thumbprint in the hillside. A section of three-rail fence lay along one side of the meadow. Scattered, spindly pine and poplar formed the opposite boundary, and at the crest of the slope, like a discarded, empty plank box, stood Jack Evans' shack. Beside it was a small corral, where one horse and one cow stood shoulder to shoulder like old friends, watching me ride towards them. When I was still a fair ways away, the man of the house strolled around from behind the shack, and the three of them observed my approach in silence.

"Good day," I said when we came face to face.

"Hello." He said it as if it were a question.

259

"You're Jack Evans."

"Nothing wrong with that."

He was maybe an inch or so taller than me – not so much skinny as bony. He looked as if he might rattle when he walked. His belt had to be cinched well up to keep his trousers above his hips, and he wore no shirt in the bright sunshine. Down the length of his left arm were the sort of crude tattoos that jailbirds draw with a pin or a sharpened bed spring. I pegged him for the sort of fellow who has been driven by drink to places where civilized men should never go.

I was eminently satisfied with him.

"I'm Zachary Beddoes," I said, and paused, waiting to see if he recognized the name. He showed no such sign.

"This ain't the kind of place you run into by accident, you know. You don't mind me asking – who told you how to get here?"

His eyes showed a spark of intelligence, in spite of his bedraggled physical appearance.

I shook my head.

"Best if you don't hear the answer to that, Jack. If you don't know it, then nobody could ever make you tell. Easier to keep a secret you don't know, don't you think? I have a job of short duration that I'd like to hire you for."

"I don't work for nobody but myself." He said it with a bit of hesitation. I had captured his interest with the hint of secrecy and intrigue.

"It's not really normal work, Mr. Evans – more like a favour I'd like you to do for me."

"Now why should I do you a favour? Mostly when people ask for a favour it's 'cause they been fool enough to get themselves stuck in trouble."

I smiled and tapped the bottle in my coat pocket with my knuckles.

"We could have a drink and talk about it, don't you think?"

His face relaxed instantly into a half smile and he ran his fingers once through what was left of his blond hair.

"Don't normally touch a drink before nightfall, what with the animals to tend to and such. Still, it might not be so bad, you know. I been working since sun-up. Should take a morning off now and then. I'm only forty-two, and I could still die young and miss all the joy in life if I'm not careful, you know?"

I tied the horses to the top rail of the little corral. I didn't remove the saddle or baggage, but I cracked open the bag of oats for them and left them enough line to reach the trough of stagnant water that serviced the cow and the other horse.

Evans led the way into the cabin and we sat on the floor in the gloomy half-light of the windowless building while we passed the bottle. It was almost humorous to see the abrupt change in his attitude once the whisky appeared. We were suddenly fast friends, there was nothing unusual about my unexpected arrival, and he had never had a suspicion about me in the first place.

His shack was a sad little place, with no furniture at all except for a couple of wooden crates, and a solid layer of dirt and straw over the floorboards. After a drink or two it didn't look so bad, however, and my host held forth with great pride about his estate.

"Won it in a card game down south, you know." He laughed brightly — already loose and a bit sloppy after the third swallow. "Next day, this guy wants his deed back, like. He's come up with some money, you see, and now he wants it back, but no chance. I wasn't giving his land back until I see it for myself. So I can tell what's it's worth, like, you know? I come up from the coast and looked it over, and I been here ever since." He laughed again, drank again. "Had good offers to buy the place, too. Five hundred bucks, even eight hundred bucks cash, but no way. They like it 'cause it's got good water, and that little canyon on the way up protects it, you know — from Indians, from the weather, all that sort of stuff."

Dedicated boozers are unpredictable. Some can soak up drink

like a sponge and never wobble; others fall over after a whiff of the cork. Jack Evans was fast fading away from rationality, and we hadn't yet talked business.

"Would you like to hear my proposition, Jack?" I enquired, holding onto the bottle for an extended time.

We were leaned up against the wall near the open door, and before he responded, Evans stared out for a while at the clearing in front of his home with a satisfied, lopsided grin.

"Seems to me," he said finally, "that when a fella takes this long to get around to talking about what he wants to do, usually it means something's gonna get lifted or someone's gonna get hurt."

Alcohol had not burned his brain entirely to cinders.

"Believe it or not, Jack, there's nothing technically illegal about what I want you to do, but I admit that if the agents of the law discover you doing it, they might not be altogether pleased."

"Hmmm. Now I don't know you or where you come from, but around here anything that makes the sheriff mad is illegal, you know?"

"I'm willing to pay you for the risk."

"Risk! Yup — everything's risky for me. I got this problem, partner. I've already been on the wrong side of the bars once or twice, you see, and every time I go back there, they seem to like me better. They want to keep me around a little longer. Money is money and all that, but I try to be pretty careful these days."

My big coat pockets were full of surprises that day. I drew out a canvas pouch with a bulge in it the size of a crabapple and dropped it in front of him with a resounding thud.

"As near as I can guess there's about a pound of Barkerville gold there, my friend, and I don't want to buy your ranch; I just want you to wear my coat and hat, take my horse, and ride down towards Fort Hope making enough noise along the way so that the news gets around that Zachary Beddoes has gone south through the canyon."

I passed him the bottle. His eyes kept returning to the pouch of gold, but the clever part of his mind wouldn't let him touch it until he had made a decision.

"I gather you aren't all that popular with the law, then, Mr. Beddoes."

"Yes sir, putting it mildly. There's been some nasty stories go around about me, I must admit. Rumours, lies, and such."

He took another drink.

"And the risk of this thing — it's like I might get a hole shot in my back or something, I suppose."

"The idea, of course, is to make the deception last as long as possible, but I would expect you to tell the truth of the situation, loud and long to anyone necessary before any shooting started. I just need a head start. Yours is a small risk, in my opinion."

When he laughed, he jerked about like a puppet gone out of control.

"They say an opinion is only just a lie that ain't been proved yet."

I laughed along with him. Between the effects of the whisky and the gold, I was pretty sure I had Blasted Jack under control. He said nothing directly, though — just ambled outside into the sunshine. After a moment, I followed.

He stood with hands on hips, head bent back, looking straight up into the sky. I couldn't help but follow his gaze, but there was nothing but blue and grey above us. I handed him the bottle, which he took without looking at me, and stood beside him surveying the countryside around his homestead.

"Once you're gone, I'll start off in a different direction, keeping my head down, so to speak," I said. "Maybe I should even take a different route right from here. What is there out behind your place, Jack? Can I get to a road going that way?"

He looked at me for a minute, stroking his cheek pensively, then walked briskly back to the cabin, handing me the bottle as he passed. He didn't go inside, just grabbed the broom that was leaned next to the door, and began to sweep an area of bare red dirt next to the corral. I didn't know what he was doing, but I already knew the man well enough not to be surprised at his actions. When a space about ten feet square was cleared to his satisfaction, he turned the broom around, and used the other end to draw a one-foot circle in the middle of the space.

"Ranch," he said.

Next, he scratched a long, winding line beside the edge of the corral, with an irregular shape attached to the end of it.

"That's what I call Frog Lake, and this here's the crick that comes out of it." At this point, I realized he was drawing a map. He trotted all the way over to my horse, and kicked at the dirt, frowning in concentration. "Now, town would be about here." From there, he walked twenty feet to where I stood, dragging his toe in the dust. "This'd be where the road goes," he pronounced. I nodded agreement, and we both drank some whisky.

When he recommenced his discourse, he spoke in a low but expressive voice, pacing his way around the cleared area, scratching with the broomstick, and occasionally pointing to the horizon beyond his house.

"If you head down here, or over here, or even through here, you get the miserablest gullies and gulches. Take you forever, and you still get nowhere. This here is swamp. You can't get too far west here. This is a dry creek bed, leads up to Frog Lake, but you don't go all the way. Maybe halfway, maybe a mile, and then you go up over the ridge, down to here somewhere, then you look for . . . Damn! Where's the road? Oughta be somewhere right here, and I got it way over there." He looked to me, apologetic and mystified, and I handed him the bottle. "Maybe if you got some paper, I could try drawing this a little smaller."

"No need, Jack. I'll just wait a while after you're gone, then go out the way I came."

"You sure? I'm good with maps normally, you know. I just got this one too big, and I now can't see it quite right."

"Let's not bother," I said. "I always seem to get mixed up trying to follow maps anyway."

He shrugged, tried briefly once more to resolve the discrepancies in his scratches and circles, then came and sat next to me. He leaned against the front wall of the shack, basking in the sunshine, and when I glanced at him a minute later, he was asleep.

The whisky sat in the sunshine, and it was as warm as afternoon tea when I took another mouthful. I considered waking him up, but it didn't seem worth the effort. He might as well sleep it off. I realized that I had made a mistake in bringing a full bottle along. I should have made do with just enough for a friendly bracer – an introductory social lubricant.

Checking my watch, I found it was eleven-thirty. "If I hadn't started out travelling today, I would be having a tasty luncheon of dog soup with my friends," I thought.

The world was beginning to feel like a rather unsteady place. I sank down onto a patch of wild grass, closed my eyes, and tried to decide whether one day's delay would seriously decrease my chances of success.

Suddenly, I found I was being shaken into consciousness by a tall, balding blond stranger with a jaw like Gibraltar. It took me several seconds to recognize Jack Evans and to remember our plan.

"If we don't get started right quick like," he was saying, "we'll have blowed our whole day, you know!"

It was almost one o'clock. My head was spinning, and I wondered how Evans had managed so quickly to be awake and sober.

"You get a move on now, Zach, if you're serious about this stunt. I've got to look to my cows before I do anything."

As he stumbled away I perceived that while he may have been awake, he was still some distance from sobriety.

Jack brought water to the animals' trough from a well behind the house, and I had him pour one bucket over my head, which helped my concentration a good deal. Leaving him to complete his farm chores, I stumbled over to the horses, and unloaded Farrell's brown horse.

"I'll leave the white one saddled. You'll ride him," I shouted.

"I can take my own horse if you want."

"No, Jack. I've been seen riding that big white, and I want everyone to recognize me — that is, recognize you and think it's me. Anyway, I'm afraid part of the deal is a trade of horses. I bought that white fellow and this brown mare fair and square, by the way. I need one to ride and one to pack, so I'll need to take yours with me."

At this he hesitated, but it was hardly a moment until he shrugged. "Oh well, Nathaniel will get you to Fort Hope safe enough; don't you worry, Zach. You've got a good horse there! Been with me a long time, you know."

Evans finished his work and buttoned up his shirt.

"I'm not actually going down the canyon," I said. "I'll go over to Fort Kamloops, then south from there."

He half smiled and nodded sagely.

"Don't you worry Zach — half the country will hear how you're ripping down the canyon, I'll make sure of that. You pay me an honest dollar, and I do the job good and proper, you know."

"That gold poke is still inside on the floor. You take it and hide it someplace good while my back is turned here," I suggested. "You want that waiting for you when you come back north. Take a bit with you now in a twist of paper if you want just for expenses."

He tottered away while I saddled his horse, and ten minutes later we were ready to go, Evans on the white horse wearing my hat and long, green coat, with the whisky bottle protruding from one pocket.

"I'll ride with you as far as that main valley. Then I'm coming back here for the night. I want you to get a head start on me."

I was telling the truth when I said this, but I also wanted to be sure he was on his way before he started drinking. I only hoped that if he passed out, the horse would continue to head south, rather than return to the Farrell ranch. I don't know whether Jack guessed my ulterior motive or not, but he spoke at some length about how confident I should be. He could be relied on to execute his part of our plan, whatever the obstacles.

"Yessir," he said, with a philosopher's distant gaze, "I'm mostly a loner these days, because of the ranch and all, but I know good and well what's involved in taking on a partnership. I had myself some good partners in my time. Phil Prescott and me was together for better'n two years when I first come north. Helped me build the house right at the start, but he had the consumption, and went south and died. Joe Willis was a good man, too. We had a claim together up on Meagre Creek, but he died too. Drowned. Good man, though. I been lucky with the partners I took on."

I declined comment on the sort of luck his partners seemed to have had, but allowed that, indeed, good fortune was sometimes more important than good judgement in choosing one's companions.

"Well, I always had to depend on luck, myself," Jack observed, "because I never had much in the line of good judgement." We both had a good laugh at that. Then he said, "You're pretty much of a loner yourself then, are you?"

"Pretty much," I agreed, then added, "I've been working with a partner or two lately, though."

"And now you divided up and went your own ways, I guess?"

"Probably. It's always hard to say, of course."

"Well, I'm glad you asked me to sign on. We'll do this job up right and proper, you and me."

As the sun reached its zenith behind us, we rode together across the meadow, to the mouth of the ravine that led down into the long horseshoe-shaped box canyon.

I had chosen Farrell's white horse purely because it would be easily noticed and remembered when people saw Evans ride past doing his imitation of Zachary Beddoes, but it was in fact proving to be a good horse. It showed no signs of tiring or protesting as Evans started it out on a new leg of the journey. His horse, on the other hand — the one I rode — sensed something unusual afoot, and kept bumping up against her former owner's leg as if for reassurance. It took most of my concentration to handle her, for I was not a great horseman to begin with, and I still felt a trifle tipsy.

Once we reached the dry creek bed, the canyon narrowed so that we had to travel single file. Then, for the last few hundred yards of the southernmost end, the baked clay hills opened out a little, and we rode side by side up to the place where I had planned to leave my new companion, but as we turned the final corner we were confronted with a frightening surprise.

Our horses strolled into the open valley at a patient walk, but as soon as we looked across the half mile of desert prairie to the opposite hillside, we pulled hard on the reins and had the animals fairly dancing on their hind hooves back into cover. Out of sight, we quickly tethered the horses to the most convenient bit of brush, scurried back up the rise on foot, and peered over. Crouched together behind a great sandstone boulder, we looked across to the place where I had said goodbye to May Sang — a quarter-mile distant. There were five men there — three mounted, two on foot beside them, examining the ground.

I muttered something unpleasant under my breath, regretting that I had wasted so much time using a bottle to introduce myself. I had never once guessed that such a remote, widely scattered community could organize and mobilize a rescue committee so quickly. Now it appeared that Evans was going to have to figure a way to manoeuvre himself in front of those characters, for this group had surely been sent out on my trail. They spent a long time there, examining the tracks and talking amongst themselves. The possibility now presented itself that they might choose to follow the lesser trail, and come straight towards us.

We both held our breath, so to speak, as we squatted, watched and waited, but I remained confident that they would ride away, would follow the route taken by May Sang and showing the larger number of hoofprints. No one had seen Evans and I when we blundered into their view. The surprising thing to me was that they were taking so long to come to a decision.

So intent was I on this observation that it startled me when Evans uttered a loud profanity. Turning to look at the animals, I saw that they had shaken themselves loose from the brittle sagebrush branches to which they were tethered, and while the dark one had evidently started for home, the white had strolled out from concealment and was foraging for dry grass in plain view of all and sundry.

Evans leaped from the hillock where we were stationed, skidded down the slope on his backside, and trotted out to retrieve the animal, but by then it was too late. As I watched, one man pointed towards us, then all turned their attention.

A moment later five men on horseback trotted down the valley, trapping us within the narrow walls of the dry creek's gorge without any route of escape.

By the time Evans came back with one horse, I had control of the other. Without speaking, and without haste, we mounted and headed back in the direction of his homestead. We were each trying our best to come up with a plan, but it now seemed clear to me that my good fortune had been used up. We reined in at a sort of bottleneck twist in the canyon, and Evans jumped down, holding his rifle in one hand, the whisky bottle in the other.

"Let's take our own horses back, Jack," I suggested. "You go on to your ranch, hide my stuff wherever you can. You can have it all. Chase that other horse of Farrell's down in this direction and try to hide any evidence that I've ever stopped up there. I'll handle things from here. I guess they've caught me, but I don't want these beggars getting any of my gold. Go on, Jack."

I was tired — too tired to fight any more.

Evans didn't show any sign of hearing what I had said. He handed me the reins to his horse, took another pull at the bottle, then went back to the bend we had just passed, where he scrambled up the cliff face about fifteen feet, and wedged himself behind a fold in the rock.

I didn't know what to do. He looked like he was preparing a single-handed counterattack, which I knew would not only be futile, but would greatly reduce my chances of being fairly treated when I did surrender. I meant to run after him to say this, but while I was trying to find a place to secure the horses, I heard the pounding rumble of the riders coming down the draw.

They never came fully into my view, for at that point my partner raised his rifle and fired five shots in quick succession. I kept our mounts from bolting, but not without effort, for the reports echoed like thunder in the enclosed space.

I managed to tether the white to some sagebrush as Evans ran up to me, grabbed the lead to his own horse, thrust his rifle into my hands, and clambered into the saddle.

"Everything's going just great, Zach." He gasped for breath, but was obviously exhilarated. "They're off their horses and running for cover. You go keep on top of them like. I'll be back in ten minutes. Don't you let them move, now. Keep them right like they're sitting!"

He was off before I had a chance to speak, riding back towards his ranch as fast as he could manage over the rough rock of the dry creek bed.

Still grimacing with anger and confusion, I followed instructions, by turns running and climbing to the perch just vacated by my overzealous accomplice. I found things as he said. Here and there, behind rocks and around corners, the five members of the pursuit party had deployed themselves so that only occasionally could I glimpse a hat, a coat sleeve, or a thatch of hair. They had bunched themselves into more or less a single group —

a sign that they were amateurs in the game of chasing dangerous men, for it made it easy for one person with a gun to control them, at least for a short period of time.

They were positioned along one side of a triangular opening in the ravine. Their horses were behind them, around the corner, hidden from my view. As I watched, the fifth member of the troop emerged tentatively from this direction, probably having just finished attending to the mounts, and I squeezed off a rifle shot which kicked up a spray of gravel not far behind his foot. I smiled to myself as he leaped and squirmed to where his cohorts crouched.

Just once did one of them attempt to return fire — a single pistol shot that sailed aimlessly off into the sky. I fired again in their general direction, and heard the bullet ricochet ominously down the enclosed corridors of stone. They stopped shooting completely. They had to aim uphill into the sun, and I don't think any of them had seen exactly where I was. Past the ringing in my ears I could hear their anxious voices, no doubt coming to the same conclusions that I had reached. I had the upper hand for the moment, but in the long run they must win, for I was as unable to move as they.

Five minutes passed. I was rather mystified when one of them chose to wave his hat around as if to draw my fire, but I obliged with a careful shot that ripped through the fabric and scared the fellow half to death. Thinking about the peculiar action, I realized that they were not aware there was no exit on the other end of the canyon, and wanted to make sure I did not slip down and ride away while they remained in hiding. It was interesting to know that they were not familiar with this piece of country, but I couldn't think of a way to turn the information to my advantage.

Finally I looked down the gorge and saw Jack Evans trotting towards me on foot. He motioned quietly for me to come, and for the first time I realized that our pursuers must still think they were dealing with only one man, possibly a man holding a hostage.

Evans still had a half smile on his face.

"I found a good, solid little tree just past that boulder there. You take your horse down there now, you see, and tie him real tight. Then, come on and follow me." He pointed down the canyon wall to a pattern of footholds that gave access to a ledge which ascended and led around the corner. "That path there. I'll go along there, and you catch up. Are they still all squirrelled down under cover?"

"I suppose so," I replied.

"Good, good. You get that horse tied down good, like. Then follow me, okay?"

As he said this he reached into the deep pocket of my long green coat and drew out two dun-coloured sticks of blasting powder.

I was shocked into momentary silence by the sight of them, but once again he was off and running before I could gather my wits enough to speak — hopping and scrambling up the vertical face of the hard clay and sandstone wall like a mountain goat.

He meant to blow them to pieces. Win or lose, I couldn't stomach that. It didn't take long for me to firm up my resolve. I had to stop Jack Evans. I could not countenance the massacre of a group of strangers who threatened me only because they meant to uphold the law.

Desperately I hoped, as I jumped from foothold to foothold, that Evans would wait for my arrival before he tossed the explosives onto the unsuspecting citizens. If they realized that it was safe to leave their cover and advanced, though, Evans might use the gunpowder before they had a chance to separate, and the bloodshed would be terrible.

My haste was too great. A third of the way up, I lost my footing and bounced and skidded all the way to the bottom. Still I heard no deafening blast, and back up the cliff face I went. This time I made it to the top, side-stepped as fast as I could along the ledge, and found myself standing on a broad rock about the size of a kitchen table. I figured that I must be directly above the five deputies, but Evans was nowhere in sight.

The quick climb had completely taken my breath away and I allowed myself a second or two to squat down and rest.

I decided to crawl over to the edge of the rock and peek over the side to clarify my exact position. I was just kneeling to begin this action when I heard a scrape and a rustle from exactly that direction. A second later a head and a pair of shoulders appeared, as one of the manhunters hauled himself from the last of his own set of footholds onto the ledge.

I found myself face to face with one of the only people in the region that I actually knew by name. Bill Atherton was as surprised as I was to renew our acquaintance in that particular spot, but I was first to recover from the shock and jump to my feet.

The last time I had seen him I had been aiming the Sharp's buffalo gun at him, and I had missed. This time it was the toe of my boot that I aimed, and it connected perfectly with the top of his shoulder and his collarbone. He was tough and quick, though, and his balance was admirable. He kept from going backwards, rolled sideways, and drew his revolver from its holster, all in one long motion. I hadn't even thought of reaching for my gun, and if his weapon had been cocked I think he might have had time to shoot me. Instead the barrel was still pointed silently forward when my second kick landed squarely on his forehead. Without a sound from his lips, Atherton flipped backwards over the edge. I couldn't see him, but I heard him skid and bounce as he tumbled down the vertical slope. Below me I heard a shout of surprise from one of his fellows, at the same time as I heard a sharp whispered exclamation to my left.

"Zach! Come on now, man!"

Jack Evans was just above and beyond me, calling impatiently. In his hand he held the two sticks of explosives — originally meant to blast stumps from his fields, and now destined, I supposed, to end the lives of five of his neighbours. The two short cylinders were tied tightly together and the two-foot length of fuse was already burning.

"Forget it, Jack!" I said. "We can't do this thing. It's not worth it — too much killing. They're innocent men down there."

"What?" he exclaimed.

The fuse sizzled slowly but steadily along.

"Don't kill them, Jack!" I pleaded.

"Nonsense!" he said, and threw the bomb as hard and far as he could over the precipice and down the canyon. "I don't even know them people! I'm not gonna hurt them! I just want to see if they tied their horses up any better than we did a while ago."

The mighty boom of the explosion was greatly exaggerated by its origins in those confined depths, and even though I was well clear, I felt momentarily deaf and dizzy as the breeze settled fine dust on my shoulders.

"Zach! Come here, Zach!" I finally heard over the hollow ringing, and I ran and scrambled to the higher ground where Evans stood. He was laughing so hard I could not make out what he was trying to say, but I looked where he pointed and soon saw the reason for his glee. All five horses had bolted at top speed for distant pastures. Two could be seen far out on the flat lands going one direction, two more had turned the opposite way, and the fifth was kicking the air and spinning about like an unbroken colt, just past the main gap opening out onto the wide valley.

Jack stood for a moment on the rocky peak like a scarecrow come to life, slapping his thighs and laughing aloud. Then he turned to me as he started back the way we had come.

"Now I got to get moving, like. Good luck, Zach! You be careful, you know. Get yourself a good spot where you can see like, and watch me now."

He picked up speed as he spoke, and I didn't try to follow him along the ledge. Just before he dropped over the edge to slide down the cliff face, he turned and shouted back once more.

"You keep watching me, partner!" and he disappeared from my sight, headed back towards our horses.

Things had been happening awfully fast, and I was still dumbfounded at how my new friend had managed to control the events, but I knew what was going to happen next. I returned to the table-sized rock where I had fought with Bill Atherton and flopped onto my belly.

The dust had mostly settled, and from my vantage point I had a pretty good view of the five confused and frightened young guardians of justice as they crawled out of their hiding places to take stock of the situation. They moved cautiously at first, peering down the canyon towards the spot where I had fired on them with the rifle. Then, once they were satisfied that no more shots were forthcoming, they began to shout questioningly to one another. When they were all present and accounted for, they began to argue loudly. One man jogged off to look for the horses, and a couple more squinted into the rays of the setting sun, trying to focus on the top of the canyon walls.

"Beddoes!" someone shouted. "Beddoes — are you there?"

Not one of the figures in this scene of grand confusion had a gun in his hand when Jack Evans suddenly rode through their midst at high speed. He screamed like a banshee and fired one pistol shot in the air as he galloped through. The gun was aimed harmlessly heavenwards, but the five fellows below me scrambled frantically for shelter. As Jack galloped out of sight, they emerged one by one, wailing and cursing and throwing their hats on the ground.

I had no doubt whatsoever that they believed Zachary Beddoes had thrown bombs at them, then escaped towards the south. If they had the courage to follow, they would receive ample confirmation that he had passed that way. Jack Evans was a memorable man.

I was confident that none of them were aware of the homestead, but I waited until they had started off towards the main valley in search of their horses before I headed back to the cabin.

As darkness fell, I was eating a supper of cheese and biscuits on the porch, and silently thanking my absent host for his hospitality.

After a long, uninterrupted night of sleep, I awoke to another chilly but beautiful morning. I helped myself to a meal, courtesy of the honourable Mr. Evans, then took the liberty of rummaging amongst his belongings until I found his razor, a small piece of shaving soap, and a wooden framed mirror. It amused me to find that my host had chosen to stash his pound of gold in a spot no more discreet than his shaving kit.

I used the razor to shave not only my face, but the entire top of my head. Clean-shaven and bald, I did not even resemble the mysterious Russian from 150 Mile House, let alone the nefarious Beddoes. I doubt that Rosh would have recognized me.

I left Evans an extra ounce or two of gold in payment for supplies I took from his home, for in addition to a few days' foodstuffs I also helped myself to a black suit and white shirt, (baggy and funereal, but sufficient for my needs), and a pair of stout leather suitcases with brass fittings.

Just before noon I finally tired of gazing at the image of my fresh pink face in the mirror, and I started my short journey north along the route I had first come, towards Clinton. I went slowly, avoiding the main wagon road as much as possible, and reached that outpost – the beginning of Gustavus Blin's other road through Lillooet and the lakes – before nightfall of the following day.

It was the beginning of what I expected to be an uneventful chain of wagon and boat passages that would return me to San Francisco.

CHAPTER EIGHTEEN

*T*HE DAY-AND-A-HALF journey to Clinton was straight-forward — even restful after the excitement of my previous week — and I arrived in that sleepy little junction hamlet with an easy, optimistic attitude.

I sold the horse that had belonged to Jack Evans and joined up with a commercial waggoner and his helper who were travelling to the lakehead at Lillooet. It was about a forty-five-mile journey, traversing mountain slopes that reached four thousand feet — a hard trip at the best of times, and particularly so late in the year, with snow already beginning to accumulate higher up. I was glad to have the assistance of the men with their wagon to transport my heavy goods, although I thought it best not to socialize too closely with the good fellows.

I gave my name as Hector Pinkus, and claimed to have lived at Quesnelle Mouth with my wife for the past three years. I purported to be a minister, and claimed that my wife had been a schoolteacher. She had recently died, I explained. Overcome by grief, I was returning to the south with two suitcases full of heavy books. The two teamsters evidently believed me, and for the most part left me to my sullen grieving.

I acted out the part satisfactorily, which took some care and concentration, for inwardly I was relaxed and self-satisfied. Remembering the start of my journey south, when I was full of suspicion and constantly bickering with Rosh, I could not help but marvel at the contrast between that mood and my present one. It felt a bit strange now to be on my own, without a companion, but I was sure I would get used to it. I had always been a solitary sort of man.

The route down the lakes was in many ways just as arduous as the road down the canyon, and after the first overland section, I was pleased and relieved to board the steamship *Champion* at Lillooet and ride it south down Seton Lake. During this passage, I introduced a new facet to the story of my life as Hector Pinkus. I allowed that my wife had died of a strange, very painful fever while reading her schoolbooks. From that time forward I felt confident that no one would be likely to touch my baggage.

It meant, of course, that I had to load and unload my own burden for each overland stretch of the journey, and there were many of these. At the south end of Seton Lake, a mile-and-a-half road had to be travelled to reach Anderson Lake, where the *Marzelle* met us. After this a thirty-mile stretch was negotiated by wagon to Lillooet Lake, where the vessel was called *The Lady of the Lake*. At its lower extreme another road began — this one thirty-eight miles, leading to Harrison Lake and Fort Douglas.

Once past Fort Douglas, I felt that I had made it back to civilization, and it was indeed only a couple of days before I was safely installed in a private room in a hotel in New Westminster, the capital of the colony. I was forced to remain there for several days, since bad weather had halted steamship travel across the straits to Fort Victoria. During this time I purchased a recent newspaper and discovered my own name therein. The publisher seemed remarkably well-informed and up to date, and he told his readers that one Zachary Beddoes had managed to create a sensation with crimes and disturbances ranging all the way from Barkerville down the Fraser Canyon to Fort Hope. Beddoes had stymied all attempts to capture him on charges of kidnapping, robbery, suspicion of murder, and much more.

I kept my head well-shaven at all times and managed to procure a Bible the same shade of black as my suit. To be on the safe side, I remained in my hotel room except when I took my meals or when I walked to the docks and enquired about weather and possibilities for passage. I heard no more mention, however, of Mr. Beddoes and his misdeeds, people here on the coast being mostly unconcerned with the wild and foolish things that went on inland, so by the time I crossed to Fort Victoria a week later, I had begun to relax.

The imminence of winter was befouling the weather, and once again I was forced to find a hotel and wait before I could travel farther. I chose a place called *The Prosperity Hotel*, owned by a middle-aged Chinese man named Ho. The hotel was clean and quiet, it was close to the waterfront, and there were no questions asked when I paid my bills in raw gold, or when the dark stubble began to grow on my face and head.

I found Fort Victoria quite a pleasant little city, and I was in no hurry to risk leaky vessels and winter storms to escape it. I still enjoyed walking along the docks, but purely for the pleasure of seeing the great sailing ships rocking at anchor, redolent of mysterious, faraway places. More than once, in a dockside public house, I watched captains and navigators deep in conversation as they encircled a table and pored over charts and maps. These were great maps — covered with strange names and tantalizing blank spaces — but as I looked at the men themselves, I doubted that I could trust them to pilot me across unknown seas. I chose instead to enjoy the amenities of Fort Victoria.

In the evenings I played cards with my landlord, Mr. Ho, winning and losing a dollar or two in a night. It was an enjoyable pastime, and the amounts wagered were a pittance to either one of us, but of course we joked as we gambled about our terrible losses, and how we would soon be ruined. I specifically remember Ho telling me once between gales of laughter that before long, I would own everything – his hotel, his wife, and his daughter included.

Our gambling saw no great sums of money change hands, but by the New Year I had used a portion of my capital to become Ho's business partner. We soon spoke to builders and made plans to expand our hotel and its services.

On the last day of January, I proposed to marry his daughter, and on the last day of February, we were married. She now wears the ring I found in Dead Ned's booty. Some questioned the brevity of our courtship, and I marvelled at my own temerity at the time, for we knew little about each other. When required to fill in documents, I was forced to guess at the spelling of her name, and wrote it as *Sue*, although I knew that was inaccurate. Our union has proved to be harmonious and contented, though. As I once mentioned to Jack Evans, I seem to be fortunate in my choice of partners.

I do not have enough interplay with occidental society here to know whether they are scandalized by my marriage to a Chinese woman, and frankly, I do not care. We are expecting our first child sometime around Christmas, and we are both, of course, very excited. If it is a girl, my wife will decide what she is to be called, but if it is a boy, I have already chosen his name.